Praise for Sean McGrady's Eamon Wearie Mysteries

"Postal Inspector Lt. Eamon Wearie loves a good mystery and in *Dead Letters,* Wearie gets a double dose. . . . This postal police procedural holds its own with the best. . . . McGrady does an excellent job of pulling the two mysteries together in a shocking conclusion. . . . Use the mails. Keep Lt. Wearie employed!"

— Jodi Stinebaugh, *The Prime Suspects*

"Lt. Eamon Wearie is not your run-of-the-mill detective. . . . *Dead Letters* is well written and proceeds along to a very interesting and surprising conclusion. It is a little unusual without being too pat. . . . In this way and in the characterizations the book is very realistic . . . hard-hitting."

— *Mystery News*

"Well-written and well-plotted."

— *Mystery Loves Company*

"Eamon Wearie . . . will remind some readers of Lawrence Block's Matt Scudder ten-or-so years before Scudder faced the central fact of his middle age and joined AA. . . . What distinguishes this promising debut is . . . the generally lively, literate running commentary on the moral lapses in American public and private life . . . and lots of caustic humor. . . . Not for the squeamish, if anybody still willing to leave the house in America in the 1990s can be so described."

— Richard Lipez, New York *Newsday*

Books by Sean McGrady

Dead Letters
Gloom of Night
Sealed with a Kiss
Town Without a ZIP

Published by POCKET BOOKS

Town Without a Zip

AN EAMON WEARIE MYSTERY

Sean McGrady

POCKET BOOKS

New York   London   Toronto   Sydney   Tokyo   Singapore

This book is a work of fiction. Names, characters, places and incidents are products of the author's imagination or are used fictitiously. Any resemblance to actual events or locales or persons, living or dead, is entirely coincidental.

An *Original* Publication of POCKET BOOKS

POCKET BOOKS, a division of Simon & Schuster Inc.
1230 Avenue of the Americas, New York, NY 10020

Copyright © 1997 by Sean McGrady

ISBN: 0-671-86942-6

First Pocket Books printing September 1997

10 9 8 7 6 5 4 3 2 1

POCKET and colophon are registered trademarks of Simon & Schuster Inc.

Cover photo © 1996 Chris Anderson/PNI

Printed in the U.S.A.

For everyone in ZIP code 11768—
especially Nick Maravell, Joan and
Sal, Mark Sanborne, Larry Smith,
Richie Doyle, and all my pals down
at Main Street and Gunther's

I guess somewhere inside of himself he was angry, very angry. You get angry about a lot of things and you, yourself, dying uselessly is one of them. But then I guess angry is about the best way that you can be when you attack.

—Hemingway, *Night Before Battle*

1

Ray Duffy came out of the mean February cold into the crowded warmth of Dixie's Guns & Ammo. It reminded him of a hardware store: wood floors smelling of linseed oil, neat rows of clearly labeled merchandise, the hunting rifles that were mounted among the antlers—not to mention all those Elmer Fudd–faced, big-assed crackers in John Deere caps. Unlike most hardwares, though, there was a humongous Confederate flag hanging from the rafters. And then there were all those *Charlie's Angels*–like posters, featuring bikini-clad babes with the latest high-tech bazookas. To Ray, Dixie's was that whole men's-world shit—the same dickheads you saw in the barbershop or buying Michelins or shelling out for lap dances at the strip clubs.

The place was mobbed, like it was the day before Christmas or something—all because they were going to change the gun laws again. Ray knew most of the crackers in the store were pissed off, thinking it was some big old government conspiracy to nuke the second amendment and their God-given right to bear arms. All that NRA bullshit. *What a crock*, Ray thought, *the way these boys are always going on about the Constitution and what our forefathers had wanted two hundred years ago. Like the world hasn't changed any since then. Like we're still a country of farmers with pitchforks.* Ray snickered at the idea as he made his way to the glass display racks holding the 9 mm action.

It was almost like a going-out-of-business sale, the way those Maryland crackers were pressing up to the counters and calling out their orders to these twerpy clerks who could barely keep up with the demand. Ray didn't know where to begin, just too many damn choices. You had your Brownings and Colts, your Austrian Glocks and Sig Sauers, your Springfields and Remingtons, your Czech CZs and Spanish Llamas. You had nickel-plated or stainless steel, you had chrome or polished blue steel. Man, he liked them yuppie guns, those sleek, slick, black Glock 17s. Nice, not like anything he'd ever shot before. At the cabin, he just had a couple of standard police issues, a .357 Magnum and a regular old Smith & Wesson .38. Solid and predictable, nothing fancy. He had to buy those guns off the street, though. Shit, just one more way a prison record forced you to make some changes in your life.

"The president's an asshole," the flannel-shirted cracker next to Ray said. "Taking away the right of law-abiding citizens to defend themselves from crazed criminals. Ain't that the truth?"

"Amen, brother," Ray said, smirking. "Pretty soon, before you know it, only the animals will have the guns."

"What a world," the cracker said, before turning to place his order.

Ray was pretty much decided on getting a couple of Glocks. He'd have to remember to get some magazines to feed into them. Then there was the matter of the big gun. What would Jack want? He'd probably want something American-made; after all, the man was a Vietnam vet. Maybe one of those M-16s, that type of thing.

The big sport models were located all the way on the other end of the store. Ray shook his head in good-natured wonderment at the sheer size of the place; shit, Dixie's must have a good six thousand feet of floor space. There was one whole aisle just devoted to combat knives. Lots of military surplus: canteens, fatigues, jackboots, army watches, holsters, ammo belts, gas masks, heavy-duty flashlights, superzoom binoculars, night-vision goggles, walkie-talkies, smoke grenades, survival packs. Shit, from the looks of things, there were a lot of people getting ready to go to war. Then there was the police paraphernalia: the cuffs, the billy clubs, the bullet-proof vests, even the fake badges to make it all seem very real. Man, there were some mighty sick people in the world, no doubt about it.

Ray soon found himself with the rifles and shotguns, admiring one of the display mounts. A big, beautiful, blue masterblaster, just the ticket.

"Isn't she sweet?" a clerk said, noticing where his attention was lodged. "That's a Vietnam tribute model put out by Colt and the American Historical Foundation. It's a special limited edition. Notice the highlighting in twenty-four-karat gold, the way it sets off the metallic blue finish. Check out the engraving. See what I mean?"

In bold capital letters, the M-16 was enscribed: OURS WAS A NOBLE CAUSE. Man, Ray liked that a lot. It was almost too perfect. "Is it a real working gun?" Ray thought to ask.

"Yes, sir," the clerk said. "But of course, it's no longer a fully automatic weapon. Because of the new federal restrictions, it's been refitted. But believe me, sir, it still offers plenty of firepower. In fact, I can't imagine anyone needing more. Unless of course you were going off to war."

"Could it be converted back to a full autoload?" Ray asked.

"Well, I suppose it wouldn't really be much of a problem. At least not for a person with any real gun knowledge."

Ray knew just the person for the job. Yeah, Deke could do it, easy. Besides, he had some other work for Deke to do, anyway. "I'll take it," he told the twerp.

"I should tell you that this gun is a little pricey because of its collector's value. It goes for fifteen hundred dollars."

"No problem," Ray said. "I also want to get two of them Glock 17s. With plenty of ammo for everything."

"It's good you came into the store today, sir," the clerk said. "By next week, these new stringent laws will make it impossible to buy more than one of these exquisite pieces at a time."

"That's why I'm here now. I know an opportunity when I see one."

"Are you a veteran, sir?"

"In a manner of speaking," Ray said, smirking.

"Will you want the special glass display case to show off your M-16? It's only a hundred extra."

"That won't be necessary," Ray said.

It took a while to get through the paperwork. There were all sorts of state fees and surcharges. "They're making it tougher all the time for good honest folk to take advantage of their constitutional right," the clerk said, clucking over the small pile of forms. Ray got a little worried when he began to study the driver's license. "I'm afraid we have a little problem here," the clerk said. Ray was ready to bolt for the door, if need be. "You've got a P.O. box here. We're going to need a street address."

"Division," Ray said, breathing a sigh of relief. "Division Street."

The clerk looked up. "I need a specific number, sir."

Shit, what was Jack's number? Ray just thought of it as the little brick house on the corner of Division and State. "Four seventeen," he said, not having a clue.

The post office box was necessary to get a copy of Jack's driver's license. So easy; just say you changed your address and send in your ten bucks to Motor Vehicles. Ray was concerned only that the dumbshit clerk might get wise to the photo on the license. It wasn't even close. He didn't look a thing like Jack, but then again, it was hard to notice anything other than Jack's massive black beard. There was no real way to know who was buried beneath it. Still, the post office box was an act of genius. The way he got all those subscriptions in Jack's name, to *Soldier of Fortune* and *Nudist Lifestyles,* not to mention the wackjob mailings the militia groups put out. Did the whole Oswald-loner-misfit trip on him.

"So how will you be paying for this, sir?"

"Cash," Ray answered.

The clerk looked surprised but otherwise didn't miss a beat. "It comes to $2,567.63."

Ray took out the roll and peeled it off.

"You can pick up your purchase in three days," the clerk said, returning from the register. "That's how long it takes to clear the background check."

"Nothing to it," Ray said.

"And here's your driver's license back. The state requires photocopies of everything these days." Ray took it and turned to leave. "Incidentally," the clerk said, stopping him in his tracks, "not that it's any of my business, but I think you made the right choice in shaving the beard. Heck, I could hardly find you in that picture."

2

There was trouble in paradise. It had started from
the moment they landed at Honolulu International.
They were met at the airport by the hotel's greeters,
who presented them with the customary leis. Mary
made a face at the ropes of carnations and orchids,
like it was the tackiest, most touristy thing in the
world. But she was probably just tired from the
thirteen-hour flight. At least that's what Eamon had
thought at first.

But things didn't improve when they arrived at the
Royal Hawaiian. Eamon thought it was absolutely
fantastic, this sprawling, Old-World honeymoon palace nestled right on Waikiki Beach. But Mary com-
plained that it reminded her of some big, pink,
out-of-control wedding cake. What was wrong with
that, Eamon wanted to know. They had just gotten
married, hadn't they? Mary told him it wasn't that, it
was just that she'd been imagining something a bit
more secluded, some private lagoon fantasy of hers.
He reminded her that they were spending only four
days on Oahu, that he had them booked on the island
of Kauai after that. The travel agent had assured
Eamon that their accommodations on Kauai would be

picture-book perfect, a seaside cottage far from the madding crowd. Mary just said, "We'll see."

Okay, Hawaii had been his idea. Mary was all set on Europe; she had gotten it in her head that it would be romantic to take that new tunnel train from London to Paris. But Eamon figured that drab, dank February weather would've taken all the romance out of the Eiffel Tower and those outdoor cafés on the Champs Élysées. If he had known what trouble his decision was going to cause, though, he would gladly be saying *bonjour* instead of *aloha* now.

Fortunately, Mary began to feel a little bit better about things after a nap. When she woke up, she said the pink room was really quite lovely, what with its regal, antique furnishings and its spectacular ocean views. Eamon was relieved. They ordered a pitcher of mai tais from room service. Things were definitely looking up. Then they made love. No problem there, either. That part was always good, from the beginning. But it was something special now to be with his bride, with the woman of his dreams. He had finally found her, after all the looking, after all the empty, restless nights.

It was the second time around for Eamon. The first excursion he chalked up to reckless, drunken youth; Trish had been nice enough, but you needed more than nice to make a marriage work. Now, Mary Seppala was the real thing, a keeper. He knew it from the first instant he'd laid eyes on her, on the courthouse steps, downtown Baltimore, working on that crazy chain-letter case. Detective Mary Seppala. Those legs that did forever. That dark olive skin. Those outrageous Liz Taylor violet eyes. That beautiful head of raven hair. A combination to set the heart forever aflutter.

They tied the knot at Mary's father's house. "If only her mother were alive to see this," her dad kept saying. Eamon's parents drove up from their retire-

ment condo on the North Carolina coast. Bunko
served as his best man. Just a few close friends and
family. Mary, true to her independent spirit, forsook
the white gown for a simple, short dress in her
favorite color, which was emerald. Bunko, the tough-
guy postal inspector, teared up when Mary said, "I
do." It made Eamon smile to see Bunko, his thrice-
married, hard-drinking, chain-smoking partner, go
soft on him like that. After the justice of the peace
finished, everybody threw rice and the couple got into
a limo and headed for the airport.

Eamon Wearie was a married man again, just like
that.

It would take some getting used to. Mary was prone
to saturnine moods, to eclipsing moments of discon-
tent. Oh, that first night at the Royal Hawaiian, she
humored him by attending the traditional luau; she
was able to sample the native dishes, everything from
the kalua pig to the lomilomi salmon to the notori-
ously insipid poi, without resorting to making faces.

The next morning, though, while having breakfast
in the Surf Room, enjoying fresh pineapple slices and
the good, strong kona coffee, they argued about the
day's itinerary. Eamon had wanted to visit Pearl
Harbor, to pay his respects at the *Arizona* Memorial,
but Mary would have none of it, saying that a memorial to the dead didn't fit in with her idea of a
honeymoon. He suggested shopping, thinking that
she might like taking advantage of the arcade of fine
shops behind the Royal Hawaiian's coconut-palmed
gardens; in fact, he had planned on surprising her, by
taking her into Chanel or Louis Vuitton to buy her
something special. But again, she made an unhappy
face. "I can shop anytime," she actually said. It was
then, sipping his coffee and looking out at the opal-
blue splendor of Mamala Bay, that Eamon began to
experience his first doubts about their union.

In the end, they compromised, deciding on a visit

to Iolani Palace, the rajlike nineteenth-century Victorian in downtown Honolulu, which had been home to Hawaii's last monarchs, King Kalakaua and Queen Liliuokalani. In the process of their tour, they got a little history lesson to boot: they learned that the first people to come to Hawaii were Polynesians in 500 A.D. who'd somehow made the two-thousand-mile journey by canoe, of all things. They also learned about Kamehameha, the first chief to unite Hawaii under one rule, and the great struggles for power that followed, as the islands became coveted by America for their resources and strategic location.

Frankly, Eamon thought the whole guided tour was one long snooze. But he was glad to have kept his mouth shut, especially after Mary proclaimed the palace the best thing about their trip so far. Afterward, Eamon suggested they buy some funky aloha shirts and check out some of the tiki bars. But Mary made another one of her faces. This time Eamon insisted. Big mistake. There they were, in their hallucinogenic new rayons at an anonymous bamboo bar, with their untouched umbrella drinks, as Don Ho crooned "Isle of Golden Dreams" from the jukebox, looking to all the world like the unhappy survivors of a tropical shipwreck.

"I'm going back to the hotel," Mary finally announced. "You can do what you want. I don't care."

She got up and walked out. Eamon didn't do a damn thing to stop her. Instead, he called the bartender over and told him to pour the umbrella drink down the drain. Then he ordered a double Jack on the rocks. That would do for starters.

He found Mary on a chaise longue on the white sands fronting their pink hotel. She was an audacious sight in her string bikini; it continued to amaze him that she belonged to him. He didn't want to lose her—no way. It didn't take him two sips of the Jack to realize that: yeah, right—like he was going to throw it all away in some coconut joint listening to a medley of Don Ho's greatest hits.

"I'm sorry," he said, rejoining her. "I love you."

"I love you, too," she said, looking at him with pained eyes.

"We should've gone to Paris," he said, stroking her black hair and eyeing a Waikiki coastline that was congested with whitewashed high-rises. "I should've listened to you in the first place."

"It's not your fault," she said. "I don't know what's with me. I've just had the most uneasy feeling ever since we arrived."

At that moment, they were approached by a startlingly beautiful island girl. She was wearing a bikini top and a vibrantly colored sarong, and her luxuriant hair was full of exotic flowers. "I am Kea," she said. "I am a descendant of Kaahupahua, queen of the sharks. I have a special gift for reading faces. Would you like me to read yours? It costs only five dollars. But it's all up to you."

Eamon shook his head as Mary reached into her purse. "Tell me something wonderful," Mary said. "I need cheering up."

Kea placed her fingers on Mary's forehead, as if she were reading Braille, as if her touch could reveal secrets of the soul. "You take everything very seriously," Kea said, pressing deeper. "That is why you are often disappointed. You are on your honeymoon. Am I not right?"

"What a guess," Eamon said cynically. "Us and everybody else on the beach."

Kea ignored him, keeping her hands on Mary. "You will be tested. You will need to be patient. And you will need to forgive. In short, you will need all of your resources. There is a reason for everything. But at first these reasons will elude you."

"Can I ask you something?" Mary said.

"The answer is that you should wait," Kea said,

way ahead of her. "You should wait until you are truly ready."

"Thank you," Mary said. "I appreciate your wisdom."

Eamon said, "Am I missing something here? What in the world was the question?" Then it suddenly hit him. "Oh, no—you're not talking about waiting to start a family, are you?"

Mary didn't answer—and that said everything.

"Don't listen to her," Eamon pleaded. "Believe me, it's all a scam. This is how she makes her living. By preying on dumb, unsuspecting tourists."

"That's not true," Kea protested. "Let me read your face. I will show you that I am not making it up."

"My wife might be a sucker," Eamon said, "but no way I'm shelling out five bucks for this nonsense."

"For you, it's free," Kea said. "What do you have to lose?"

"I don't know about this."

"Don't worry," she said, placing her hands on him. "Now you will learn the truth."

Her hands were surprisingly cool and dry. But she didn't keep them there long before pulling away. "What's wrong?" Eamon asked. "Why are you stopping?"

"You are surrounded by death," Kea said coolly. "The dead are all around you."

Mary let out a tiny gasp. "Oh, my God," she said.

"That's because I'm a postal inspector who just happens to work out of the dead-letters office," said Eamon.

"Whatever you say," Kea said, walking away.

"Nothing is going right," Mary said, watching the girl move on to her next unsuspecting couple.

3

They met in the Pratt Street Pavillion, an upscale mall on the murky gray waters of the Inner Harbor. They bought slices of pizza and sat down at one of the many free tables in the atriumlike interior. Ray thought it was a joke the way they'd spruced up the downtown, putting in all these shops and restaurants for the tourists, taking advantage of the harbor and that dumb old ship, the U.S.F. *Constellation,* close to Camden Yards and the science museum and the aquarium and all that crap. Ray knew what the real Baltimore looked like, and it wasn't so pretty, all those blocks of tenement row houses, all those boo boys with their crack pipes, all that white trash sitting on their stoops with paper-wrapped bottles of Thunderbird. Deke was always going on about how it was the niggers that had wrecked the town, but Ray knew that wasn't it at all. Black and white never entered into it. It was just about money—either you had it or you didn't. Thems with money made their way into the nice green 'burbs outside of town, same as it always was.

The mall was quiet on a midweek afternoon in early February. Just the suits and other money junkies taking five for a sandwich or a cup of coffee. Ray watched Jack eat his three slices of pepperoni pizza with some amusement. The man was a pig, slobbering the grease all over his grungy black beard and getting tomato sauce on his thermal undershirt, looking like some half-starved lumberjack or something.

"I still don't know about any of this," Jack said, chewing on a hunk of crust and sounding like some whiny retard. "I mean, it's all so risky and everything."

"Look," Ray said, trying to reason with the putz again, "at least this way you have a chance. If we pull off the job, then at least you'll have the bread to get out of town. Create a new identity for yourself. Believe me, the change will do you good."

"You make it sound so simple," Jack said. "But maybe I'll beat the rap. You never know. My lawyer says we got a better-than-even chance."

"This the same guy who's soaked you for every nickel you have?"

"Yeah, maybe you're right," Jack said resignedly.

"Believe me, you keep listening to that pud-brain lawyer of yours, not only are you going to be dead broke but you're going to be living the swanky life in Leavenworth or even Marion."

"My lawyer says that even if we lose, they'd never send me to one of those maximum-security places. I'd probably be going to one of those federal correctional institutions. That's a whole level down. Maybe even one of those Club Feds, like with those Wall Street–Milken guys, with the tennis courts and everything. That's what my lawyer says, anyway."

Ray knew Jack's lawyer was right about that, but he had to keep applying the pressure, all the same. Otherwise, Jack might try backing out of the whole deal. "Shit, the feds will probably make an example of you, Jackie boy. Show everybody what they do with a government employee who goes on the take. I wouldn't want to be in your shoes, no sir. They send you to Leavenworth, then you'll find out why they call that sucker the 'hot house.' Oh, yeah, those boys will be lining up to take a shot at you, pardner."

"What do you mean?" Jack said, sounding all nervous again, the way he always did when Ray started talking about life behind bars.

"C'mon, Jackie-boy, do I got to spell it out for you? When those cons find out that you used to work for the government, they're going to be unzipping their flies all at once."

"Jesus, don't talk that way," the poor slob said. "I was just a damn postal worker, for God's sake. All I did was destroy some mail. It wasn't even real mail. It was just some advertising crap. I had to dump the stuff. There was no other way for me to keep up with the quotas. You can't imagine the kind of pressure the managers were exerting on us."

"But they caught you, Jackie-boy. All on tape. All recorded by security cameras. All over, Jackeroo. You might as well just say your good-byes now. Because it's going to be a long time before you ever see daylight again."

"My lawyer says eighteen months, tops. Maybe that's the smart thing now. Just ride it out. Do my time. Then I come out and I can start all over again."

"Get real, my friend. Start over with what? With what money? And where are you going to live? That's just for starters. And who the hell is going to hire you? You'll be an ex-con, the lowest of the low. Nobody will go near you."

"I just don't want to compound things now," Jack said. "It could get out of hand, you know."

"Listen to me, if we don't pull this job, then you'll see what out of hand is all about. Believe me, even if you decide to ride out the rap, you're going to need cash reserves. Prison ain't going to be cheap for somebody like you."

"I don't think I follow you," Jack said, getting another one of those worried looks in his eyes.

Ray was going to play it for all it was worth. Time to push the deal through. "I'm just trying to look out for you," Ray said, trying to put just the right note of concern in his voice. "And that's just what a fish like you is going to need in the joint. Somebody to look out for you. And that's going to cost you, believe me. I saw it done all the time on the farm. You get some big biker dude to keep the niggers off your back. Think of it as a kind of life insurance policy. You pay the premiums and you get to stay alive."

Ray didn't bother to tell Jack that he'd done his own paying out at the farm in Hagerstown. But it was worth it. Deke kept his word and no harm came to Ray. He got his mom to put the monthly installments in a bank account in Deke's name. She gave him some trouble until he explained the alternative. And for once, the hag just shut up. It was weird now that his mother was dead, the way there was no one checking up on him, no one asking all those nosy questions and keeping him halfway honest. He almost missed the old bitch—what a laugh.

"Are there any alternatives?" Jack asked. "I mean, what if you can't come up with the cash to pay for protection?"

Ray laughed. "Why, sure there are alternatives, Jackie-boy. You could always become somebody's wife. You find yourself an influential con who can provide a nice little home for you. And on Tuesday and Saturday nights you close your eyes and pretend that you're Cinderella. But let's face it, Jackie-boy, you ain't exactly wifey material. Who'd be hard up enough to want you? You got those ugly black whiskers and you haven't exactly been keeping to your exercise program."

The poor slob looked like he was about to start blubbering. Ray had him just where he wanted. "You could always try putting up a fight. Absolutely, why not? Sure, you could try to resist those nigger posses with their homemade knives. Of course they'll take their shanks and cut your fat Butterball ass into finely sliced deli turkey."

"Stop it," Jack said, close to tears. "I can't handle any more."

As the slob mulled over his options, Ray took a moment to check out the scenery. In a way, he liked the unrealness of malls, that whole artificial quality. A climate-controlled environment with plastic plants and spritzing fountains. The way they were always so brightly lit, all friendly and beckoning, a whole shoppers' dream world. All designed to make you part with your hard-earned cash. Man, you had to admire the warped genius who came up with the idea of shopping malls. Now there was a dude who understood all about control factors.

As far as Ray was concerned, the best thing about the mall at the Inner Harbor were all those tasty-looking office girls. Man, he liked their smart clothes and their jazzy haircuts, these serious bitches in their Wonderbras and nylons and spiked heels—the kind he could never get close to. They'd always walk by him like he didn't exist, leaving behind their little bursts of perfumed sex. Not much had changed since high school, that was for shit sure. The way people were always ignoring him, underestimating him. He was thirty-five now. Somehow it didn't seem like so much time had passed. It wasn't so long ago that he was at Muldeen High, waiting for Jill at her locker. It seemed like she was the only one who hadn't laughed at him. Her prissed-out cheerleader girlfriends were another matter. But Jill, with her big, sensitive green eyes and long, straight chestnut hair, had that whole artsy-fartsy thing going for her. Man, this was a girl who made pottery and shit like that.

"All right," Jack said, interrupting Ray's reverie, "I've been thinking about it and I've decided that you can count me in."

"I never had a doubt, Jacko," Ray said, snapping

out of it. "I knew you'd come around to my way of thinking. Everybody always does in the end."

"But what if we get caught?" Jack asked, suddenly going all weak-kneed again.

"Let me worry about that," Ray said with authority. "I know what I'm doing here."

"I know, I know," Jack said. "This ought to be easy for an old hand like yourself. I keep forgetting who I'm talking to."

"It's not like this is some kind of bank we're talking about. Believe me, we waltz right in there and waltz right back out. Not like there's any guards to worry about. We don't even have to dynamite a safe. Nothing to it, Jackeroo."

"How many banks you hit in your career, Ray?"

"Ten or eleven," he said, lowering his voice confidentially. "Shit, I'd still be doing them if it wasn't for that mouse-turd partner of mine. Little rat-nosed snitch."

Jack shook his head empathetically. The poor slob was such a sucker, believing Ray to be a big, old master thief. Stroke of genius to borrow Deke's rap sheet. No way he was about to tell Jack what he'd really been in for. That was his own personal business. Ray knew better than to trust anybody with his secrets. He had a score to settle, and he didn't care who got hurt in the crossfire. All that mattered was that Ray found her. Thinking of her had helped him get through the whole Hagerstown experience. Jill was out there somewhere, and if he knew anything, it was that she was probably thinking of him at this exact same moment, too. They were destined to be reunited. Then, and only then, could he ever make it right between them. She would have to listen then; she would have to give him a second chance.

"I'm just glad I'm working with such a professional," Jack said, "somebody who's got all the angles covered."

"It was just a good thing that you bumped into

me," Ray said, smirking at the thought. "A real lucky break."

More like fate, that was what it was. Making small talk in that bar. Not really paying much attention until the slob mentioned that he used to work at Postal Depot 349. Suddenly Ray's ears pricked up. *No kidding,* he said, trying to sound casual. So Jack told him all about working the sorting machines and conveyor belts, like Ray could give a damn. But he made like it was the most interesting shit he'd ever heard. Ray bought him a drink, and then he bought him another, just to keep him talking. Ray knew only one important thing about Depot 349: it was where those fucking postal inspectors worked out of. But Jack didn't seem to know anything about that stuff. He said those guys weren't regular postal employees, that they worked apart from everybody else, in their own special suite of offices high above the loading docks. Ray wanted to know more, but he couldn't keep Jack to the subject at hand. He just kept going on about all that dead-letters shit. Not only did Depot 349 handle regular mail, but it was also the nation's largest destination for all those old, moldy dead letters. The putz thought it was utterly amazing, these football fields of undeliverable letters and parcels, as if Ray could give a shit. But he didn't interrupt him much and he kept buying the drinks, and pretty soon Jack was telling Ray how he'd really got fired from the job and about how he was running low on cash on account of all his legal bills. It got Ray to thinking. And it wasn't long before a plan began to form in his mind.

They left the Pratt Street Pavillion and took a walk over to the aquarium. No particular reason. Just seemed like a good place to continue their discussion. No way they were going to shell out fifteen bucks to get in, though. Ray took one look at the school buses waiting outside and a lightbulb flashed inside his head. He just told the cashier they were bus drivers who needed to take a quick look inside for a missing kid. Man, the shit people bought into.

So there they were in some humid tropical-habitat thing, with all these parrots and rubbery-looking trees getting sprayed every few seconds with warm water because it was supposed to mimic conditions in a rain forest or some such nonsense. As far as Ray could tell, the only thing slightly interesting were the piranhas, which swarmed in this fake muddy river. They stood on one of the wooden observation bridges for a better look.

"Check it out," Jack said. "Those are real man-eaters. I'm surprised at how small they look. But, gosh, look at the teeth on them. You can actually see the fangs on those little bastards."

"I want you to draw me a map of Dead Letters," Ray said, trying to get back to the business at hand. "I want it to be very detailed. I don't want you to leave anything out. I want to know exactly where those postal inspectors are."

"How come you always want to know about the inspectors? What's the deal there?"

"I just don't want them interfering with our plans," Ray said.

"You don't have to worry about them," Jack said. "They're not going to be anywhere near where we're going to be."

"Just draw the fucking map, Jacko."

"I wonder if you can eat piranhas," he said, not paying attention. "I mean, without the teeth, they almost look like catfish. Boy, I sure like fried catfish. Especially the Cajun way, blackened all to heck. That's the absolute best."

The putz was always thinking with his belly. "Forget the fish fry for a moment," Ray said. "Besides the map, we're going to need a couple of your old postal uniforms. So we can slip in relatively unnoticed."

"You ever have catfish over at the Little Bayou?

They serve it with fried bananas. I kid you not. Hot peppers and bananas. It's much better than it sounds."

Ray was starting to lose it. "Screw the stupid bananas. I need you to pay attention for a minute, you fat fuck."

That shut the turd up, all right. They left the rainforest exhibit to check out the big tanks of weird-looking sea life. It was the usual aquarium crap. There were plenty of those exotic rainbow-painted fish. Then you had fish that were horse-faced and dog-faced. You had fish that looked like porcupines and lions and zebra. You had chameleonlike rascals that could change their color to blend in with the scenery. Ray liked those the best, especially the ones that could disguise themselves as rocks; these fish just sat there in the background, unmoving brown lumps that were practically unnoticeable. He watched as this little guppy parked himself in front of one of those living rocks. The guppy never knew what hit him; the rock fish swallowed him whole, just like that. Man, Ray could identify with that approach. Sit back and bide your time. And strike when they least expect it.

"Have you ever tried eel?" Jack asked, as they paused in front of a tank of electric eels. "Much better than it sounds. The best is at the sushi bars. No kidding. They fry it up real nice. I'm telling you, it's surprisingly tender and sweet. Like chicken or something."

Ray made a face. "People are always saying that everything tastes like chicken. They say frog legs taste like chicken. They also say alligator tastes like chicken. Even rattlesnake is supposed to taste like chicken. Bunch of shit, as far as I'm concerned."

"Well, I'm telling you that fried eel tastes a little bit like chicken. I ain't lying."

"I bet if I fried you up," Ray said, snickering, "you'd taste a little bit like chicken, too."

They left the eels and stingrays for a look at the

sharks. It was the main event, the big draw. Everybody wanted to get a look at the three or four killer sharks that were cutting back and forth through the big swimming pool. Ray and Jack made their way to an observation deck two stories above the pool.

"You ever have shark meat?" Jack said. "Just like steak, I kid you not. The best way is to barbecue it. Pretend it's prime rib or something and slather it with A.1. sauce."

"You're such a putz," Ray said.

"I'm not sure I like your attitude," Jack said. "In fact, I'm not so sure I even want to be involved in any of this anymore. You're always picking on me and—"

Before Jack could get in another word, Ray had grabbed him by his belt and forced half his body over the observation deck's guardrail. Suddenly Jack was dangling face-first over a pool of restless killer sharks. Ray, holding onto Jack's legs, wasn't about to let him drop, but he wanted to give the putz something to think about. All that time in the weight rooms of Hagerstown had finally paid off.

"Oh, Jesus," Jack bawled. "Please pull me back up. Oh, Jesus, don't let go of me."

Ray was aware that his antics were pulling in a crowd. People were pointing up at them with some interest. As if it made a fucking difference. "I think you have a rather simple choice to make here," Ray said, choosing his words carefully. "Either you play along with me, or else you're the lunch-board special, Jackie-boy."

"Just help me back up," he pleaded. "I promise I'll do anything you ask."

Ray savored the situation for just a moment longer before pulling Jack to safety. The big oaf was all shook up, red in the face and gasping for breath. It was too bad that he still needed him alive. It sure would have been fun to watch those sharp-toothed bastards go to work on him. Well, it didn't much matter. The putz was fish food any way you looked at it.

4

Things definitely improved once they arrived on Kauai, which was nicknamed the Garden Isle. To Eamon, it might just as well have been the Garden of Eden. Their charming thatched cottage was nestled right on the fine-grained shores of the jeweled Pacific. Eamon's travel agent hadn't oversold it at all. They were perfectly removed from all the other units in the four-star Polynesian resort village. Best of all, it was far away from the whitewashed towers of Waikiki, scene of their earlier anxiety.

Of course, this slice of heaven didn't come cheap. But Eamon hardly minded paying the three hundred dollars a day, especially when he took note of the transformation in his bride. Mary went from being a tight-lipped, unwilling hostage to an ecstatic honeymoon participant. Their seclusion amid all that volcanic splendor had brought out another side to Mary—a wild, untamed sexuality that thrilled him. All of her inhibitions had apparently been left behind in the pink chiffon of the Royal Hawaiian. Out on Kauai, in the remoteness of the western part of the island, they skinny-dipped and made love on the pristine beaches. One day, they even hiked back past the sugarcane plantations into the emerald hills and stumbled upon a forgotten waterfall. There, they frolicked in a clear pool, under a steady cascade, like in some outtake from that old TV show, *Fantasy Island.*

Eamon couldn't get over his luck. Not only had he married the woman of his dreams, but the sex was great, too. It made him feel glad to be alive, absolutely. It was wondrous to meet your match, to be fulfilled. He knew not everyone was so lucky. In fact, he was sure most people never found what he was experiencing with Mary, and no one had to tell him about the terrible frustration that lay behind all that unrequited love.

He built a small campfire on the beach one cool, moonlit night. They bundled themselves up in sweaters and passed a bottle of wine back and forth. It was beautiful and mysterious under the stars at the end of the world.

"I wish it would never end," Mary said. "I wish we never had to go back."

"I know what you mean," Eamon said. "I'm not exactly looking forward to returning to Fells Point and those two complaining cats. That's not even to mention Pinkus."

"I wanted to talk to you about him," Mary said, referring to Daniel P. Pinkus, Eamon's tenant for the past six years. "I really think we should give him notice, now that I'm moving in."

"It's going to be tough," Eamon said. "You don't know him. He's going to take it hard. He's a bit odd. He really feels it's his place, you know. Not only does he take care of the cats for me, but he cleans house and grocery-shops and does all the cooking, besides. And, to top it off, he's always early with the rent."

"If it's all right with you, I'm going to give him notice the minute we return. I think we really need the privacy."

"I can't believe it's almost over," Eamon said. "I can't even imagine returning to work. To walk back into that sordid old world again."

"What were you working on before we left?"

"Lately, it's all been cyberporn," the postal inspector said. "Bunko and I have been going after pedophiles on the internet. Scumbags who've been using these new computer bulletin boards to troll for kids. It's a whole new ball game with this electronic mail. Stuff didn't even exist ten years ago. God only knows what's next."

"What kind of people do these pedophiles turn out to be?" the homicide detective asked. "Are they usually monsters?"

"No, worse than that," Eamon said. "Usually they're just ordinary people with extraordinary secrets. I can't tell you how many times it's a popular teacher or an outgoing Rotarian or a well-liked pediatrician."

"Yes, the banality of evil," Mary said, nodding her head knowingly. "That's how Hannah Arendt termed it after looking into the eyes of Adolf Eichmann, the Nazi Gestapo leader."

Eamon was always surprised by Mary's breadth of knowledge; he'd never heard of Hannah Arendt, but no way he was going to let on. "Is it the same way in your line of work, too?" he asked. "Do the killers always turn out to be unremarkable?"

"Actually, we see a lot of economic crime," she said, considering it. "We get our fair share of drug murders and bungled robberies. But we also see something else on a regular basis, something a bit more disturbing, really. I'm talking about the career criminal, the sociopath who couldn't care less. These sickos are really something to see, Eamon. These predators kill and rape and mutilate without a scintilla of conscience. They just aren't living in our world, as far as I can tell."

"Maybe it's the way they were brought up. Most of them have never gotten a break, have never known a normal, loving home environment. A good deal of them have been physically abused. Not to mention family histories that are rife with substance abuse and chronic unemployment."

"I don't buy it," Mary said rather forcefully. "I used to wonder about all that sociological garbage, too. But, let me tell you, when you meet these beasts up close and personal, you realize real quick that they would've turned out the same warped way, no matter what. These people just don't *feel* or *think* the way normal people do. Believe me, it has nothing to do with their upbringing. These men were sociopathic as little kids. These are the same delinquents who were torturing neighborhood pets and extorting lunch money from their classmates in kindergarten."

"I'm not so sure," he said, trying to fathom it in the serene moonlight of Kauai.

"Think of it another way, then," Mary said, still arguing her point. "Think of all those kids who come from violent, impoverished, dysfunctional homes who turn out all right. Think of that. If what you say is true, that these sociological factors play such a big role, why is it, then, that so many kids come out of those impossible situations just fine?"

He loved her tenacious, argumentative mind. Just talking to her was a kick, such full-fledged competition. They both had fathers who'd been cops, so they were used to the shop talk, to seeing the world in terms of good guys and bad guys, of black and white. Eamon had the sneaking, undeniable suspicion that his new wife was just a little bit smarter than he was. It didn't bother him at all. After all, he was the lucky fellow who got to put his arm around her in the cool Hawaiian night. There was no one else, just the two of them in the glow of the moon and the dying campfire, just red-hot embers at the end of the world.

"So what's on the itinerary for tomorrow?" she asked in a sleepy voice, her head resting on his shoulder.

"I've got a little surprise for you," he said, delighted that he'd been able to keep it from her.

"What is it?" she said, perking up. "I thought we've already done everything there is to do. We've kayaked on the Hanalei River. We've gone horseback riding. We even did that snorkeling cruise to the reefs. I mean, what on earth is left, Eamon?"

"Well, now we're going to take a helicopter tour of the island," he announced happily.

"Oh," she said, her enthusiasm draining away.

"I thought it would be something to remember," he said, trying to rally her.

"It's not that," she said, sounding nervous.

"Oh, no, you're not thinking of that crazy fortune teller again." Every time he'd wanted to do anything with the slightest risk factor, she'd get panicky, thinking of that strange face reader they'd met in front of the Royal Hawaiian. "You had the same bad feeling before we went snorkeling, remember? And look how that turned out. We had a fabulous time."

"Maybe we shouldn't press our luck," she said. "I still can't shake what that Kea woman said. That stuff about how death was all around you. It's so spooky. Why did she have to say that?"

"Who knows," Eamon said wearily, realizing he was fighting a losing battle.

5

Deke always made Ray nervous. It didn't matter that they were no longer sharing a cell in the joint. The man could still scare, even if all they were sharing these days was a red vinyl booth in a Fells Point diner. Deke had started ranting and raving from the moment he sat down. It seemed there were some Japanese motorcycles parked outside.

"Dang, I'd sure like to know which faggots own the sushi specials." Deke scanned the diner with typical menace in his gray eyes. "Like to kick their fruity asses. Show them what's what. This is still the United States of America, damn straight. Goddamn yuppie scum buying those rice burners."

Ray knew better than to express a contrary opinion. Deke was the coldest, meanest dude alive. Ray had seen him slit a black guard's throat with a filed-down toothbrush just because the poor son of a bitch had said good morning to Deke on the chow line. Being that he was a member of the White Supremacists— and concerned about his steel-balled reputation— Deke went berserk. It was over in less than thirty seconds. Of course none of the other cons snitched. One less hack was nothing to get too upset about;

even the nigger posses didn't see it as a black–white thing.

A tired, bedraggled-looking waitress handed them menus. "You know what that bitch needs, don't you?" Deke said after she left. Ray just nodded, waiting for him to calm all the way down. The menu seemed to do the trick; Deke pored through the choice-heavy document like he was going through court transcripts. Ray understood, though. It hadn't even been a full month since Deke got his walking papers. He still wasn't used to life on the outside—all those choices, all those possibilities.

"I'm going with the Tex-Mex platter," Deke told the waitress after a goodly amount of time. "And give me a plate of them jalapeño peppers on the side. And a couple of beers, too."

"What kind of beer?" she asked, her pen at the ready.

"Beer is beer," Deke said, and the waitress had the good sense not to debate him.

Ray ordered what he always ordered: a double bacon cheeseburger platter. In fact, he basically just lived on burgers and pizza. He couldn't remember the last time he had a vegetable, at least anything other than a slice of onion or tomato. Of course, he also supplemented his diet with those supervitamin drinks that he whipped up in the blender at home.

"Dang, nothing like a beer," Deke said, taking his first greedy draft. "The only thing I ever regretted about my time in the joint was missing out on regular suds."

"What about regular pussy?" Ray asked.

"I got my share," Deke said, smiling like a pervert. "Some of them queens could make themselves up real nice. Mascara and panties and everything."

"Shit, you couldn't pay me to do those fuck boys," Ray said, forgetting for a moment about Deke's rule against the f-word and the s-word.

"Watch your dang mouth," Deke said, glaring, "or I might just have to watch it for you."

That was a slip Ray wouldn't make again. He forgot how weird Deke got about those two words. Something his mother taught him or something. Still, Ray couldn't see it. Not doing without pussy on a regular basis. Sure, he usually paid for it, but in some respects that was the best way to go. Girls made like they liked it, moaning and shit, the whole nine yards. Made him feel good, at least for a little while. That was the one thing you couldn't get on the farm. You could get everything else at Hagerstown. You wanted a pint of Wild Turkey, no problem. Shit, there were boys with heavy smack habits in the joint. All you had to do was have the cash. Shit, you could even buy a real working gun, if that was what you really wanted and if you were willing to do the heavy additional time that the violation brought. Yeah, you could buy drugs and hardware and even a little ass if you wanted. Prostitution was a big business, with pimps and enforcers, with hacks looking the other way. The problem was, Ray wasn't much interested in the kind of ass they were selling.

"Things sure are different on the outside since the last time I was out," Deke was saying. "Seems like all the cars look the same now. Nothing stands out anymore. Know what I mean? And the women all got that short Peter Pan hair. I notice that. None of that long, sexy, to-the-waist stuff that I used to like. Goddamn world."

"When was the last time you were out, Deke?"

"The time I busted out of the Maryland Pen. That's the one located on Forrest Street, right downtown. Gosh dang—the summer of 1979. I'd just turned thirty then. I remember it like it was yesterday. A sweet, sweet memory, brother. One of those memories that sustained me, if you know what I'm saying here.

"Anyhow, and I won't go into details here, I escaped through this air vent in the laundry. It wasn't like I'd planned it, really. It was more like I saw my opportunity and grabbed it by the balls. It was a beautiful, beautiful night, brother. Real warm but not too sticky yet. And the funny thing is, instead of hightailing it out of the city, I made my way to this disco. Called Penny's Place, if memory serves correct. Walked right in there in my prison blues. Nobody even blinked. And I started dancing with this little tittie queen. And, believe me, pardner, it didn't take me too long to get her in the alleyway. Told her I had some weed or some other lie—I forget now. Busted her all up, believe me. All them years without the female organ, as it were."

Ray knew Deke meant he raped her and probably left her for dead, besides. Deke was the coldest of the cold. But he had his uses, of course. And it wasn't like Ray couldn't imagine Deke's frustration. Deke had been put in a reformatory when he was fourteen or some such shit. And the man had probably been out, altogether, no more than three years since that time. He was closing in on forty-eight years old now. And he didn't look so good, truth be told. There were sad, dark bags under the menacing gray eyes now. His mangy blond hair was thinning badly up front, even if he did hold it back in a ponytail. And he'd lost some weight in the last year or so. Not only that, there was something about his skin, the way it had gone slack, like it was just hanging on him, the way all his tattoos seemed deflated. Deke just didn't look the same. Not that he wasn't still a mean motherfucker. Not that he didn't still have that hard, wiry look. Not that those colorless prison tattoos still didn't unnerve a person. Ray knew there wasn't too many people who could endure the pain of homemade art. Deke had the sign of the beast—666, right from Revelations—carved over his heart. There was a bunch of other stuff, too. There was a headless Statue of Liberty. There was a pair of dice showing snake eyes. There were the usual swastikas and skull and crossbones. Not to mention the official Harley-Davidson insignia. No, the man still looked evil mean, that was for shit sure. But still, Ray thought he looked different, somehow.

"Tasty," he said, digging into his plate of Tex-Mex. "Can't get over how good the food is since I got out."

The man has no taste buds left, that's what it is, Ray thought. He shook Tabasco all over the slop. It was just your usual refried beans and ground beef, but you'd never know it from the way Deke was going on about it. "Give my compliments to the chef," he actually told that poor bedraggled waitress. And then he was popping those hot jalapeños like they were Milk Duds or something. "Incidentally," he said, shoving more slop into his face, "I got that special order for you. She's a full-working piece now, brother."

Ray knew he was talking about the Colt M-16. "Where's she at?"

"Already put it in the trunk of your car, pardner," he said, smiling wickedly. "Nothing to worry about."

"How'd you know which car was mine?" Ray asked, wondering how he got the trunk open, besides.

"I'm keeping my eye on you," Deke said, winking.

Ray looked at him sharply, wondering how much more he knew. The man was full of surprises, no denying it. He was going to have to be a lot more careful around Deke. He should've known better than to underestimate him.

"So what are you keeping from me?" Deke said, continuing to smile like a fiend. "I'd hate to think that my bosom buddy was holding out. Gosh, that sure would be hard to swallow."

Ray couldn't wait to put some distance on the motherfucker. "I'd never hold out on you, Deke. You know that. We're like brothers, man."

"Then what's the heavy artillery for?"

"I'm just preparing myself. Just in case. You know, in case something happens my way."

"Then who's your new friend, then? The big, fat, hairy bear I see you around with? You planning something with him?"

Shit, he knew about Jack. The man was good at sniffing out things, that was for shit sure. He had to get Deke off the subject. "No, I ain't planning nothing with that jerk, believe me. But I do got something for you. A big-time job, the kind of thing you're good at. I need someone taken out, removed from this world."

"Oh, yeah?" Deke said, interest shading his face. "Who's the chump?"

"A real son of a bitch," Ray said, feeling the anger rise in him, the way it always did when he thought of that dumbshit postal inspector. "The prick that's responsible for me doing hard time. Believe me, it's personal."

"This the guy that sent you to the farm? The guy who made you serve all your federal time at Hagerstown?"

The prick had arranged for Ray to serve out his time in state prison when he could've been sent to one of those cushy Club Feds instead. Ray's lawyer couldn't believe it. The state had him on aggravated assault, there was no way out of that. But he would've done only six months at the farm, tops, if it weren't for the postal inspector butting in. The prick gets him on a bunch of counts of sending obscene and threatening mail. Doesn't understand anything. Doesn't have a fucking clue about him and Jill. Thinks he was harassing her. Like Ray would hurt the woman he loves. So instead of letting him serve out his time at the fed resort in Montgomery, Pennsylvania, the prick makes sure that Ray has to serve his federal time at Hagerstown, one of the nastiest of the state holes. Without Deke there to protect him, Ray would not have made it through the first week.

"Here, take a look at this," Ray said, taking out the newspaper clipping and handing it to Deke. "I want him dead, the hardest way you know how."

"Well, ain't she might tasty-looking," Deke said, eyeing the picture of the happy couple. "I definitely want me some of that yummy pie."

Ray couldn't believe it when he saw the wedding announcement in the *Baltimore Sun*. At first he was just angry, reminded of all that Lieutenant Wearie had cost him in his life. If that prick hadn't entered into things, why, him and Jill would still be together, for one thing. And he never would have had to do all that hard time on the farm. Two whole wasted years, years that passed like slow death, just dreaming of the day—the day when he could reclaim what was rightly his. And then to come across that announcement, to see that smug bastard's face again and to realize that he hadn't got what was coming to him. Well, now it was payback time, you'd better believe it.

"Dang, he's marrying a cop," Deke said, reading the newspaper copy. "Says this Mary chick is a homicide detective, of all things. How about that? Well, it seems we already got something in common. We both know a little something about killing people."

"I don't care about her," Ray said. "I just want Wearie taken out."

"Says she's keeping her last name," Deke said, like he didn't hear Ray. "Now isn't that just like one of these women of the nineties?"

"You'll also notice that it says they're honeymooning in Hawaii right now. They won't be back for another week yet. Wearie's got a little place in Fells Point."

Deke took out a pouch of tobacco and a pack of papers. Rolling his own cigarettes was just one more holdover from the joint. "Let's make it a twofer," he said after a while. "Two for the price of one. It'll be more fun that way, seeing that I've never delivered a cop before."

"Whatever," Ray said. "So long as you deliver Wearie to his maker."

"I'm telling you, I'm going to enjoy this, brother. I'm going to tie him all up and do his little pudding pie right in front of him. Yes, sir, I'm going to make him watch and then I'm going to cut his throat."

"I don't want to know about it," Ray said, reaching into the front pocket of his jeans for the roll of C-notes. "I'm giving you five G's now. And five more when you complete the job."

Ray passed him the fat roll under the Formica table. "Dang, it's nice doing business with you," Deke said, smiling obscenely. "I see this as the first of many such mutually beneficial transactions."

Fat chance, thought Ray. *I'll be long gone by then, motherfucker.*

Ray sure hadn't liked giving Deke all that money. But there was no other way, really. He needed Wearie taken care of. Otherwise, there was a chance he'd be able to tie him to everything later. Wearie was the last of the loose ends, as far as Ray could tell. He sure wouldn't want to be in that postal inspector's shoes. Deke would show no mercy, that was for shit sure. Ray would sure be glad to get away from Deke. There was no way he could know about the cabin. Not a chance. Ray had bought the place while Deke was finishing up his time on the farm. Man, it just gave him the willies thinking about Deke and how much the man already knew. How'd he know which car to put the rifle in? Deke must have been following him around. So he probably knew about Ray's apartment in Fells Point as well. He probably was trying to figure out Ray's net worth. Deke knew Ray's mother had left him some money, and it would only be a matter of time before he'd start applying the pressure. Guys like Deke never let up. They squeezed and they squeezed until there was nothing left. But Deke would never find Ray at the cabin, and nobody else would either. That was the beautiful part.

Ray started thinking about Jill again. Sometimes it

was hard for him to get a good picture of her in his head. She was beauty and purity itself, man. So different from all the sluts he usually found himself with. It was weird but he found it hard to even imagine her in the physical way, with his hard body on hers. He could think about practically every other woman like that. But they were all sluts and whores anyway. With Jill, it was so different, the way they could talk, really talk, the way those conversations could just go on and on and you would really feel alive and special. Everything was better when Jill was around. The sky was bluer, the sun shined brighter, even the burgers tasted better. There was only one Jill. And without her, there was really no other reason to go on. Life was gray and dead and endless without her presence. He tried to keep his special memories of her alive, to call them back, to remember and savor all the details. He especially liked to call back the night that they went to the movies together, just like a real couple, just the way it was supposed to be. He felt proud walking into the theater with his arm around her, the way other people were enviously checking out his woman. It was the finest night of his life, like magic or something. After he had tasted that, it became impossible to go back to his ordinary, crummy old life again.

He hoped Jill would like the way he was looking these days. No longer was he some dumpy, out-of-shape nobody. Even after they let him out of Hagerstown, he kept up with the weights, joining one of those fancy fitness centers. He definitely liked checking out the leotards and thongs over there, all those sweaty sluts. It made him horny just to think of all that flesh action. Those bitches wanted it just as bad as he did, even if they didn't like admitting it. He needed to get laid. It had been a week since he'd paid that ugly street bitch for the blowjob. It would be good when he could stop paying for it. With Jill, it would be a whole new experience, with the love and the sex going together, the way it was all supposed to be. Still, he was real horny right now. He mulled over his options. He could always go back to his apartment and take out the old magazine collection or put a videocassette on. But jerking off could sure get old in a hurry. Of course, he could go down to the park and scope out some runaway. You almost always found some pathetic, vulnerable young kid sitting by her lonesome on one of the park benches. These girls were always broke and sad and far from home. All you had to do was talk to them like you cared about them, maybe buy them some food, whatever it took to earn their trust. Then he'd get them to come back to his place with a promise of some pot or a free bed to sleep on. No big deal. Then you slipped a Mickey into their drink or something and did whatever you wanted while they were passed out. It was amazing the kind of powerful drugs you could buy over the counter. At Hagerstown, he'd listened and learned, and now he was an expert in the science of pharmacology, along with a few other interesting things as well.

Still, going down to the park to nail runaways was work. It meant being nice to them and listening to all their tired, unhappy shit. He'd have to go through the motions, at least until he could get them back to his place.

In the end, Ray decided to just find himself another street bitch. Paying for it just seemed like the cheapest way to go, all things considered.

6

Daniel P. Pinkus's obsessive-compulsive disorder was worse than ever. He desperately needed to get his doctor to refill the Prozac, which had been such a help in the past. But Dr. Wilkenson insisted that Pinkus come in for a full workup before he'd write out another prescription, just to make sure that prolonged use of the drug hadn't caused any adverse effect on his liver or kidneys. But that was the last thing Pinkus needed to put himself through. Why, the worrying and waiting for test results would've destroyed him. Not that he wasn't already a mess. The OCD had taken over his life, turning each day into a torturous, ritualistic nightmare.

He could not wash his hands enough. Microscopic germs were everywhere, no longer invisible to his eyes. Not only were they breeding in the bathrooms and in the cats' litter box, but they were taking over the refrigerator and the countertops and the floors. No matter how much he scrubbed himself and the house, they'd reappear, taking up residence on his toothbrush or in the soap dish or on the towel he used that morning. He changed the linens every day, he bought latex gloves by the dozen, and he washed his hands until they bled. All to no avail. The germs and the voices would not leave him alone.

The voices were the worst part. All the sick, sick words that assaulted him at all times of the day. Relentless thoughts about disease and death. A litany of AIDS, cancer, heart attacks, and new flesh-eating viruses. He suffered constantly, in a state of perpetual, crippling anxiety. He fretted about leprosy and syphilis and Ebola and *E. coli,* no matter how absurd it might seem to himself, even. The voices never let go of him, haunting his sleep, following him to the ends of consciousness.

If that was not enough, he was further tormented by fitful, fearful visions. He didn't want to hurt anybody, especially not himself, but sometimes the voices whispered the unthinkable. Often they started up when he was in the kitchen getting dinner ready, while he was using the cutlery. Or sometimes it happened when he was clipping some interesting story out of the newspaper, using the scissors. It was horrible, absolutely horrible. He couldn't handle a sharp object these days, whether it was a steak knife or a sewing needle, without the demonic voices urging him on, telling him to just do everyone a favor. Why, oh why, would they tell him to hurt himself like that?

Oh God, he didn't want to think about it. He just had to get some more Prozac, somehow. Then the voices would subside, would be rendered harmless again. He wondered what OCD people did in the old days before the advent of the wonder drugs. Did they just pick up that gleaming kitchen knife then? Was that the only way to alleviate the pain? Was there no other way to dull it, to make it go away?

He had to think of something else, he just had to. Eamon and Mary would be home from their honeymoon soon. He hoped it would all work out. He didn't want to leave the little row house in Fells Point, home sweet home for the last six years. He liked the fact that Eamon was never around, always at that silly job of his. Pinkus had finally gotten things just the way he wanted them. Why did Eamon have to go and marry this Mary woman? Why, they hardly knew her. Pinkus knew Pacino and Brando were upset, too. Mary was not a cat person, you could just tell. And she would probably have her own way of doing everything. Who even knew what kind of odd habits she might have? Maybe she wasn't clean enough. He didn't even want to think of all those new germs in the house. God, it was going to be difficult getting used to someone else. Eamon hadn't even considered his feelings. He just went and married this strange woman without even asking his permission.

But maybe everything would turn out all right, Pinkus thought, trying to think of the good side. This Mary was a policewoman, after all. At least they would always feel safe in the house now. And, who knew, maybe she would turn out to be a positive influence on Eamon. Because it wasn't like Eamon didn't need some help. All that drinking and carrying on. He used to be so bad in the old days, bringing home all kinds of horrid strays. How many times had Pinkus got up in the morning and found himself face-to-face with another one of Eamon's one-night stands? It happened all the time. These terrible girls who were always half naked, frying up bacon and eggs in the kitchen. And they always just took food from his side of the refrigerator, without asking or anything. No manners whatsoever. Pinkus couldn't even imagine where Eamon met these girls. Oh, well. Maybe this Mary woman would be a change for the better at that.

Deke almost missed life on the inside. On the outside, he was nobody. But in the joint, he was important. Being a White Supremacist meant a certain amount of respect. Rules applied. People knew better than to mess with him. Even the bulls understood the value of a clique system. But out here, in the real world, he was treated like everybody else, like all the other Marty Morons.

Someday he would have to learn to stop calling the guards bulls. It was a throwback to the old days. He'd been negotiating his way through gladiator school since he was fourteen. Now you called the guards hacks or maybe even supercops. But when he came up through the ranks, they were always bulls, for better or worse. And mostly for the worse. Deke thought that a lot of them bulls belonged in the cages with the cons. They were no better, really—uniform or no uniform. Dang, some of them bulls were total psychos, brother.

Still, there was a lot he missed about the joint. There weren't a whole lot of decisions to make, like on the outside. Bedtime and mealtimes were set, nothing to think about. You wore blue denim every single day, just like the next guy, no better and no different. It was a life, like it or not, that you could count on. Tuesdays were melted cheese sandwiches for lunch and meatloaf for dinner. Thursdays were ham and cheese and spaghetti. You didn't have to worry yourself with making all these dumb choices all the time. Same with the TV. You just watched what was on, whatever the niggers had already chosen among themselves. Deke didn't mind. At least you always knew where you stood.

Freedom was a damn hard thing to get used to. Deke still got up at five-thirty A.M. every morning, buzzer or no buzzer. It was just one of those things. And he still made coffee the old way, with a packet of instant and warm tap water, even though he could've bought a kettle now. And in terms of clothes, he just made do with white T-shirts and blue jeans, same as always. But it was all different anyway, as much as he tried to keep it the same. He missed his brothers, the camaraderie, the sense that you were one of many. Outside, he felt like a loner, that he was invisible to everybody else. Dang, people just looked right through him, like he didn't damn well exist.

At night, it was hard to sleep. He missed the sounds: the low, hushed voices; the mass snoring; the clanking of beds; the flush of toilets; that strange, constant trickling of water; the total lack of silence. Dang, it was all that he'd ever known. Ever since the boys' diagnostic center. Fourteen years old, the damn judge saying, "I hope you get the help you need, son." His foster parents not even showing up at the hearing. And then things going from bad to worse to forget about it. Raping that older kid to show him what's what, to survive, brother. Getting rung up on that one. Going from the diagnostic center to Baltimore City Correctional. So what if that joint was medium security. He was still only fifteen at that point. But then he was mixing it up with older cons, learning the ropes. He had to knife that son of a bitch at BCC—no choice there, brother. It was either him or Deke. All them years being tacked on, though. Another black robe telling him that it was for his own good. Never had a chance, never even had a proper lawyer. Always some wet-behind-the-ears public defender telling him to plead guilty, not to waste everybody's time.

Then, at long last, he finally got chewed up and spit out of the system. But by that time, he was twenty-five years old. He'd already spent almost half his life behind bars. What did he know about getting a job or getting along with the Marty Morons out there? Not much, brother. Fortunately, he met up with some of his former cellmates, and they helped set him up. Joined a cycle gang. Part of Satan's Circle now. Learned how to fix bikes, not to mention riding them, even. Got semiregular work in a Harley shop. Became a full-time hog and a part-time dealer. Sure, started in with the drugs, the whole biker scene. The hole-in-the-wall bars, the slutty skanks, the methamphetamine, the kick-ass fights. Prison had sure taught him well; nobody had to tell Deke how to take care of himself in a bar scuffle. You released your blade and tried to put the other guy into that other world. 'Cause if you didn't finish the job, you could bet he was going to, brother. There were no losers in a hog contest, just casualties; that was a fact.

He went from dealing meth to hot-wiring cars. Then he was hitting mom-and-pop joints and all-night liquor stores. It was like a natural progression, a sense that it was all destined to happen in the way it did. Finding himself in that bank, that stupid old man reaching for his gun, like déjà vu or something. Like a bad dream he'd been having since childhood. The old guard lived, but it didn't stop them from throwing the book at Deke. This time they put him in supermax, over at the Maryland Correctional Adjustment Center, which was pretty close to full-time solitary confinement. Dang, they kept the lights on twenty-four hours a day. You got one hour a week in the exercise yard. You ate alone in your cell. The bulls made your life hell; it was the way they retrained you. Deke put in four long, hard years at MCAC. Then they made the mistake of thinking he'd been rehabilitated and transferred him in the Maryland Pen. That was where he made his big breakout. But if he had it to do all over, he'd never have crawled through that air vent. After they corralled him again, they put him back in MCAC. And for the next ten years, he rotted away with almost no human contact. The bulls wouldn't even talk to him. No TV, no radio, no human voices. It changed a man. It filled him with a kind of hate that was hard to explain. Every time you thought you'd hated enough, you surprised yourself and found another wretched layer of the poison. It turned out a man could reach all the way down into himself and find the strength to hate indefinitely.

Deke was grateful later on, to be sure, when they sent him to Roxbury and then on to Hagerstown. Dang, he'd been in every joint in the state of Maryland. But after his second stint at MCAC, he was all done with trying to escape. Life was about survival, no more, no less. He did his time, careful to stay out of trouble, which just meant he wasn't getting caught at it anymore. Not that it much mattered. The parole board was not about to make an exception in his case. But, finally, after maybe thirty years in the joint, they had no choice. He'd served his full time. Deke was forty-eight years old and dying on account of his liver. The prison doctor said he had some kind of bad hepatitis. He told Deke not to drink on the outside and to take it real easy. One day at a time, the quack said.

Ain't that a hoot, Deke thought, taking another hit from the pint of bourbon. He was in a fancy-smancy Lexus driving to that postal inspector's place in Fells Point. These new cars were really something; so much had changed since the last time he was out on the road. He couldn't get over the wipers, how you could select different speeds and everything now. It sure came in handy on a night like this, with an off-again, on-again kind of rain. Every few seconds, the wipers swiped the drizzle off the windshield, bringing a smile to Deke's leathery face. Modern technology, brother, it sure was something. The only thing that didn't seem to change was how easy it was to borrow somebody else's car; must've taken him all of thirty seconds to get behind the wheel of the Lexus.

He liked that up-to-date heater, too. You could select just the exact temperature you wanted. He thought it might be broken, though, the way he had it up to eighty-eight degrees and by the fact that it didn't seem all that warm to him. He was getting a little sick of this cold, wet February weather. Maybe when he got done with that postal inspector and his honey, he'd go down to Florida for some R&R. Because he sure hadn't been feeling like himself lately. Maybe that quack in the prison infirmary hadn't been lying about that hepatitis stuff after all. Heck, what was he thinking? He was getting soft, that's all it was.

He had to get a grip on it, had to concentrate on the business at hand. He wanted to take a look at the postal inspector's house, just to get a good feel for the layout. Later on, it might be useful. Maybe he'd mess the place up a bit, just to screw with their heads. Get them thinking scared, get them off balance. Maybe the inspector's wife had left some of her underthings behind; dang, he could do a real number with her panties and bras, give that nineties chick something to think about right there. Not taking her husband's name, damn cunt.

As Deke pulled alongside the curb, he wondered what Ray's angle really was. That boy seemed real secretive lately. Deke was sure he was up to something. But he wasn't too worried; he'd get to the bottom of it, one way or the other. Then again, maybe it was all about revenge. Maybe Ray had learned to hate like Deke. Maybe he'd reached down in the bottom of his being, too, and found the same bad muck Deke had.

The house was dark, just the way it was supposed to be. He took out his special locksmith's tools, picks you could buy at almost any hardware nowadays. It took him no more than a minute of fiddling before he had the door open and he was feeling for the light switch.

Deke loved breaking into a house. You were entering someone else's private domain, finding out about all their little secrets. He'd start with the living room and kitchen, the more public spaces, as it were, before working his way into the bedrooms, where all the good stuff was sure to be. He was practically sexually excited at the prospect of snooping through their bureau drawers. You never knew what you'd find there. Were there dirty magazines about? Did they smoke reefer? Did they have a vibrator buried under the undies? It made him feel like some sort of detective, the way he gathered clues and figured things out. He wasn't just breaking into their house, he was coming into their damn lives, brother.

Deke was standing in the living room, admiring

how neat and tidy the whole place was, when a light snapped on down the hall and somebody called out, "Eamon? Mary? Are you back already?" At first Deke was a little surprised, but the thought of getting out of there never entered his mind. Surprise had already turned into anticipation, the way it always did with him. A moment later, some scrawny guy in a bathrobe was looking at him real funny and saying, "Who are you? Do I know you?"

Deke said, real calmlike, "I think you got it all backwards, friend. I think it is I who doesn't know you."

This seemed to throw off the scrawny runt. "Well, I don't think I understand," he said, all flustered-like. "I'm Daniel Pinkus and this is my house."

"Well, I'm glad we got that all straightened out now," Deke said, enjoying it that much more.

"Are you some friend of Eamon's?" the runt said. "Is that what's going on here? Because it wouldn't surprise me in the least."

Deke just smiled at the unlucky stranger and reached for the nearest thing, which happened to be a knifelike letter opener that had been left on the coffee table.

7

It wasn't an inexpensive proposition, at two hundred dollars per person, but Eamon thought the forty-five-minute helicopter tour of the island of Kauai might offer up the memory of a lifetime. Mary was far less enthusiastic, as she seemed unable to forget that strange face reader's chilling words.

"You can't spend your life worrying about every little thing," Eamon told her when they arrived at Burns Field. "Besides, nothing's going to happen to us."

"Doesn't anything faze you?" Mary asked as they entered the small terminal building.

"Not a damn thing," he said, his voice rich with confidence.

"Do you believe in God?" Mary asked.

"What a funny thing to ask," he said, pausing in front of the ticket counter. "But as you know, I'm your typical guilt-ridden Irish Catholic, even if I haven't been to confession in years. Still, I have my faith, such as it is."

"But do you *believe?*"

"I believe that we have a flight to catch," he said, grinning and turning to face the ticket agent, an attractive blonde with an eye-fluttering, how-can-I-help-you? smile.

The agent took his VISA card and asked if they would mind signing the release papers. "It's for insurance reasons," she explained.

"Why, have there been any problems?" Mary asked, looking alarmed.

"Oh, no, not at all," the blonde answered, as she held her gaze on Eamon. "Captain Bob is the best."

"Captain Bob?" Mary repeated, unbelieving.

"Excuse me, I mean Captain Dover," she said, still lavishing serious attention on Eamon. "In fact, he's just outside waiting for you. Use gate two; it'll bring you right onto the tarmac."

As they approached the gate, Mary said, "Did you see the way that woman was looking at you? I thought her pupils might explode from all that effort."

"Come on. It wasn't that bad, was it?"

Mary rolled her eyes. "I'll bet you're just used to women looking at you like that. Tell the truth now."

"Well, I confess I haven't exactly been neglected," he said somewhat sheepishly.

"Let me guess: you were the high-school quarterback and dated the prettiest cheerleader. It's been that way always, hasn't it?"

"I have to correct you there," he said, smiling at the thought. "I was the second-string quarterback. But I must admit to dating my fair share of cheerleaders."

"And did you step in and win the big game in front of several thousand cheering local fans?"

"Actually, yes, now that you mention it. Last game of the season against our arch rival, Ward Melville. It was homecoming day. The whole deal. Our starter, Jay Harper, got injured in the first quarter. I threw four touchdowns coming off the bench, including the game winner with only six seconds left on the clock."

Mary rolled her eyes again. "You're serious, aren't you?"

"I was born under a lucky star, darling."

"There's so much I don't know about you," she said, shaking her head.

He knew what she meant; after all, they'd known each other only six months before tying the knot. But, thinking about it, it was strange how everything seemed to work out in his life. It had been that way always, as far back as he could remember. It was like someone was watching over him, guiding him and protecting him.

Captain Bob was waving for them in front of a sleek, new-looking Agusta A109 twin-engine helicopter. He was a slightly overweight, khaki-clad fellow with a sunburned, unshaven face. *"Aloha, malihinis,"* he said, greeting them. "That means welcome, newcomers. Are you all set for the ride of your life?"

"Where's everybody else?" Mary asked, pointing to the big, empty, sleek copter, which looked like it could hold seven or eight passengers. "Do we have it all to ourselves?"

"Oh, no, we're not taking the Agusta," said the genial pilot. "Since there wasn't much of a demand this morning, we'll be climbing aboard Little Nellie."

Little Nellie was right behind the sleek Agusta. Mary's face dropped at the sight of the no-frills three-seater, but she held her tongue. Eamon had to admit that it was a rather ancient-looking single-rotor craft, not the thing to instill confidence. Captain Bob insisted that they strap on bulky orange life vests, explaining that it was a new regulation for copter tours passing over water; Eamon only wondered why Captain Bob didn't don one.

Little Nellie made some racket lifting off, wheezing and cranking and *ka-chopping* until somehow finally managing to become airborne. Eamon thought there might be NASA rockets that made less noise and commotion. But whatever trepidation they initially experienced soon dissipated as they sped forward over a paradisal green world. They flew close to the ground, overtaking fields of sugarcane and pineapple and macadamia nuts, close enough to make out the farm workers and harvesting machines, until Captain Bob hit the throttle and sent them soaring up, up, up and away. Suddenly, in one exhilarating burst of speed, they were several thousand feet up, with a wild, topographic view of the island, making out deep blue rivers and sun-splashed hills and rugged coastline. Kauai was a kaleidoscope of terrain and weather patterns; cloud-blurred mountaintops reigning over rainbow-misted valleys, patchwork fields coming right up to the lip of the white-crested Pacific.

Captain Bob did his best to give a running narration, shouting over the constant chatter of the whirlybird. As they entered the Waimea Canyon, he told them that it was thirty-six hundred feet deep, two miles wide, and ten miles long. "It's the Grand Canyon of the Pacific!" he yelled back, clearly enthralled with the sight himself, even though he'd obviously flown through it countless times. They followed the Waimea River, coming right up alongside the awesome canyon walls, chasms of Arizona reds and browns looking every bit like a match for the real Grand Canyon. It really was something, and Mary squeezed Eamon's hand from the sheer wonder of it all.

Minutes later, they emerged from the spectacular canyon to the thrill of the Na Pali coast. The sheer, breathtaking cliffs looked down on bleached, peopleless beaches and crashing surf. Eamon thought it looked just like the craggy coast of his ancestors, that same bright, mossy, emerald green.

"Let's take it down for a better look!" Captain Bob said over the clatter. As they descended, the chopper suddenly started to shake violently. "Oh, shit," Captain Bob said, as the whole instrument panel blinked red. They were several hundred feet above the raging water when the chopper's blade completely stopped *ka-chopping*. "Oh my God!" Mary screamed.

It was strange, but as they went into that heart-stopping nosedive, Eamon became absolutely focused. It felt like slow motion to him, like something he still had control over. Only one thing mattered in the eerie calm: getting his wife out. That was all he knew as Little Nellie spiraled down.

They hit the water hard, jarred like toy people. The front windshield shattered and ocean water began to pour into the cabin. Eamon knew they didn't have a second to lose. Before he could even check Mary, who was still moaning from the impact along with Captain Bob, he knew he had to get the copter door open, give them a way out. He braced himself and kicked it with everything he had, coming up against the unmovable gravity of the ocean. He kicked again and again, furiously, until it gave, and then he was helping unbuckle Mary, getting her out, pushing her away to safety. Captain Bob said he was all right, told Eamon to get out, too, that he'd be right behind him.

Mary was bobbing in the rough sea in her bright orange life vest, just a few yards from the copter. *Thank God, thank God,* he thought, seeing her, realizing it was all going to be okay. The shore was not far, only fifty yards away or so, easily swimmable. Suddenly, though, Mary was screaming something and pointing behind him. He turned, only to see that the copter was sinking, with only its tail exposed and with Captain Bob nowhere to be seen. Something had gone wrong, terribly wrong.

Eamon struggled to free himself from the bulky confines of his vest. He had to get the pilot out before the copter sank completely. With his heavy-soled shoes supplying propulsion, he dived down to the copter's cabin, carefully maneuvering himself past the huge bent-up propeller. Fortunately, the water was absolutely crystal clear and Eamon had no trouble getting to him. He was still seated behind the controls, totally submerged. Eamon had no idea if he was dead or alive—bubbles were coming from his open mouth—but he immediately made out the problem:

the pilot's seat belt was jammed. Eamon grabbed at a shard of broken glass and cut through the nylon to free him.

But if someone asked him what happened next, Eamon would have to truthfully say that he didn't remember. He knew he was running out of air and that he was struggling like crazy to get Bob through the hatch, but after that it was a total blank. The next thing he knew, he was somehow bursting to the surface with the pilot, gasping for breath. And then somehow he and Mary worked in tandem to bring the pilot's seemingly lifeless body to shore, where they gave him mouth-to-mouth and somehow managed to bring him back, gurgling and spitting up gallons of seawater.

But somehow they made it, even if they were bruised and shaken. Somehow they were all alive. Somehow, somehow. It just reaffirmed Eamon's faith, his belief in God and the ineffable. It was deep and unshakable, an abiding sense that nothing could harm him or those he loved and that everything would always work out in the end. He knew others might think him naive, but it was the way he had chosen to live his life, confidently and optimistically. He refused to give in to fearfulness and negativism, to a vision of a world bereft of hope.

Best of all, that dumb old fortune teller had been all wet. The dead had no special claim on Eamon. He stood on the hot white sands of the Na Pali coast with his wife, a living, breathing testament to his strong-willed beliefs.

8

Jack hated shaving his beard. He hadn't been clean-faced since he'd been in the Marines. But damn that Ray, he like totally insisted. First, he had to pare it down with the scissors, and then he must've gone through four or five of those double-edged razor blades getting the rest of it. It actually hurt, the way it burned and left his skin looking all scratchy red.

Damn, his face was like a baby's bare ass now. A baby with a bad rash, at that. Jack must've been crazy listening to Ray. That guy was going to wind up getting him in even more trouble than he was already in, if that was possible. He wished he could back out of the whole thing. But he knew Ray would never allow it. He was such a creep. Why had Jack even confided in him in the first place? Bumping into him in that bar, what a mistake.

At least Ray knew what he was doing; Jack had to keep reminding himself of that. A person didn't go to prison without learning some things along the way. Sure, Ray was weird and creepy, but he also knew how to take care of business. Why, everything about the guy was professional. Making Jack draw those maps of Dead Letters and getting him to shave his beard so he wouldn't be easily recognizable to his former co-workers. Now that was smart, not the kind of thing *he* would come up with. And then having the both of them wear his old postal uniforms so they'd have no trouble blending in. Maybe he didn't like Ray much, but he had to admit the guy was always thinking, always one step ahead of everybody else.

Ray was coming to pick him up in just another couple of hours. Jack was getting more nervous by the minute. And when he got nervous, he got hungry. He'd already eaten a whole Sara Lee cheesecake. But that was nothing for him, just a light snack nowadays. He'd simply had too much time on his hands since they'd fired him. There was nothing to do but eat and watch television. He went into the freezer and picked out a Hungry Man entrée for the microwave. Minutes later, he was in his living room scarfing down Salisbury steak and mashed potatoes and watching the *Jenny Jones* show. Jenny was reuniting this guy and this girl who'd shared a one-night stand but who'd subsequently lost touch with one another. The girl was eager to get together with her old lover after the show. She told Jenny that he'd been the best, most memorable night of her entire life. But there was a slight problem: the guy couldn't remember her.

Jack couldn't even imagine having sex these days. First of all, there probably weren't too many women who'd look twice at him, considering all the weight he'd put on. But it was more than that: it was the whole making a human connection, extending himself like that. He just felt empty, like there wasn't anything left to give to somebody else. After his wife had left him about five years back, Jack had sort of just given up, not having the necessary energy to participate anymore. The only thing that really hurt was missing watching his little boy grow up. The kid was eleven now—and who knew how old he'd be when Jack finally got out of prison.

That was the only reason why he was pulling the

job. He wanted to make sure his kid was provided for while he was put away. His ex could rot in hell for all he cared, but no way was he going to take it out on the kid. He deserved better; after all, he had his whole life ahead of him. Jack had been trying all along to be a good father, remembering birthdays and holidays and always being early with the child support, even though he figured Bernadette was poisoning his son's mind against him anyway. But it wasn't the kid's fault that his mother was a lying, cheating adulteress.

Ah, Bernadette wasn't that bad. Jack even kind of understood now why she got mixed up in that affair with that dumb garage mechanic. She was just going crazy from not having any life. All Jack ever did was go to work and then come home and park himself in front of the TV with a six-pack. She used to call him a slug, and you know what? She was right. Because they never did anything together—never went anywhere or did any of those fun couple things that everyone else was always doing. Still, it sure felt sucky to catch them in bed like that.

But he got over it. And in the end, he even forgave Bernadette. Because basically, he didn't care. He really was a big, fat, passive slug. He was never the same after 'Nam, anyhow. It probably would've been best for all concerned if he'd just been shipped home in a body bag. Nobody gave a damn anyway. He found out how true that was when he got back to the States. He was such a dummy, thinking he was this big American hero. Thinking that being a decorated combat veteran meant something. How could he have been so stupid? But what did he know? He was only eighteen when he enlisted in the marines. Wanted to make his old man proud. Wanted to show everybody that he could do something right for a change. Going through basic training on Parris Island, becoming this total paranoid killing machine. It was unbelievable, but it turned out he was a pretty darn good soldier. It was only later, after his tour of duty, after he'd been stateside for a while, that he began to experience doubts. Then came the nightmares, when he started remembering their faces, every single blessed one of them, every last kill.

He couldn't hurt a fly now. He was just a hopeless couch potato now. He was ashamed of himself. He used to be in the damn corps, no joke. Ray probably wouldn't believe it. Oh, the creep knew that he was a vet, but he had no idea that Jack had been a member of Marine Force Recon, the elite within an elite. He'd been somebody once. Others had looked up to him, depended on him. It was a long time ago now, but that didn't mean it hadn't happened. He charged hills, crossed leech-infested rivers, crawled over bodies, breathed napalm, laid it on the line.

Semper fuckin' fi, man! The marine motto. *Semper fi.* Always faithful.

Now he was a big, fat nobody. After the corps, he looked for a civil-service job. He just wanted to forget, to make it all go away. Became a postal worker, just like every other vet who was suffering flashbacks. Nobody wanted to remember anything. Everybody just wanted to become automatons, to lose their humanness completely. And what better way to do that than working the sorting machines at the United States Postal Service's Eastern Seaboard Midregional Bulk Management Depot?

Postal Depot 349, also known as Dead Letters, was the largest processing facility on the entire East Coast. Jack was what they called a bulk-mail sorter. It was his job—along with hundreds of other automatons just like him—to make sure the conveyor belts and computerized sorters and optical scanners were running smoothly. This was sometimes a challenge, considering that over three million pieces of mail came pouring in every single freaking day. Sometimes it could be a real horror show, especially when the older machinery malfunctioned, causing delays and stressing out the managers, who were constantly worried about their efficiency ratings.

Still, it wasn't so bad, really. It was a secure job with benefits. It allowed him to marry Bernadette and to have the kid. They bought the little place in Federal Hill, a nice middle-class existence. God knows he should have been happy with it. But he was still tormented by those nightmares, haunted by the faces of the dead. He couldn't get away from them. They were everywhere. They appeared in the leftover milk of his cereal bowl, they materialized over his favorite TV shows. He sought help at the VA hospital, but all they did was sponsor these bogus rap sessions with other miserable, guilt-plagued vets.

It seemed like work was the only place where he could truly escape. Most of the day was sapped by mindless drudgery: screening and separating letters, parcels, and flat packages on the belts. The bulk-mail sorters were responsible for everything that got rejected by the optical scanners; half the mail nowadays had bar codes and was never touched by human hands. But there were still plenty of people out there practicing "poor address hygiene," which was postal lingo for basically failing to use standard abbreviations and proper ZIPs. Twenty human sorters could handle about fifteen thousand letters an hour, as opposed to the forty thousand pieces one computerized decoder could dispense with.

As far as Jack was concerned, it was good, brain-numbing assembly-line work. He was able to lose himself in the stupendous monotony, to shed his demons in that deafening roar of belts and machinery. In most ways, it was a great job for a vet suffering from post-traumatic stress disorder.

Often, during his lunch hour, Jack would borrow one of the motorized scooters to head back into Dead Letters itself, into an off-limits treasure trove of postal riches. Because not only was Depot 349 the largest regular processing facility on the coast, it was also the final resting place for most of the nation's undeliverable mail. Inside, the place was so huge it had stop signs and traffic lights. Dollies and forklifts made their way down huge passageways that had actual street names. It took a full-time janitorial crew of twenty to just mop the floors. They even had a guy—swear to God—whose only job was to change burned-out lightbulbs. Jack could never get over that one. But Dead Letters was its own strange world, full of weirdness and mystery. Because it certainly wasn't just bins and hampers of misaddressed letters. It was much more than that. Jack didn't even know where to begin. It was like the Louvre or the Smithsonian or something. The place was a total freaking museum, full of rare artifacts and genuine history.

For example, two of the original Pony Express stagecoaches were on display in the holding room. There was even a fully restored mail boat, a steamer from the 1860s that had gone down on Lake Michigan. Who knew how these things had made their way to Dead Letters? All Jack knew was that he couldn't get enough of that old stuff. That was why he'd spent all those lunch hours back there, losing himself in a cobwebby, bygone world. He liked to read the letters, too. Especially the real old ones, going back to the early 1900s. Before all the wars. When things were still relatively peaceful and news still came wrapped in an envelope. It helped to eavesdrop on these turn-of-the-century people, to enter their hermetically sealed world. It pacified Jack, allowing him to get out of his own screwed-up head for a precious while.

Not too many other people, though, were interested in that yellowing pile of mail from yesteryear. Most were like Ray, just wanting to know about the stuff that could translate into big bucks. Because valuable merchandise was always turning up at Dead Letters. Lost shipments of laser printers and Xerox copiers. Mislabeled crates of fine cigars and champagne. A lot of it was damaged goods that the insurance had already paid out against. Waterlogged Oriental rugs that just needed to be dried out. Battered-looking electronic equipment that was easily fixable. Shipments of crystal and porcelain that were only partially broken. That kind of thing.

In fact, it was only when Jack started telling Ray about the goodies that he started to show any interest at all. Jack should've known better than to talk to some stranger in a bar. But it had been some while since anyone had bothered to listen. And there was Ray, buying him drinks and acting like some kind of concerned friend. So Jack told him all about how his wife left him and how he got fired and how they were pressing charges against him. And Ray made like he could really sympathize with Jack's predicament. He seemed to have no trouble understanding how things could suddenly take one of those bad turns for the worse.

So Jack, like a big dummy, told Ray everything. He explained about how those eyes in the sky had caught him dumping and destroying mail. It just wasn't fair. It wasn't Jack's fault that he was put in that position in the first place. And it wasn't like he was getting rid of real mail. These were just bundles of magazines and advertising supplements. He had no choice in the matter. Jack's clipboard-toting supervisors were putting totally unreasonable demands on his sector. These anal-retentive managers were concerned only about their all-important efficiency ratings. They didn't give a damn that Jack and his co-workers were coming under increasing pressure to just hold the line. There were severe staff shortages brought on by downsizing. At the same time, a lot of the older machinery needed to be replaced. So there were just too many demands being placed on too few people. But did the managers cut them any slack? Fat chance. Their raises and promotions were directly linked to the numbers.

The whole place had become a powder keg of anxiety and pressure. The job that Jack had once looked forward to going to had become its own kind of nightmare. The managers never let up. They were constantly threatening the bulk-mail sorters, never letting them forget for one minute that their jobs were on the line. And no way Jack could chance getting fired. He had the alimony and child support to worry about, besides all the regular bills. The only way they could keep pace was by dumping the nonessentials—mostly junk mail and congressional franking—into these huge empty trailers that had taken up permanent residence outside Depot 349. They didn't do it all the time, just when they were absolutely overwhelmed. When that happened, they drew straws to see who'd have to do the actual dumping. Unfortunately, Jack wound up pulling that dangerous assignment one time too many.

How was Jack to know that the Postal Inspection Service had installed security cameras all over Depot 349? It was all on account of an investigation by some congressional subcommittee that was looking into why it took so long for the mail to be processed at the Baltimore facility. So they caught Jack red-handed, right on the old videotape. They made him the fall guy for everything. What the hell could he do? They had him dead to rights. The only way out was to inform on his fellow sorters. But no way Jack was going to rat out his friends. It wasn't their fault that they were being asked by those Nazi managers to make impossible quotas. He kept trying to explain it to those government morons—that the problem was with the managers and generals, not with the damn infantry. But those federal prosecutors just didn't want to hear it.

Even Ray couldn't believe how totally unfair it was. He could see how that stressed-out work environment had led to all of Jack's troubles. No wonder, Ray said, there'd been all those disgruntled ex–postal workers who'd gone on killer rampages. It was always in the news, some fired postal worker strapping on an assault rifle and marching back into his old place of employment to exact revenge on his supervisors and anyone else who just happened to be there. Then Ray asked Jack if he had it in mind to get even with the bastards, too.

But Jack didn't want anything to do with revenge. He'd left all of that terrible rage in 'Nam. No, his killing days were over. He just wanted to be left alone, to do his time in peace. After all, he did break the law. It was his sacred oath as a postal employee to protect the mail and serve the public. Even if all he did was dump a bunch of advertising crap. Even if there were plenty of others doing plenty of worse things. Why, there were guys at the depot who were actually going through the mail looking for cash. Sure, it was a whole little side business, rifling through birthday cards and whatnot, trying to intercept Grandma's ten-spot to little Johnny. You wouldn't believe the stuff going on out there.

Then Ray said it sounded like he was still angry. And Jack had to admit that he wasn't exactly happy about the whole situation. The way the feds were setting him up as the scapegoat. The way his legal bills were piling up and eating away at his life's savings. The way nobody seemed to care.

Ray told him he was stupid to be such a patsy. He said Jack wasn't thinking right, wasn't seeing things. He asked about the Dead Letters part again, where all the good loot was. He wanted to know exactly what else was back there. And so Jack rattled off all the stuff he could think of. It wasn't until he got to the part about Sector 1040 that Ray's eyes lit up. Jack explained that 1040 was where they brought all the IRS's undeliverable refund checks. You were usually talking about deceased taxpayers or people who'd moved without leaving a forwarding address. Anyway, 1040 was only a temporary holding station for the refund checks; after a last-ditch effort was made by the Claims and Inquiries clerks to locate these missing taxpayers, the checks were then sent back to the IRS for decommissioning.

Ray wanted to know how much refund money might be in 1040 at any one time. Jack had to think about it. At least hundreds of thousands. Maybe even millions. Jack really couldn't be sure. Ray said it didn't matter. Either way, it sounded like enough to him.

No, Jack never should've gone into that bar. There was some lesson there about not being so quick to confide in a stranger.

Ray would be arriving anytime now. Jack was getting more nervous by the minute. He wondered if he should allow himself another Hungry Man dinner. After all, he didn't want to be too sluggish when they hit Dead Letters. Ray kept emphasizing the importance of keeping to their timetable. He was such a control freak, really. The way he was always telling Jack what to do. What a bully. Always calling Jack a fat slob or a dumb putz. Who made him God? Jack decided to put another Hungry Man in the microwave.

He cut into chicken cordon bleu in the glow of late-afternoon television. While he waited for Ray, he'd gone from *Jenny Jones* to *Oprah* to *Sally Jessy Raphael*. He was hooked on daytime talk shows. He could never get over the people who went on them. All these seemingly average Americans confessing to all sorts of amazing stuff. *Sally Jessy* had on mothers who stole their daughters' boyfriends. There was a lot of yelling and screaming. One daughter kept calling her mother a "no-good whore tramp." Another said her mom was "a lousy cook and a lousy lay." There was a lot of anger and even some tears. But Jack noticed that the one thing nobody felt was embarrassment. They just kept yelling and screaming and trying to get the audience's attention. This was their one little moment in the spotlight and they were sure as hell going to make the most of it. Jack could understand that. It took a lot to get noticed in this world.

Jack rubbed at his newly shaven face in the late-afternoon glow. He used to think that the daytime talk shows were such a joke. In the old days, he wondered how people could get caught up in such craziness. Like sleeping with your daughter's boyfriend. Or being reunited with a one-night stand on national TV. But now he could see how strange things could just sort of happen to a person. Maybe after he got out of prison, he'd go on one of those shows, too. Maybe Sally Jessy Raphael would want to do one on big, fat, dumb ex–postal employees who wind up turning to crime after meeting the wrong guy in a bar.

9

Inspector Lita Sanchez sat at her gunmetal desk in the harsh fluorescence of the command post entering a report into the flickering gray cyberspace of her IBM terminal. Because it was after five on a Friday afternoon, most of the other postal inspectors had already made their getaways. The only other person about was Frank Shoe, who had his feet up on a nearby desk as he thumbed through the newspaper.

Even Del Masterson, their foul-mouthed, hardnosed boss, had cut out early today. Thank God for Fridays, Sanchez thought. She really couldn't stand Del. The former FBI big shot kept a bottle of Wild Turkey in his filing cabinet and usually started drinking at lunchtime. Lately, he'd been coming on to her, slapping her fanny for no good reason and saying, "How's it going, sweetcakes?" She was thinking about filing a sexual harassment complaint. She just hated to cause trouble, though. After all, she was the only female inspector at Dead Letters. It was important that she learn how to handle these things herself, to show no weakness. Maybe Eamon and Bunko would know what to do about Del; she'd have to seek their advice when they got back from vacation.

Well, correction—only Bunko was on vacation. Eamon, that big banana head, was on his honeymoon. Why did he have to go and get married like that? He'd spoiled everything now. Sanchez had liked that boy from moment one. They'd had some fun, rockin' times together before this other woman entered the picture. But even Sanchez had to admit Eamon's new wife was quite the looker; in fact, she got real jealous seeing that wedding picture of her in the paper. Not only was Ms. Seppala drop-dead gorgeous, but she had to be smart and tough and all that, too. Because they didn't make a woman a homicide detective without putting her through the paces first.

Damn you, Eamon, she thought. *You big banana head, you.*

Sanchez stopped processing her report. Every time she started thinking of that boy, she got all flustered and annoyed. They had dated steady for a few months last year, but then they had this big huge fight—not that either one of them could remember what it was about—and before they could even begin to patch it up, he met this Mary Seppala person. Sanchez still liked him a lot, even if he was married now. Eamon was just such a good-looking boy, with that thick, dark, curly hair and those blue, blue eyes of his. And he was real good in bed. He knew just how to touch a girl, and he always said all the right things afterward.

Maybe she could have an affair with him. After all, she was still going to be seeing a lot of him. Then she got a look at her serious, determined face in the reflection of the IBM screen and had to laugh. What on earth was she thinking? She had to leave the poor boy alone now. He was taken, and that was that.

She was tired and just the teeniest bit lonely. It was the end of another long week, and another boring, dateless weekend loomed ahead of her. There didn't seem to be anyone on the horizon, some new handsome prospect to moon over and dream about. Maybe she'd come on to Bunko. That would sure make

Eamon jealous. Oh, yeah, there was a good idea. She could throw herself at a degenerate gambler and boozer who was twice her age just to get Eamon's attention. Still, if she started batting her eyelashes at Bunko, it might give Eamon something to think about. Oh God, she had to stop with this deviousness.

She saw Frank Shoe sneaking looks her way, trying to conceal his interest behind the sports pages of the *Sun.* She wasn't quite that desperate yet. Shoe had a wife and four adult kids and was only two weeks away from retirement. He was also a terrible worrier who was convinced he would never live long enough to collect his first week's pension check. Lately, every time he had a little indigestion, he thought it was the beginnings of a massive coronary occlusion. And if a heart attack didn't claim him, then he was sure he'd get hit by a bus or something. That was why Shoe had been staying later and later at work. He seemed to think that it was the safest place for him.

Lita Sanchez got up and walked over to the command post's only window, a long slat of double-paned, soundproof Plexiglas that peered inward, providing a small, unsatisfactory glimpse into the crazy, chaotic world of Depot 349. Though, at the moment, it seemed especially quiet down there in those cavernous reaches of belts, bells, and buzzers. It was strange, but she didn't see any of the sorters and mechanics up and about. For a moment she became concerned, but then she realized that they were changing shifts. That had to be what it was. No other explanation fit.

Ray was in a trance, the way he always was when Jimi Hendrix wailed out "Voodoo Child" from the tape deck. He needed something to dictate the mood. He needed to get into that weird, disconnected place. He didn't want to think about being in his mother's old '78 Impala with Jack. He just wanted to immerse himself in a rush of sound and speed, in a frenzy of guitar.

But Jack kept interrupting. The dumb putz had all sorts of inane questions. But Ray just let it go right through him. Jack was just a means to an end, that was all. He had outlived his usefulness. Ray just ignored him. All his questions would be answered soon enough. He turned up Hendrix to the max as he got the Impala up near ninety miles an hour. He was just starting to get where he needed to be.

"But you're going too fast," Jack whimpered. "You're going to get us killed."

Ray smiled at the clean-shaven stranger in the postal uniform next to him. He was in his comfort zone now. It was only a matter of time now.

As usual, he wondered what Jill was doing right at this very same second. But it was real hard to come up with an image. He didn't even know which state she was in, where they were keeping her. He hated all the know-nothing people who were trying to keep them apart, who didn't understand their relationship. In the joint, they wouldn't even let him write her letters. They just took her somewhere, and now they wouldn't even let him see her anymore. But he was going to find her and save her. He knew she loved him. It was just that she didn't know it yet. Before, she'd needed time. But now, she'd had that time. Now she was probably ready for him. Before, it had just upset her. The whole making-a-commitment thing. She was just scared of her own feelings for Ray. After all, she had never known real love before him. He felt a flash of anger thinking of some of the losers she had kept company with. That long-haired singer guy, Keith Zane. What a con artist. Pulling the wool over Jill's eyes with his sensitive-as-shit act. Worming his way into her life the way he did. Poor Jill was far too trusting and naive. She had no clue about the kind of shitheads who were out there.

Just thinking of that Keith guy put him in a state. Brought so many bad feelings back. Not that he blamed Jill exactly. Those long-haired pretty boys with all their clever, pretty talk. He should've taken care of that turd when he had the chance. If that guy hadn't screwed with Jill's head, then it would've been a whole different story. Everything had been going so great, too. Just the fact that Jill had moved back to Muldeen after all those years away. After being out in California doing all that artistic kind of stuff. Was a set designer or some such shit. But then she got homesick or something. Moved back in with her parents. It was just an unbelievable piece of luck. Ray and Jill were both thirty-two years old and living at home. And neither one of them was married. It was almost too perfect. Even Ray's sourpuss mom approved of the idea. Because the first moment he laid eyes on Jill again, he set his mind on one goal: to make her his.

Ray had never forgotten Jill Summers. Not fucking likely. Not with all those pictures he'd tacked up on his bedroom wall. One day, he just showed up at cheerleader practice and pretended to shoot the bitches for the school paper. He made the most of his opportunity, sitting there in the bleachers, taking aim at the kick line. The weird thing was, he tried to snap the other girls doing splits and other crotch exercises, but with Jill, he just focused on her amazing, angelic face. She wasn't like the others; she was so pure and delicate, man, and he wanted to keep her that way in his head.

But Ray was too much of a dork to approach her in high school; he could never seem to work up the nerve. Not that he didn't try to keep an eye out for her, though. He knew her schedule by heart—from what time she got up in the morning to what bus she took to what period she had French. He was just making sure that she was okay. He was like her guardian angel or something. Except she didn't know it.

And then they just sort of lost touch. She went out to Berkeley, that big hippie school in California, while he enrolled at the local community college. He was going to major in accounting, but he didn't last more than a couple of months. Jill, on the other hand, got her degree and even went on to some kind of graduate-school thing. He was proud of her, the way she took her studies so seriously. At some point, he decided to put his true feelings down on paper. He wrote these long, wild letters to her—trying to explain what she meant to him and all that shit—but for some reason, he never mailed them.

After he dropped out of that dumb community college, he took a job at Moe's Tobacco Shop, which was this little all-purpose stationery store that sold everything from yo-yos to rolling papers. It was real nowhere, but the owner wasn't around much, so Ray just spent most of the day flipping through skin magazines. At night, to get away from his chain-smoking, yellow-stained, bathrobe-beautiful nag of a mother, he locked himself in his room and hiked the music up. He escaped in Hendrix and Deep Purple and Black Sabbath. To complete his exit from this world, he took hits from his three-foot-long wonder bong.

Ten years of this shit went by like nothing, really.

And he'd probably still be at it if Jill hadn't walked into Moe's on that spring day three years ago. At first, she made like she didn't remember him, but he knew she was just nervous, too. It turned out she was working up the street in this art gallery–framing store. She started to come into Moe's almost every day. She was always needing pens and paper and envelopes and shit like that. Ray bided his time. He was just a helpful, friendly, reassuring presence. When he finally asked her to go to the movies, he made it sound real casual, real incidental-like. How could she possibly refuse? It would just be two old friends catching a flick at the multiplex. Friends who obviously dreamed of a whole lot more together.

"That's it!" Jack was yelling. "That's Dead Letters!

C'mon, snap out of it already! Or else we'll miss the exit!"

It was awesome, really, the way it was all lit up in the lonely February twilight. It was like some kind of miniature city. In the distance, Ray could see huge mail trucks lined up alongside the loading docks. It was easily the biggest single structure he had ever laid eyes on; it was like the Pentagon or something, the way it just went on and on. There was even an airfield on the outskirts, flashing its blue runway lights. Even the freaking parking lot was something to behold: it would've taken a good half hour just to walk from one end to the other. Ray slammed the brakes in the middle of its floodlit reaches.

"What's the big idea?" Jack demanded. "We got to park closer than this. We're going to be carrying heavy mailbags."

"I want to show you something," Ray said, opening the car door and getting out. He didn't bother to turn off the engine. This wasn't going to take long.

The dumb putz followed right behind him. "Damn, it's cold," he said, blowing winter breath. "I don't even have a damn overcoat. C'mon, what's the big secret already?"

Ray opened the Impala's roomy trunk. There was nobody about, just a handful of frost-coated cars this far back in the lot. Jack came over for a look. "What the hell?" he said, glimpsing the hardware. "I told you no guns. You promised nobody would get hurt. I'm telling you I won't be a part of any of this."

"Don't worry about it," Ray said, reaching into the trunk for one of the Glocks. "Because you're not a part of anything anymore."

Before the realization could fill Jack's face, Ray had brought the gun right to Jack's temple and fired twice. It didn't sound like much out in the cold wasteland— like a couple of firecrackers or something—but it was a smart little gun, all the same. Ray liked the fact that it was so light and easy to handle.

It was a good thing that Ray had kept to his fitness program; otherwise, it would've been impossible to lift the fat slob. Still, even with all the regular bench-pressing, Ray found it a challenge getting the body in the trunk.

Ray realized this was only the second person he had ever killed. The first one almost didn't count. His mother had lung cancer and was going to die anyway. But the old nag had sure taken her sweet time about it, that was for shit sure. Ray just couldn't take any more of her bitching and moaning. Besides, he needed the money from the sale of the house. So one night, he just put a pillow over her head. She really didn't even struggle that much. A couple small little kicks of the feet, that's all. The way Ray looked at it, he did her a favor. She was starting to look like real shit with all that chemo. They didn't even do an autopsy. Big surprise there. Like anybody was going to care about his pathetic, lonely old mother.

He got back in her old Impala and put it in drive. He looked at his watch and saw it was five-thirty P.M. He had exactly twenty-five minutes to make everything right. The whole thing had to be done between shifts; otherwise, he was sure to be overwhelmed by enemy forces. He bore on with a new determination. They had it coming to them, that was for shit sure. Sending him to the Hagerstown zoo without so much as a second thought. Taking his girl and fucking with his head the way they did. What did they think he was going to do? Just forgive and forget? Just drop off the face of the planet or something? Fat chance, mother-fuckers.

There were several different ways into Dead Letters. Fortunately, Jackie-boy had drawn a fine map. The first thing he had to contend with was this giant tractor-trailer snorting outside his designated entrance. He pulled right behind it and got out and walked right up to the truck's cab and knocked on its door. "What the hell you want?" some grizzled face said, rolling down the window. "Your fucking soul," Ray said, looking up at the startled bastard and clicking away with the Glock. You couldn't even hear the shots with the noise of that diesel.

Then he cautiously made his way around the big truck, up to the loading dock, where there were two other oblivious nobodies stacking boxes on dollies. It was like when he was a kid and used to play army. It was no more real than that. They didn't even have the time to cry out or to clutch their chests. It was even easier than he thought.

He grabbed one of the empty dollies and rolled it back to the Impala. It was the only way to move Jack. It pissed him off that the dumb pulphead had bled all over the trunk lining. Well, there was nothing he could do about it now. He strapped on the M-16 and the extra magazines. Then he pulled blubber boy out of the trunk and onto the dolly. He just had to get him halfway inside Dead Letters, to make it look right. Last but not least, he took that paperback book and stuffed it in Jack's back pocket. It was something Ray had read about. How a couple of those stressed-out postal psychos had been found with a copy of *The Catcher in the Rye* on their bodies. Ray just thought it was a nice final touch.

He came in through the wide, metal-pulled entryway, into a mind-deafening racket of machinery. He shoved Jack off the dolly and made a mad charge into the heart of enemy territory. There were about five or six of them working the conveyor belts. He raised the M-16 and let her rip. The damn magazine was spent in just a few seconds. He didn't even come close. He was only thirty feet away. With all the noise, nobody even seemed to know they were being fired upon. He quickly reloaded, shoving in another thirty-round magazine. The damn gun was real jumpy in his hands and seemed to fire high. He could hear the bullets pinging about in the machinery and ceiling. Again, he missed everything. Damn it, he knew he should've had some practice with it first. This wasn't like the damn Winchester he had at the cabin. That thing held steady and sure, even if it was a ton heavier.

Ray moved in closer, and by the time he reloaded again, they'd spotted him. Now it didn't matter. He got into a good solid stance and started pumping away again. This time he hit pay dirt. They were like deer in the headlights, unable to move. But again the magazine was spent too fast. The problem was, he had it on full automatic. He only had one more mag, so he switched the M-16 into a semiautomatic mode. Two of them were making a dash, trying to get away. But this time, Ray had control of the weapon and had no trouble mowing them down.

Now he took out one of the Glocks to finish the job. A couple of them were still gasping and heaving. He tried to avoid stepping in all that blood; the last thing he needed was to leave a set of tracks that couldn't be accounted for. One of the living dead looked right up at Ray and pleaded for his life. But Ray didn't let it throw him. After he put the last one out of his misery, he went back to Jack's blubbery carcass. He dropped the M-16 next to him and then placed a Glock in his gloved hand. Really, man, it was all too fucking beautiful.

There was only one piece of unfinished business left. He made his way to the elevator that would take him right into the postal inspectors' headquarters. It was only too bad, he thought, that Eamon fucking Wearie was going to miss out on all the fun. He got in the elevator and pushed the button marked Command Post. As he ascended, Ray took the opportunity to reload the other Glock.

Lita Sanchez thought it was odd that somebody was taking the elevator up to the command post at this time on a Friday. She just assumed that one of the other inspectors had forgotten something. She herself was calling it a day. In the momentary void, waiting for the door to open, she wondered what to do for dinner tonight. She felt like being bad and picking up a bucket of fried chicken. But then she just as quickly discarded the idea. She was going to have to lose a couple of pounds if she was ever going to attract another man. It was all Eamon's fault, she decided. If he hadn't married that woman, they'd still be together and she could've had fried chicken tonight without worrying about her figure.

When the elevator opened, somebody grabbed her and twirled her around, all in a lightning instant. All she knew was that someone had his big, hairy forearm hard against her neck and a gun pointed to her head. "Don't try a fucking thing, bitch," the smelly breath said. He was pushing her back into the command post. She was having trouble breathing and her legs felt weak and collapsible. He didn't loosen his grip for a second.

Frank Shoe was the only other person in the command post. He looked up from his newspaper with startled disbelief. "Don't be a hero," the smelly breath told him. "Or I'll fucking kill her."

"What . . . what . . . do you want?" Frank stammered out.

"I want you to tell me where I can find a friend of mine. Maybe you've heard of her. Jill Summers—does that ring a fucking bell?"

All the postal inspectors knew who she was. She'd been on the receiving end of hundreds of threatening, obsessive letters. Sanchez remembered the case well. The stalker was some sicko named Ray Duffy. That was who had the gun to her head—had to be. He had even tried to make good on his threat to kill Jill Summers. That was why Eamon and Bunko had petitioned the Postal Inspection Service to come up with their very own witness protection program, to be modeled right along the same lines of the Justice Department's. All because of Ray Duffy. They knew that when the sicko finally got out of jail, the first thing he'd do was try to extract some revenge. Eamon and Bunko had just wanted to give Jill Summers a fighting chance. In fact, she was the first person ever placed in the Postal Inspection Service's Witness Protection Program.

"So you know my girlfriend, do you?" Ray Duffy continued. "Well, where the fuck is she? Because if you don't tell me, this bitch is as good as dead."

Sanchez felt like she was going to pass out. She wanted to say something, to tell Frank not to divulge Jill's whereabouts. Duffy kept his choke hold on her, though. Her eyes filled with tears from the excruciating pressure. She wished Eamon or Bunko had been there. She just knew somehow that Frank Shoe wasn't going to live up to the situation.

"Just a minute," Shoe said, turning to face his computer. "I have to call it up."

"Well, you've got ten fucking seconds, asshole," Duffy snarled. "One, two, three, four . . ."

Sanchez could hear Frank frantically tapping in the codes. She knew he wasn't going to make it in time. It wasn't Frank's fault, though. She forgave him and everybody else in the world and said a little prayer to the Virgin Mary. She didn't so much as hear the gun go off as she felt the searing heat in the back of her brain. *So that's what it's like to be shot,* she thought in that last, strange nanosecond of consciousness. Then she began to tumble down a deep, deep well of seemingly infinite darkness.

10

Jill really didn't mind working the counter at the post office in Nalcrest, Florida, but sometimes the retirees who made up her customer base could be quite finicky about the way they sent their mail. Then again, it made sense when you considered that most of the retirees in Nalcrest were once letter carriers for the postal service.

"It's some books for my son," Saul Roth said, placing the parcel on the counter. "Give me the price for first class, then tell me what it'll cost me book rate."

Jill punched it up on the automated scale. "Two dollars more for first class."

"Oh, that's a tough one," he said, furrowing his brow. "You know how those bozo clerks handle fourth-class mail. Tossing it around like it was a sack of potatoes. I kid you not, Miss Winters. The lack of respect for lower-class postage is downright appalling. No wonder there's so much breakage and spillage."

"What's it going to be, Saul?"

"First class," he said. "After all, what's a few more dollars when you're talking about peace of mind. Sure beats winding up in the dead-letter office."

"I'll make sure it goes out with the noon express."

"I appreciate that, Miss Winters. Not that my good-for-nothing son will give a damn one way or the other. You have a nice day now, sweetheart."

The older men often called her "sweetheart" or "kiddo" or "baby" or even "toots." By now, she was used to it, and it didn't bother her because she knew it was very much a generational thing.

Mrs. Hulbert was next. "Listen darling, I'm going to need a roll of stamps. Give me something nice. Perhaps some flowers or even some red hearts. You know, it's Valentine's Day. Just nothing too stodgy. No dead presidents or dead inventors. So boring, you know."

Mrs. Hulbert came in every day. She was one of Jill's regulars. She must've gone through four rolls of stamps a week. Like a lot of the older folk, she spent a good deal of her time writing letters. There were her children and grandchildren to think of, of course. But she also made a point to keep up with her old friends and neighbors from Wisconsin. Sometimes that remembered world seemed much more real and alive to Mrs. Hulbert than Nalcrest itself.

"You would not believe the snow this time of year," she said. "It has to be *experienced,* darling. I can tell you, Sheboygan is not for the faint of heart. I get the shivers just thinking about it. Still, there's something nice about snow in the wintertime, don't you think, dear?"

"I wouldn't know," Jill said carefully.

"Oh, I always forget, you're a native Floridian. It's funny, though, that you'd wind up with a last name like Winters."

Jill was almost used to her alias now. And she was even starting to get comfortable with the sleepy little town of Nalcrest. At first, it seemed like the end of the world, but over time, its snail-paced way of life had grown on Jill. In a way, she cherished the warm, piney safety of the boondocks of central Florida. It was more than just a necessary haven; it was home now, for better or worse.

"You poor dear, you've got Sheboygan skin," Mrs. Hulbert said with a touch of concern. "Don't you ever get out for a little sun? Darling, it's the one thing we have plenty of—sunshine and shuffleboard."

"Believe me, Mrs. Hulbert, I'm just fine," Jill replied with a touch of irritability. "I've got life just the way I want it."

"You need to get out a little bit more often. I worry about you, darling. When was the last time you even went out on a date? Look, I'm just an old widow who's not getting any younger, but I'll bet my social calendar is more full than yours. Such a sweet young girl. And nobody in your life. Such a shame."

Jill seemed to have that particular well-meant conversation several times a day. The retirees of Nalcrest were always bringing up their eligible-bachelor sons and grandsons. But, really, as she tried to explain to anybody who'd listen, she wasn't looking for a relationship right now. In a way, it was a good thing because there really wasn't much to choose from in off-the-beaten-path Nalcrest. The locals hadn't nicknamed it the "town without a ZIP" for nothing. The closest real town was Tampa, and that was over an hour away, easy.

It really wasn't that bad, though. Oh, it was a strange little burg, all right. No place that just catered to retired letter carriers was going to be entirely normal. For example, they didn't allow dogs in Nalcrest. Which made a certain amount of sense when you thought about it. No dogs, no snow, no nothing to remind the retirees of their former occupational hazards. Also, there wasn't any home delivery in Nalcrest. Everybody had a post office box, which they rented for the grand total of three dollars a year. That was the thing about Nalcrest—it was meant to be affordable. William C. Doherty, after serving twenty-one years as the president of the letter carriers' union, founded the community in 1963. It was his dream to create an inexpensive refuge for his postal brethren. Today, bungalow apartments in the low-slung, nondescript, whitewashed buildings went for about three hundred dollars a month. Jill thought they were okay, really. Palm trees and man-made duck ponds added some much-needed charm. Of course, Nalcrest's cheap rent meant that there was quite a long waiting list of former letter carriers trying to get in. But basically the only way an opening presented itself was when someone died. Because it wasn't like people to leave Nalcrest on their own. Owing to her own rather special set of circumstances, Jill had been offered one of the coveted apartments. But in the end, she decided to rent a trailer on nearby Lake Sahatchee.

And even though the locals liked to refer to it as the town without a ZIP, Nalcrest did indeed possess its very own five-digit code: 33865. In fact, because of the nature of her work, Jill was getting quite good at recognizing ZIP codes from all around the country. Oh, clerking in a post office wasn't the most glamorous work in the world, but it paid the bills and gave her a reason to get up in the morning. Not that she didn't miss working on movies. She was good at set design, and it was interesting, constantly challenging work. You never knew what they were going to ask you to build next. On her final film project, she helped to construct a whole futuristic space settlement for a low-budget, imitation *Star Wars*. Set design was far more than just coming up with the drawing-board vision; it also meant implementing it, from buying the materials to supervising the construction crew to making crazy last-minute substitutions to creating movie magic from a pile of ordinary two-by-fours.

She'd done sets for westerns, even worked with Clint Eastwood once. There was that submarine movie where they did a pretty nifty job of capturing the paranoia and claustrophobia of closed spaces. Once she was asked to build a replica of the Eiffel Tower—just so it could be blown up by make-believe terrorists. She prided herself on being able to think on her feet. Set design meant being an artist and a businessperson and a master conciliator, all wrapped up in one. You had to be instantly creative and fiscally prudent and always ready to compromise if you were going to tackle the eye-popping demands of most Hollywood productions. One time, they gave Jill's crew a week to completely remake the sets for a nineteenth-century costume drama. "Just bring it into the late twentieth century, babe," the twenty-three-year-old director told her. Another time, they wanted Jill to re-create all of Fabergé's bejeweled Easter eggs. In this instance, she was given three whole days to come up with the fabulous fakes.

But Jill really liked seeing her name in the rolling credits, to know that she'd accomplished something, even if it was in the service of something as superficial as celluloid.

But that life in California was over forever. Even though she should've known better, she'd got caught up in L.A.'s fast-lane lifestyle. She did her share of designer drugs and slept with her share of vanity-impaired actors. She even wound up having an abortion, something else that was never going to happen to her. By the time she'd moved home to Muldeen to help her mother take care of her ailing father, she was a battle-scarred Hollywood veteran.

It was awfully strange to find herself unmarried and living at home at thirty-two. Her dad had Alzheimer's and her mother could barely cope with it. She'd made the right decision coming east; there was no doubt that they needed her, and in some karmic twist, it turned out that she really needed them, too. She took the job in the framing store, just to keep busy, to help put a little bread on the table. It was almost unbearable to watch her father's wonderful, vital mind waste away, to realize that such things could be taken from a person. Human beings were more about dignity than most of us ever cared to realize.

It was probably the most vulnerable time in her life ever. So many of her friends from the old days, from high school, had moved away. Not that she really wanted to hang out with a group of ex–pom-pom girls. And the people she'd known and worked with on the West Coast had all but vanished from the face of her existence. The famous actor who'd gotten her pregnant and insisted on the abortion sent her a computer-signed Christmas card.

So it was at this lonely juncture that she bumped into a former classmate working in the local stationery shop. For the life of her, she couldn't remember Ray Duffy. But he seemed to have no trouble recalling her. How was she to know what kind of weirdo he really was? At first he was polite and sympathetic, anxious to engage in small talk. She really didn't think much of it when she agreed to accompany him to the movies. She thought she'd made it quite clear to him that it could never go past the friendship realm. Besides, she was seeing Keith Zane, even if theirs was a casual, no-strings-attached relationship. But she couldn't seem to get through to Ray. He heard only what he wanted to hear. That night after the movies, she tried to let him down easy. "You're a great guy," she said, trying to soften the blow, "but this really isn't something I want." But all he seemed to hear was that he was a great guy.

The next day, the phone calls began. He seemed desperate to see her. And he wouldn't take no for an answer. Finally, she had to take the phone off the hook. Then he started writing letters and sending expensive gifts. She tried to refuse his attentions, but that just seemed to enrage him further. The letters grew stranger and more intense. It was only the beginning.

She shuddered, chilled from the memory of it.

But there was no way to run from your memories. No witness protection program to hide from your past. She'd have to settle for changing her name to Winters and landing in the sleepy, practically comatose little town of Nalcrest.

But she really didn't mind the alligators and the mucky ponds and the mucky heat and all the nameless, faceless strip malls. It was safe down here in the heart of Florida. Of course, she was still getting used to the elderly drivers who never shut off their turn signals and who labored to achieve the minimum speed limit. It was a small price to pay for sanctuary, she reasoned.

Jill liked to take her lunch outside, on a bench in the bland, concrete-poured town square, under the spindly palms and high February sun. Often she was joined by the postmaster, Teddy Ernst. Jill's sandy-haired, boyish-faced boss was divorced and just a couple of years older than her. There was something about him that really appealed. He was pleasantly handsome in a comforting, boy-next-door kind of way. But it was more than that. There was something sweet and unaffected about him, something that even managed to burrow its way into her frozen heart. Let's face it, in the old days he would've been somebody that she could've imagined spending some serious time with. She knew he was interested in her, but she was still reluctant to get involved with anybody. She still wasn't ready, even after all this time.

"I've been thinking about it," Teddy said, putting his tuna sandwich down, "and I think it's high time you and I went out together. We're the only two people under sixty-five in a sixty-mile radius."

"I don't know," Jill said, trying to avoid Teddy's watchful brown eyes. "What if it doesn't work out? You realize we'll still have to work together."

"Don't worry," he said, trying to cut through her defenses with a stab of humor, "if it doesn't work out, I'll just fire you."

It was difficult to trust a man again, that's what it was. That's why the whole thing with Maria got out of hand. Going into Tampa on that lonely, rainy weekend looking for God knows what. Stumbling from bar to bar, high on vodka martinis. Making the mistake of entering that ladies' club. Dancing with Maria, just wanting to feel the warmth of someone again, of just anyone who could pass the barest muster. Jill was wasted, but that didn't wholly explain why she wound up back at Maria's place. Part of it was loneliness and curiosity, of course. But she was also sad, horny, and slightly scared. The whole faulty human spectrum.

Maria and her had a little thing for a few months. They drank cheap jug wine and listened to k.d. lang and cooked veggie meals together. In bed, they touched and whispered secrets. Jill was pretty sure she wasn't a lesbian, but that didn't mean she hadn't wanted it. Jill didn't even think it was morally wrong. Because she really didn't believe in God and all that crap anymore. After her father got Alzheimer's and Ray tried to kill her, she stopped believing in ancient fairy tales.

"How about a movie?" Teddy asked. "That's a pretty harmless way to begin."

Jill winced. "I wish you hadn't suggested that."

"Hey, then skip the movie," Teddy said. "Why don't you just come over to my place for some meaningless, empty sex."

"Is that all you're interested in?"

"No, really," he said, backtracking, "I want to get to know you first. I just want a chance to enter your life."

Jill took another bite of her mushroom-and-alfalfa-sprout sandwich. She thought Teddy was sincere enough, but she was still gun-shy, no doubt about it.

"Hey," he said, changing subjects, "did you hear about the latest postal massacre? Yeah, it seems some former mail sorter went nuts with an M-16 and killed—I don't know—ten or eleven people or something. Typical, though. Former Vietnam vet. The whole murder-suicide deal. Wiped out everybody, then blew his own brains out."

"When will it ever end?" she said, shaking her head. "Did they say where it happened?"

"I forget now," Teddy said. "It's hard to keep track of all these psycho jobs. I think it happened up near Washington or something. I can't be sure now. Heard it on the radio while I was showering. Didn't get all the details."

"I suppose it doesn't really matter," Jill said. "As long as it didn't happen here."

11

It was standing room only in St. Paul's Cathedral. Eamon and Bunko were in the back, mired in a sea of dark suits and even darker emotions. Up front, a crimson-robed priest spoke about God's will and those things that remained beyond the scope of human understanding. The six mahogany caskets that were laid out before the candlelit altar brought the point home.

The front pews were a terrible scene of naked hysteria. Black-veiled women sobbed, as children too young to know what it was all about tugged at their mothers for explanation. Teary-eyed older kids looked down at their polished shoes, trying hard not to lose it. The red priest rambled on about a golden heaven full of haloed angels and big, fluffy clouds. Eamon had a hard time imagining it.

The last time he'd been in a church was for another funeral. It was always the same. Some doddering old cleric mumbling out the Latin. The organ playing strains of "Amazing Grace." A sense of the unreality of living, as well as of dying. The living mourned for the dead, of course, but they almost inevitably wound up mourning for themselves, too. Everyone was held accountable in the great, hollow-sounding, stained-glass cathedral of eternity. Sinners couldn't help but beg for forgiveness when confronted with their own withering mortality.

Eamon was not immune, either. All those years of Catholic school and Sunday mass had left him vulnerable to the ancient, somniferous rituals. He repeated the sacraments along with the priest, as if he were mouthing the words from an old, barely remembered dream that still had the power to haunt.

Then the priest asked the confirmed to partake in the Eucharist. Eamon, feeling out of sorts, stayed seated with Bunko. At a great remove, he watched them go forward for their taste of wafer. Instead of comforting him, the rites of his church seemed drained of meaning, mere vestiges of a lost kingdom. He wasn't himself, though. Right after he found out that his tenant, Daniel P. Pinkus, had been killed in a bungled burglary, he got word about the Dead Letters massacre. Ten dead and one other in critical condition. To make matters worse, if that was even possible, he learned that Lita Sanchez was the patient in the critical-care unit. His ex-girlfriend was in a coma and not expected to pull through.

He'd stepped off the plane from Hawaii at BWI only three hours ago. He was tan and rested and completely bewildered.

The service seemed interminable. The red priest promised resurrection for the faithful and described again the version of heaven put forth by Revelations. This paradise of God was full of golden thrones, golden harps, golden crowns, even golden bowls of incense. Eamon had heard it all before. For the first time in his life, it sounded like a bunch of gilded nonsense.

Afterward, Eamon and Bunko stood in the crowd outside the church in the chilly rain, watching the pallbearers usher the flag-draped coffins into the waiting hearses. Three kilts played mournful bagpipes, as television cameras made easy sense of it.

"Hard to believe," Bunko said.

"I just feel empty inside," Eamon said.

"What's strange is that I knew Jack McCallum," Bunko said, taking out a flask from his raincoat. "He never struck me as the kind of guy that could do something like this. Seemed like a big softy, really."

"Live and learn," Eamon said sourly.

Bunko took a slug of the bourbon, then passed it Eamon's way. "Well, if it makes you feel any better," he said, "everybody's got to die sooner or later."

"Thanks," Eamon said sarcastically. "That really helps."

"Nobody gets out alive," Bunko said again, as if in a trance. "That's all you've got to know."

Their next stop was Frank Shoe's house, where the family was sitting shivah. The last time they'd been there, it was for their regular poker game. This time, the food was better and the mood was a lot worse. They helped themselves from a buffet that included matzoh balls, chopped liver, bagels and lox, gefilte fish, rye and challah breads, whitefish salad, potato pancakes, cold beets, roast chicken, sweet-and-sour, roast beef, and several versions of stuffed peppers.

The dining room and kitchen were flurries of activity, as middle-aged women ran to and fro, fretting over everyone and every little thing. The two postal inspectors took their plates and ate standing up in a quiet corner of Shoe's living room. Some of the family members had opted to sit on the uncomfortable-looking wooden boxes that had been brought in for the occasion.

"Damn shame," Bunko said between bites. "The man had only two weeks to retirement. Thirty years with the service, for God's sake. Never even got to collect a dime of his pension. Remember how he was always saying he'd die before he'd ever get to enjoy that money?"

"Turns out the man was a prophet," Eamon said glumly.

"Ain't right," Bunko said. "I still don't understand why Jack McCallum even goes up into the command post."

"He probably held a grudge against us. You've got to remember it was the inspectors who caught him dumping mail."

"So you never told me how your honeymoon went," Bunko said, choosing the inopportune moment to change subjects.

"Great. At least nobody died on it," he said, thinking of how lucky they'd been to make it out of that helicopter crash.

"My vacation in Vegas was beautiful," Bunko said unconcernedly. "I actually came out on top this time. Made two grand and met a fabulous woman whose name already escapes me."

"Lucky you."

"Life goes on."

"For some, it does," Eamon said, noticing Shoe's two daughters hugging tearfully on the couch.

It was at this happy point that their boss, the thick-necked, red-faced Del Masterson, joined the party. He held a highball glass full of the brown stuff and had an ugly, malevolent look in his swampy eyes. "Hi, girls. Long time no see."

"Just terrible, isn't it?" Bunko said.

"Just be glad we weren't in the office that afternoon," Masterson said. "Our fucking lucky day."

"That's some way to talk," Bunko said admonishingly.

Masterson said, "It's too bad about Sanchez, though. Now there was a sweet-looking young thing. I don't mind telling you that I had my eye on that honey pot."

"She's not dead yet," Eamon said.

"Whatever," Masterson said.

"Go to hell," Eamon said.

"Do I have to remind you that you work for me, Lieutenant Wearie?"

"Del, that's not something I'm likely to forget. Believe me."

"Would you just look at these damn Jews," Masterson said, taking in the mourners in the living room. "Sitting on a bunch of fucking boxes. What's with these people, anyway? Got some mighty odd ways of doing things, if you ask me."

"Yeah, like our church is really normal," Eamon said to the anti-Semite.

Shoe's wife came over to accept their condolences. Eamon had seen her only a month ago, but the difference was nothing short of astonishing. She was a ghost of her former self, drained of her life force and looking darkly, sadly ethereal; it was enough to make Eamon wonder if she was going to make it.

Bunko suddenly began to cry when he saw her. "Oh, Beverly," he sobbed. "Oh, Beverly, what shall we do?"

"There, there," she said, comforting Bunko. "We'll find a way."

Masterson was clearly uneasy with this raw show of emotion, but Eamon, whose own feelings seemed permanently stanched, was grateful for something so true, so real.

It was a day and night of funerals. That evening, Eamon and Mary attended Pinkus's wake at a local funeral home. It was a sad, threadbare affair. They found themselves in a small, dark, frankincense-reeking chamber with Pinkus's father. Nobody else bothered to show up. In fact, Pinkus himself was not even present; the casket remained empty, pending the outcome of the autopsy.

Pinkus's father looked like he could've been his

grandfather instead. He was a wizened, silver-toothed, jaundice-skinned, white-haired Baptist from Macon, Georgia.

"Thankee for coming," he said. "I thought he would surely have liked a wake, seeing how he'd been studying that Catholic theology. He was an odd boy, my son."

Pinkus was a strange character, Eamon had to admit. Before coming to Baltimore and before enrolling in the seminary, he'd spent ten on-again, off-again years at Chapel Hill studying animal behavior. Someone should've studied Pinkus. He seemed to subsist entirely on student loans and government grants. Eamon couldn't recall his ever having a real job. There was nothing normal about the guy. He suffered from a terrible obsessive-compulsive disorder; he was constantly cleaning the house and himself. He never seemed to go anywhere. Most of the time, he just stayed home with Pacino and Brando, Eamon's two obese cats, whom he doted on. Pinkus hadn't even died in a normal way.

Apparently, he surprised some burglar and was knifed in the ensuing struggle. The police were still sorting out the details. It seemed, though, that the killer made off with a television set and a VCR, which struck Eamon as rather peculiar. He just couldn't understand why somebody who'd just made the mistake of knifing somebody in a botched burglary wouldn't just hightail it out of there. Why didn't the guy just leave well enough alone at that point? Why did he bother with an old, practically worthless TV? The cops theorized he was some crazed crackhead looking to barter his next fix. But there were other things that bothered Eamon as well. Why did he gut the two cats the same way he did Pinkus? It wasn't like Pacino and Brando would have done much talking to the police.

"He was surely fond of you, Mr. Wearie," Pinkus's father continued, as Mary held on to Eamon's arm in the electric candlelight. "He always mentioned you in his letters. I don't know if you knew, but Daniel was adopted. And he always had real trouble making friends. People seemed to treat him like an outcast. I reckon it was because he was a mite different than most folk. Anyway, I want you to know that my son was most grateful for your friendship, Mr. Wearie. He thought you to be a very fine person, sir."

Mary's face was by now wet with tears. But all Eamon could do was shake the old man's hand and tell him that he was very sorry for his loss.

12

Ray paid cash for his air ticket to Tampa, but he had no choice but to use a credit card to rent the car. Fortunately, the Barbie-doll rental clerk took Jack's American Express without even blinking. "Happy driving now, Mr. McCallum," the hairdo said, waving after him in the dreamy Florida sunshine.

Didn't matter that Jackie-boy had been plastered all over the news the last few days. Just proved that notoriety was harder to achieve in America than most people thought. Slaughtering ten people in a postal depot didn't cut it for some reason. The public was more interested in the glamour crimes, in taking out a president, say, or maybe being one of them serial-killer freaks who dismembered little boys or prostitutes, something in that vein.

Like who really remembered the guy who took out twenty-one people in that McDonald's restaurant out in San Ysidro, California, ten years ago? A forty-one-year-old out-of-work security guard by the name of James Oliver Huberty, and the only reason Ray knew it was because he researched it. Went over to the big old library on Cathedral to see if he could learn anything of interest. Those mothballed librarians couldn't have been more helpful. He learned that the worst mass shooting in U.S. history took place at a Luby's Cafeteria in Killeen, Texas, where twenty-four people got theirs from George Jo Hennard, a thirty-five-year-old berserko who was armed with a Glock and a Ruger. In fact, Hennard used three magazines apiece for the two guns, spitting out a total of ninety-six shots before shooting himself in the head in the restroom.

Ray found the details especially interesting. Everybody was unemployed. Everybody seemed to be between the ages of thirty-five and forty-five years old. Most of them killed themselves before giving up. Ray even made note of the guns they used and the amount of ammo that was expended and how long the shooting sprees lasted.

The worst postal rampage ever took place in the Edmond, Oklahoma, post office. A part-timer named Patrick Henry Sherrill went nuts with a couple of .45-caliber pistols, taking out fourteen of his fellow employees. Sherrill had gotten a poor job-performance rating from his supervisors just the day before. He was also a former marine, just like Jack.

Ray decided to make the Edmond massacre his benchmark. He figured it was important not to surpass Sherrill's fourteen-body total. After all, he didn't want to bring any extra scrutiny to Jackie-boy's antics at Depot 349. He'd succeeded there all too well, taking out only ten but leaving that little girl postal inspector still alive. The newspapers said she wasn't supposed to pull through, but even so, it was a worrisome, nagging little concern. When Ray found out about it, his first instinct was to go to the hospital where she was and finish the job. But then he thought better of it. His first order of business was to be reunited with Jill. Later, if anything went wrong, he could come back for the postal bitch.

Man, he already liked Florida, though. Nothing

wrong with all that warm sunshine, that was for shit sure. He sped along a chalk-white highway en route to some little place called Nalcrest. There wasn't much to look at, just orange groves and billboards for alligator farms. Still, for the first time in like ages, he felt a real sense of possibility glimmering in the afternoon haze.

He pictured Jill on the screened-in porch of her house, waiting for him. She was sitting on a rocking chair in a white dress, sipping lemonade or iced tea. It wouldn't be long now. More than anything, he wanted to look into those sensitive, moony green eyes again. Tenderly, he would stroke her long, straight chestnut hair, caressing her into submission. Everything had to be worked into real slow. Then he would kiss her very gently and let her know that all was forgiven now. They could take all the time in the world. There wouldn't be any of that awkward, rough groping stuff. He would carry her into her feminine, pink bedroom and lay her on the big, brass bed. He'd begin by spreading little kisses on her firm, juicy tits and then he'd work his way down to her perfect, perfumed snatch. Jill was the first woman he wanted to eat out. All the others seemed like such nasty sluts. But with Jill, he'd show her he could be a good, attentive lover. He knew it wasn't just about stamina, even though he had plenty of that to spare, too.

His hands felt sweaty on the steering wheel. It had been such a long, hard wait. He just didn't want anything to go wrong now. He'd come too far to be disappointed. He hoped she'd be pleased with all the effort he'd made. After all, it had taken a lot of doing to prove his love.

In her wildest dreams, Jill hadn't ever thought she'd wind up living in a trailer park. But she'd come to accept her edge-of-the-world existence at Peaceful Waters, which was snug on the shores of Lake

Sahatchee, a former home to Seminole Indians and Spanish trappers. It was a cool blue oasis that reminded Jill of the lakes up north, the way it was rimmed by a soft bed of pine needles, the way the light refracted off it, vivid and golden, giving off a rich sense of the autumnal.

The trailers were another matter. Laundry hanging out to dry was a permanent fixture, as were the oldsters in their sun visors, sitting on folding chairs under their trailer awnings. Still, there was something homey and safe about Peaceful Waters, as if they were so far removed from the hustle and bustle that nobody would even think to bother with them.

Usually when she got home, Jill got her sketch pad and headed down to the water's edge, to enjoy the early twilight and to capture some of that wicked chiaroscuro. But this day, she pulled her car up to the little pink trailer and saw that somebody had already been there. A bouquet of red roses and a box of chocolates had been left for her outside her door, causing her heart to sink all at once. The mere sight of this small romantic offering brought back that bad time full force. Ray had been awfully big on flowers and candy.

Then she remembered it was Valentine's Day. She felt instant relief. That was just like Teddy, she thought. He'd said something at work about how he was going to surprise her when she least expected it. Still, after all that had happened to her, she was leery of any such attention. She thought she'd made herself quite clear to him about that. Besides, just the fact that he was her boss made the whole idea untenable. But she had to admit Teddy was a sweetie, just to be thinking of her. God knew there weren't too many other people out there carrying her in their thoughts.

She took the goodies inside. Her trailer, which rested on blocks, was only three rooms big. It wasn't much, really, but it had all the amenities, full electric and running water, everything except an air conditioner. She was surprised that Teddy hadn't attached a card. Obviously, he didn't think she had too many other suitors.

She decided to give him a call, just to thank him. Actually, maybe she'd invite him over. She had some cold beer in the fridge. They could get a pizza and eat it outside on the picnic table. Later, if everything was still going smoothly, she could take him down to the lake, to one of her secret places. Oh, what was she thinking? It was crazy. But there was something about Teddy she trusted. She liked his disheveled, good-natured appearance, the way he didn't seem to be trying too hard, as if he was content with who he was. He had a heck of a nice little tush, too. But it had been quite a while since she'd been alone with a man. She didn't know if she was ready yet.

Then again, she'd been ready enough to get involved with Maria. But that was different, that was safe and comfortable in its own nutty way. Jill unsnapped a cold beer and put some music on the CD player. The beer felt good on a warm, placid night. She plopped down on the couch and lost herself in the haunting echoes of the Cranberries. She finished the first beer and reached for a second one. A long shadow fell over her tiny trailer. It was going to be just another boring, lonely night. She was on her third beer when she started imagining Teddy without his clothes on. Maybe she was ready, at that.

She tried calling Teddy, but she wound up getting his machine. She decided not to leave a message. She'd try again in a little while. First, she'd take a shower, cool herself down. Two cold showers a day was the rule rather than the exception in Florida. Usually, she took the second one just before bedtime, but tonight was different. Tonight she shaved her legs and sprinkled herself with baby powder. Tonight she dabbed herself with Chanel and wondered about what she'd do for birth control, if it came to that. Because she wasn't on the pill anymore—and that certainly hadn't been a worry with Maria. There was probably some all-night drugstore where she could buy condoms.

Using the medicine-cabinet mirror, she applied lipstick for the first time in ages. It was Maria who had given her the cosmetics, no doubt hoping she'd take a hint. In the old days, before Ray, she'd enjoyed making herself beautiful, getting ready for a night on the town. But in the last few years, she never bothered with anything more than soap and water. She'd even sheared her long, Godiva-like hair in spite and anger. She didn't want any other men to get ideas about her. Even if she lied to herself about it, making believe that she'd cut it short because it was easier to manage.

Her phone rang while she was finishing with the eyeliner. She hurried to pick it up, thinking it was Teddy, her not-so-secret admirer. "Hello," she said. "Hello? Hello?" she repeated into the staticky void.

A moment later, she heard the dial tone. But somebody had been on the other end, waiting and lurking, she just knew it.

Ray used to do that all the time. But it couldn't be him, that simply wasn't possible. She shivered at the thought in the warm night.

It had to be Teddy. God, he was just another male cretin. How could she have been so wrong about him? In the future, she'd stick to women. They were easier to figure. In the meantime, she went back into the bathroom to wipe all the gook off her face.

Ray couldn't believe the dump Jill lived in. A goddamn fucking trailer park, for shit's sake. Man, that girl needed him big time, even if she didn't know it yet. He was going to take her away from all this, to a new, improved life. She'd definitely like the cabin and all that fresh, clean country around it. Nobody was apt to bother them out there. They could raise their kids and shit without any interference from asshole neighbors or what have you. Every so often, they'd go into town for supplies, but that was about it. Jill was going to just love it.

He was almost ready to make his move. He was pretty damn excited, but he was trying to keep his emotions in check. He had a plan and he meant to stick to it. He'd already called Jill from a roadside phone booth, just to make sure she was there and had gotten his Valentine's Day presents. He'd taken the liberty of spiking the chocolates, in case she was a little uptight about everything. This way they could just ease back into it again. This way there wouldn't be an attitude-adjustment problem.

Ray had already driven by the trailer park several times. Part of it was just getting himself ready in his mind. It was like in the old days when he used to drive by Jill's parents' house in Muldeen. He'd cruise by there to see if Jill was home, or to see if that Keith guy's car was parked in the driveway. He'd drive by maybe ten or twenty times in a day, just to take stock of the situation. It was important to know what you were up against. Sometimes late at night, he'd see the lights on in Jill's bedroom and he'd feel this real nasty pain in his innards.

There were times when he blamed her for everything, for not giving him enough of a chance. Shit, there were moments where he almost hated her. It pained him something terrible when she didn't take his calls or answer the door, even though he knew very well that she was home. It was weird the way you could love somebody but still want to hurt them a little, just to make them take notice. Sometimes he even harbored thoughts of revenge. But mostly he just loved the stupid bitch.

It was confusing the way lots of different kinds of feelings were, like, swirling in him. But he still needed Jill. Because without her, it was almost, like, hopeless. Then there wouldn't be even the possibility of something better.

He thought he was almost ready to ride over there

now. He took one last look at himself in the rearview mirror. He put a comb through his hair, even though it was only bristles, anyway. He kept it the Hagerstown way now. He just thought the buzz-sawed look made a statement about how he wasn't going to take shit from anybody anymore. He bought a special new shirt for the occasion, though. Actually, he had some trouble finding something cool, just because of his neck size from all the working out. He looked sharp, though, if he said so himself. He gave himself the thumbs-up in the rearview, then turned the key in the ignition. It was time to get it done.

13

The nurse told Eamon to talk to Lita Sanchez naturally, as if it were just an ordinary day in her life. This wasn't so easy, considering that she was in a coma and that her head was bandaged and that there were tubes coming out of her mouth and nose.

"It's me, Eamon," he said, taking hold of her small hand. "I'm praying for you, kid."

He didn't know what else to say. What was he supposed to do? Try to cheer her up? Fill her in on the latest office gossip? Tell a joke or two? He couldn't seem to get past the bandages, past the horror of her immediate predicament. The Lita he knew was a feisty, blue-collar gal who took no guff. But that was just what she showed at work. He'd gotten to know the other side of her, that soft, private core that surprised you with its girlishness and playfulness. They'd had some sweet times together, just hanging out watching the world go by. She was the kind of girl with whom you could rent a pile of videos on a rainy Sunday afternoon and call out for pizza. She was easy to please—and nowhere was this more true than in bed. She seemed to cry out at his every touch. It was dumb, but she really made him feel like a man, like he was her strong protector. He'd loved her in a way, and if Mary hadn't come along, he'd probably still be with her.

"God, this is hard," he said, beginning again. "I hope you can hear me, Lita. I want to tell you something that I probably should've told you a long time ago. I'm sorry . . . I'm sorry for how things worked out with us. I really liked you. No, that's not right. I loved you, that's the real truth. For some reason, I didn't know how to handle it at the time. I think I was kind of afraid, you know.

"I kind of felt you wanted me to be your hero. Like I was supposed to protect you and take care of you. And there was a part of me that just wanted to run from that. I didn't feel I was up to the job. I was having a tough enough time just taking care of myself. But I'm sorry, because we should've talked about it, should've dealt with it. Instead of me just taking off the way I did.

"Anyway, that's pretty much what I wanted to say. I hope you'll accept my apology at this late date. I think you're a terrific person, Lita, and I need you to come out of this. I mean, I know things can't be what they once were between us, but we can make it into something else, something good in its own way."

He had no idea if she could hear any of it. It seemed like she wasn't even breathing. The only way to tell she was alive was from the blips and bleeps of the respirator. But buried beneath the bandages and the tubes was his old lover and friend. He wanted to cry, but he just couldn't. The Wearies simply weren't made that way. There was just the terrible nothingness, all bleak and empty and hollow. He longed for the release of tears, for any kind of absolution at all.

He squeezed Lita's lifeless hand one last time. He wasn't going to tell her, but he was sorry for one other thing, besides. He was sorry he hadn't been in the command post that terrible Friday. Because if he had been, you could bet Lita Sanchez would not be lying in this strange, purgatorial state, somewhere between life and death.

Deke had found a perfectly wonderful tittie bar downtown. He was with his kind of people, enjoying his kind of times. Moby and Dix were hogs and they understood the world in the way of the hog. Dang, they were the kind of fellas you could really talk to, really get down with. He had just finished showing them all the tattoos he'd gotten in the joint and they were suitably awed.

"That's some nice body work you got there," Moby said.

"You're a living piece of art," Dix said, "that's what you is, boy."

Moby was the porky one with the ponytail. Dix was the hard-bodied leather dude with the Fu Manchu. Deke kept getting them confused in his mind. The drinking was starting to take its toll. For some reason, he just couldn't do the Wild Turkey the way he used to.

"Well, I appreciate the compliment, fellas. But I can tell you I'm most proud of the Harley-Davidson insignia that I got at Baltimore City Correctional. There's a man in there who's a regular Michelangelo."

"There ain't nothing in this world as fine as the sound of a Harley at idle," brother Moby said.

"Except maybe the sound of that V-twin engine with a single crankpin going at a full throaty roar," said Dix.

The topless waitress came by with some more beers and shots of Turkey. Deke waved his friends off and gave the skank another twenty. He was going through the money Ray gave him pretty fast. It was about time for him to pay another visit to that postal inspector's house. Nail that son of a bitch so he could collect the last half of his fee from Ray. First, he'd have to find Ray, though. That boy was nowhere to be found. But wherever he was, Deke knew he was coming back.

Because Ray was surely aware of the consequences to do otherwise.

"I like the Dyna Wide Glide myself," Moby was saying. "Now that's a sweet highway bike with its two-point engine isolation mounting system. It's got the foot pedals way out front for even more comfort. Not only that, it's got that bobtail fender and comes in Inca Black Pearl, which is the nicest paint job going, if you want my opinion."

"I'll take a Fat Boy any day over that," Dix said.

"A mighty fine chopper," Deke agreed. "Looks a lot like the '49 Hydra Glide, which was another classic machine. Me, I wouldn't mind one of them Heritage Softail specials. Got them wide whitewalls. Staggered dual fishtails. Now that's a bike only God could've made."

Deke got a warm feeling inside thinking about Harleys. He remembered that time when he made the pilgrimage to their museum in Pennsylvania. This little old woman gave the tour—and, dang, if she didn't know her bikes. Deke couldn't stump her at all, even though he threw every question he could at the old bag. She was something else, though. If he could have picked out somebody to be his real mother, that's just who he would've wanted.

Dix and Moby had their attention fixed on the floor show. Some ugly, chubby bitch humped a pole to some loud, new music that Deke didn't care for. He liked Hank Williams and Johnny Cash, stuff that you could follow the words to. The new crap just gave him a headache. He got downright annoyed every time he turned on the radio. Damn impossible these days to find a real country-western station. Don't even try to tell him Garth Brooks is country music. Heck, he was sick and tired of everything, if anybody cared to know. He was sick of the way he was constantly being shunted aside, like he didn't count, like he was this invisible nobody. People just saw this old tattooed guy in blue denim. They couldn't seem to get past that. If you didn't look like you had a million bucks in your pocket, you might as well just forget about it. The whole country was filthy with this attitude.

Deke got steamed just thinking about it. But what did it matter anyway? He had a sneaking feeling that he wasn't going to be around much longer. He sure wasn't feeling like himself. He either felt way too warm or he got these bone-numbing chills. He couldn't even pee anymore. He kept drinking and drinking, but nothing seemed to come out. And he was constantly sweating. It was as if the alcohol were seeping out through his pores. His red Willie Nelson bandanna was soaked through and through. He tried not to dwell upon what was happening to him, but sometimes he couldn't help but get stuck on the bad thoughts, thinking about his own demise and that big, ungrateful, uncaring world going on about its business as if he'd never existed in the first place. That's when he'd start to get real upset and want to take a bunch of them bastards with him. It seemed as if it was the only way he ever got anybody to take notice of him.

The skank with the itty-bitty titties and the tight-assed attitude came back to their table. "Are you *gentlemen* through? Or should I bring you another round?" the skank said, making a disapproving face.

"Sister, you sure have a sad, unfortunate manner about you," Deke said. "I guess it's on account of the fact that you got them small tits and don't like yourself too much. But, dang, that ain't our fault."

After the skank left in a huff, Deke turned to his new buddies, Moby and Dix. "Boys, it's been swell. I sure have enjoyed the pleasure of your company. That's no lie—and to prove it," he said, dropping a hundred bucks on the table, "let me buy you both a steak dinner tonight. I won't take no for an answer. I wish I could join you, but I'm a working man. I got places to go and promises to keep."

"Shit, you're the best," Moby said.

"Fuckin' A right," said Dix.

Deke shot them a look. "What did I tell you boys about watchin' your language around me?"

After they mumbled out their apologies, Deke took his leave. He was in a hurry to get to that postal inspector's house. He felt a burning need in him. The liquor was mixing with the sickness, and the sickness was mixing with something from the long-ago. His head was hot and feverish and he probably should have been in a damn hospital bed. But he had the hunger now and it yearned to be filled, no two ways about it.

Deke stepped outside into a neon night. He didn't even know what time it was. He had come into the tittie bar around noon, if he remembered rightly. The Block, Charm City's answer to Times Square, was one big, bright, flashing Sodom. He felt a little disoriented in the garish light of all those LIVE-NUDE-XXX marquees. For a singular moment, he thought about relieving his tension in a jack-off booth. But then he remembered that postal inspector's new wife. She'd do just fine.

He forgot what the hell he'd driven over in. Couldn't remember where he parked, couldn't even remember the vehicle. He saw his buddies' Harleys glinting at the curb, offering up transportation possibilities. But he quickly realized that would be breaking his own personal code. As they were fellow hogs, he wouldn't be able to live with himself, no sir.

He was blowing on his hands, trying to keep warm and think of some alternative, when God smiled on him. Some junior dickhead in a BMW pulled right up alongside of him. Some young suit-and-tie talking on his big-deal car phone. Deke just swung his car door open and grabbed the startled dickhead by the lapels and threw him onto the pavement. Kicked him in the damn skull until his fancy glasses were scrunched and there was blood coming down his face. Then he stomped on that fruity phone of his and gave him a few boots to the wiener, just for good measure.

Deke got right behind the wheel and hit the pedal and peeled out. Dickhead had left some music in his CD. Some damn opera thing, some bitch who could break glass. Deke couldn't figure how to turn it off, so he finally just smashed it in with his fist. He needed quiet now, he needed to start replaying the special memory scenes. He always started with that magical afternoon when he was fourteen and surprised his foster mother, Mrs. Lewis, the prim and proper church lady. He forced her on the bed and hiked up her thick, starchy skirt and gave her something to think about. The best part was when his foster father came home unexpectedly and got a good gander of Deke putting it to his wife. Their eyes met in that white-hot moment, and that was the most Deke ever enjoyed himself.

Deke knew early on that all the rules that everybody else played by just didn't apply to him. He knew plain well that there weren't no God and heaven and hell and all that fiery-pitchfork stuff. Once you knew that, it was a whole different ball game, brother. It was just a matter of needing and taking, then.

He rushed through his special memories, just like he was rushing through the stop signs and red lights. He was almost there. The power surged in him. He was in charge now, and the world glittered with sick, sick possibilities. He wanted another yummy taste before he died like any other animal, like any other senseless creature. He needed, and now he was going to take once more, and one more time after that, and again and again, so long as he kept on living and needing.

He came down the postal inspector's street and felt immediate, stinging disappointment when he happened on the sight of them leaving their house. They were holding hands and coming down the front steps. Damn, now what was he going to do? He could follow them to see if an opportunity presented itself. Or he could just come back later. Or . . .

Or he could just run them down and get it over with. He slammed the gas. They'd already spoiled everything anyway.

Eamon and Mary ate their dinner in silence in the kitchen. They couldn't have eaten in the dining room or the living room, even if they had wanted to. Those two rooms, along with Pinkus's bedroom, were cordoned off with crime-scene tape. The house felt gloomy and sinister, haunted by the evil that had taken place there.

"Of course, we'll have to move," Mary said, over the tiny breakfast table. "I can't live here after what's happened."

Eamon nodded. Mary had made a lovely spaghetti dinner, but all he could do was pick at it. He kept refilling his glass with red wine.

"I want to get out of here right away," Mary said. "I don't think I can stand another minute."

"But it will take a while to put the house on the market," Eamon said.

"I can't wait that long."

"What do you propose we do in the meantime?"

"I suggest we move in with my father for the duration. Unless you have a better idea."

Eamon was silent. It was probably the only solution for now. He couldn't take any more either. To think what had happened to poor Pinkus and those two cats here was beyond Eamon's comprehension.

"I learned something else upsetting today," Mary said. "I checked with the homicide team handling the investigation and they told me that the animal who killed Pinkus also raped him. They did a rectal swab and came up with a positive for spermatozoa."

Eamon poured another glassful of wine. He could barely process this new piece of information, coming on the heels of so much other insanity. If only he'd been home that night. If only he'd been at work to help Sanchez that day. It was almost like he was not supposed to be around for either tragedy, as if they were somehow related. But how could that be?

"There's more," Mary said. "Pinkus was probably killed by an ex-con. It's the way he was knifed with the letter opener. He was what prisoners call 'zig-zagged.' Amateurs stab people by sticking the knife in and pulling it back out and maybe repeating the process. Hard-core prisoners stick the knife in and zigzag it in an attempt to rupture as many vital organs as possible."

"How educational," Eamon said, taking another swallow of the wine. "Did this sociopath also *zigzag* the two cats?"

"Actually, he did," Mary answered.

Eamon grimaced. "Did they find any fingerprints?"

"No, they speculate that he was wearing gloves. Not because it was a smartly executed crime but because it was quite cold that night. They're now checking into recently released prisoners whose pathology and history might match the brutality of this crime."

Eamon got up to get another bottle of wine. He was about to dig the corkscrew in when Mary said, "Do you really need any more?"

"As you might imagine, I'm a little depressed," he said. "I need something to get me through this."

"I'm here for you, Eamon," she said, looking up at him with patient, concerned eyes. "You're shutting me out. Talk to me."

He put the corkscrew back down and rejoined her at the table. "I don't even know where to begin, Mary. I feel so helpless and lost and pained. I feel I let Pinkus and Sanchez down. Somehow I feel personally responsible, even though I know that's crazy. I mean, it's not like I could've done anything to prevent it."

"It's not so unusual for people to feel that way after they lose someone they care about. We're not used to things' being beyond our control like that. It plays havoc with our sense of an orderly universe. We want to believe that we can make a difference, that nothing is foreordained."

"I can't believe I have to go back to work tomorrow. To pretend that it's just a normal day."

"You never told me how it went at the hospital today. Are the doctors at all hopeful?"

"Nobody has a guess," he said, picturing Sanchez with the bandages and tubes again.

"You were close to her, weren't you?"

Eamon didn't reply; it seemed like too much to get into right now.

"I think you need somebody to talk to," Mary said. "I'd like to recommend the priest at my church. Father Joseph is a decent, thoughtful man. I think he might be helpful to you right now."

"I can't take it anymore," Eamon said, suddenly rising from the table. "Let's take a walk, anything. Let's just get out of this miserable, reeking house."

They grabbed their coats and walked hurriedly past the yellow police tape and the living room that was still stained with Pinkus's blood.

They were outside on the sidewalk debating in which direction to proceed when Eamon heard the gunning engine and the toppling garbage cans. A BMW had jumped the curb and was coming right at them. There was no time to react and no place to turn. They were caught between parked cars and spiked iron grating as the BMW barreled at them. Eamon threw Mary over the hood of one of the parked cars. He had no time to save himself, though.

He just leaped as the car hit him, trying to avoid the full brunt of the impact. He was hurled in the air like a juggling pin, but he came down like a human being, landing on his head and making a sound like a cracking coconut.

He tried not to black out, but he was fading in and out of consciousness. He could feel the wet, warm blood, the sense that he was leaking away. He heard sirens. But where was Mary? Was she okay? Everything was swirling and tracing like when you were very, very drunk. He heard the worried, half-whispered speculation of bystanders. Then somebody was putting a towel or something under his head. But what about Mary? He was being lifted onto a stretcher. He struggled to stay with it, to keep his eyes halfway open. Then he heard Mary's voice. "I'm here," she kept repeating. "I'm here." Everything was wet and fuzzy and getting darker, but it no longer mattered. He hadn't let her down, thank God.

He caught a wavering, unfocused glimpse of the wreck as he was being ushered into the ambulance. The BMW had hit a tree; it looked like a mashed-up accordion with air bags. He heard a policeman say, "Some drunk. No, he's fine. It's the drunks who always survive these things." He wanted to tell him that the guy wasn't a drunk at all. He had seen the maniac's face. He was aiming right at them. But even though Eamon was trying real hard, he couldn't seem to get the words out of his mouth.

14

Jill was feeling more alone than ever Valentine's Day night. Her whole life seemed like such a miserable waste. Here she was in a trailer park in the middle of Retirement Central, with not a friend in sight. She wasn't living anymore, she was sleepwalking through a life. How else to explain her clerking in the Nalcrest post office? Her time, her energy, her very lifeblood were given over to dispensing stamps and weighing packages. At night, she listened to lonely music and sketched lonely charcoals of Lake Sahatchee. What was the fucking point anymore?

All the things she grew up dreaming about were so far out of reach that it wasn't even funny. All she ever really wanted was to marry Mr. Right and have some kids and a nice house. No matter how hard she denied it to herself and others, that was the pathetic truth. Even when she was out there in La-La Land doing the careerist fandango, she never stopped thinking that she was going to meet that special someone. She was going to turn thirty-six in a couple of months. Not only her biological clock was ticking down—so were her last remaining hopes.

She'd finished the six-pack from the fridge and now

she was popping the chocolates Teddy had left for her. She just wanted to be sad, to reach down into her very being and wallow there. She had the Cowboy Junkies' "Trinity Session" on the CD player. It was moody, soul-affecting music that squeezed its particular sadness out of the harmonica and the mandolin. Jill and Keith used to listen to it all the time at his place. They'd drink a little wine, smoke a little dope, make a little love. She missed him, just because he was a good guy to hang out with.

Keith wasn't the be-all and end-all, but he was cool in his own sloppy, half-assed way. He was grunge before there was grunge. He wore untucked flannel shirts and rarely bothered to shampoo his floppy, Lennonesque hair. But he played an acoustic guitar with divine inspiration, and there was something mellow and unhurtful about him that she just liked. Of course, he was totally unreliable and totally promiscuous. Not that it really mattered. Because after Ray entered the picture, Keith just ditched Jill big time.

Ray started by slashing Keith's tires and worked his way up to bashing in Keith's beloved twelve-string. Not long after that, Keith explained to Jill that he was a lover, not a fighter. She could hardly blame him for bailing out. But with Keith out of the way, Ray refocused all of his attention right back on Jill. He must've written ten letters a day to her. They were so crazy, going on and on about what a beautiful angel virgin she was and how she was the only one pure enough and untainted enough for him. He wrote that he couldn't live without her and that he was looking forward to initiating her into the beautiful world of lovemaking. He was some piece of work, all right. He even made a point of *forgiving* her for seeing Keith. Because he realized it was only her way of making him jealous. What a sick puppy.

She scrawled RETURN TO SENDER on all his letters, but that just seemed to make him write more. Then one night, he came over to her parents' house and put an ax to the mailbox. That's when she finally went to the police for an order of protection and brought the postal inspectors into it. They all took the matter very seriously. The Muldeen police made a point of patrolling by her house every hour on the hour. Lieutenant Wearie, that nice postal inspector, brought charges against Ray for sending obscene and threatening mail. They did everything within their power to stop him. But it was her dad, her poor, Alzheimer's-deteriorated dad, who really saved her.

She never would have believed it if she hadn't been there. Her dad had gotten to the point where he didn't even recognize Jill or her mother anymore. He could no longer bathe himself or even go to the bathroom without help. Her mother was a saint, a long-suffering saint. It was wretched to watch her once strong, able-minded father reduced to diapers and bibs and absolute incoherence. Everyone told them they should just put him in some kind of home. But Jill's mother was resolute. And a good thing she was, too.

The night Ray broke in, her mother was out playing bingo. He just kicked the front door in. Jill didn't have a chance to dial nine-one-one; he came at her like blind fury. Before she even knew what was happening, he had his hands around her throat. Ray told her if he couldn't have her, then nobody could. She was sure she was going to die. The one thing she hadn't counted on was her dad, who'd wandered haplessly into the living room as she was turning blue in the face. For one strange, unbelievable moment, he became his old self; it was like some light just snapped on. Suddenly he said in a strong, commanding voice from the past, "Unhand my daughter!" And then he was charging at Ray, grappling with him, stopping him.

After Ray fled, her dad returned to his Alzheimer's-impaired state. In fact, he never recognized Jill as his daughter again. He died during Ray's trial, much to their relief, she was ashamed to admit.

Jill started to feel a little funny, as if the beer and the chocolate hadn't mixed right. Hardly noticing, she'd picked her way through almost half of Teddy's Valentine's candy. She supposed it served her right to have a tummy ache. The Cowboy Junkies were doing their version of Hank Williams's "I'm So Lonesome I Could Cry." Jill's thoughts drifted to her old life in California. She suddenly missed the glossy men and the Chardonnay-and-Brie parties and the careless money. Even a set designer did all right out there. She'd driven a bright-red Miata convertible and lived in a mission-style house in the hills. What she wouldn't do to be back there now. What was she thinking when she begged the postal inspectors to put her in some kind of witness protection program? Might just as well have committed suicide.

At the time, though, it seemed like the only way. She was so shaken by Ray. She was so sure he would never go away, that he would make it his life's business to track her down. But now she didn't know. When he got out of prison, he probably just latched on to someone else, taking his frustration and torment out on some other poor, disbelieving soul. He was probably out there now, stalking that new, special someone.

Jill was suddenly starting to feel really sick. It was more than just her stomach, too. She was getting really woozy and trippy, like she'd smoked a lot of dope or something. She wondered if there was something wrong with the candy. She felt so disoriented.

Just then the trailer door flew open. At first she thought she was hallucinating. This supersize version of Ray came bursting in. Now she was sure she was dreaming. This Ray was twice as big and muscular as the real Ray. He also had this hard, military crew cut. Her body felt like Silly Putty, all soft and negotiable. She just sat there on the couch, unable to react and just waiting to wake up. Strangely, the Cowboy Junkies continued to play in the dream.

The first thing Ray did was count the missing chocolates. He said, "I almost forgot what a sweet tooth you have. You're going to be out for a while. But don't worry, I'll be here when you wake up."

"I'm glad you're not real," Jill said, giggling crazily. "Or this could be really scary."

"I've missed you so much, Jilly," he said, coming over to her on the couch. "You wouldn't believe how I've been counting the days."

Then he tried to give her a hug. That's when the dream creature felt so real that Jill began to scream out in terror. This was some fucking nightmare. Before she could scream too much, though, Super Ray had wrapped her mouth in duct tape.

"That's just for now," he said, looking at her lovingly. "The drugs are obviously making you over-react. They were in the chocolates. It's a combination of sedatives. But I think you might've taken too much of the shit. So it might be a good idea for you to barf up some before we leave."

She was shaking her head now and crying, but he didn't seem to notice. "Sometimes those same drugs will make a girl real horny." His words seemed to come from far away, like from the other end of a long, black tunnel. "Not to worry, we got plenty of time for the old snake dance later."

She wanted to run, but her legs felt like they were made out of Jell-O. Her arms and hands fared no better. She tried to hit him with all her might but only managed to slap at him weakly. He pulled her up from the couch and said real slowly, "I totally, fucking love you, Jill. I always have. And I always will." Then he pulled her into him and hugged her very tightly. She felt his large hands come to rest on her bottom. Her jellied flesh barely had the strength to cringe.

"You're going to love Pennsylvania, Jill. Have you ever been out that way? Great country up over Harrisburg. Mountains and rivers and shit. Wait'll you get a look at the cabin. Man, you're going to love it. We're going to make babies there and live a real normal life without anyone fucking it up."

She could barely keep her eyes open now. "Hey, don't go to sleep on me yet," he said, dragging her over to the tiny bathroom. "I want you to try to upchuck, if you can." He ripped the tape off her mouth and helped her over to the toilet. Then he stuck two big fingers down her mouth, which started the upheaval. "Good, that's the kid," he said, stepping away. "Keep at it. I'm just going to pack a few things for you. You're going to need some clothes and shit."

She'd never felt worse. Never mind that Ray had somehow found her. Never mind that her dream nightmare was a real nightmare. She felt chilled and feverish, all at once. She kept trying to throw up, but nothing seemed to come out after the initial burst. She would've liked to stick her head in the toilet and drown herself. But it took too much energy to do that. She needed to think, to come up with a plan, anything. She felt so heavy-headed, though, so freaking out of it. She needed to do something to save herself. But how? She had no power to fight Super Ray. He'd make mincemeat of her. She had to give herself a chance, somehow. She saw her lipstick on the sink, from before, when she was making herself beautiful for her imaginary date with Teddy. She could write something, leave some kind of clue, if she could just reach it. She was tottering at this point, on the brink of oblivion.

"You almost through?" he said from the background. "Because we really ought to be going. It's a long ride to Pennsylvania."

With every last ounce of her unfocused, jellied strength, she grabbed for the lipstick. It was no small triumph to come up with it. Now what? She saw the toilet paper. That would have to do. She was able to write Ray's name and the first three digits of a Pennsylvania ZIP code before he barged back in and caught her with the lipstick.

"What the hell's going on here?" he demanded.

She brought the lipstick up to her mouth and made like she was trying to apply it.

"Oh, I get it," he said, falling for it perfectly. "You were trying to make yourself beautiful for me. Don't you worry about that now, kitten. We'll clean you up later."

Super Ray bent down and lifted her off the bathroom floor like she was a prop-department dumbbell. "I've already put your clothes in the car," he said. "I couldn't find any suitcases so I used some garbage bags. I hope you don't mind. Man, we have so much catching up to do. Shit, you wouldn't believe what the last few years have been like for me . . ."

She couldn't stay awake a moment longer. The will to fade away was stronger now than even the will to live. She sank away into the heavy, druggy depths, into a sea of bad dreams. She welcomed it, though. Because there was no nightmare that could compare with the reality of Ray.

15

"**Y**ou know, it sounds like you were actually quite lucky," Mary Seppala's father said to Eamon. "You really could've been killed, leaving my daughter to be a young widow."

"That's what the doctors told me, too," Eamon said glumly. "That I was one lucky fellow."

They were in the living room of Mr. Seppala's house. Eamon lay back in a big old recliner with a pillow propping up his battered, swollen head. He didn't care what anyone said; he didn't feel so lucky. It was true he hadn't fractured his skull, but it was also true that the doctors had to shave him bald and thread ninety-eight Frankenstein-like stitches up the middle of his scalp. Oh, he was a sight, all right. He had two nasty shiners, and his body was one massive purplish bruise. This was not to mention two dis-lodged teeth, or the fact that a concussion forced him to spend the night in the hospital.

"Get you another one, son?" Mr. Seppala asked amiably, pointing at Eamon's empty beer.

"I don't see why not," he said, ignoring his doctor's advice not to mix alcohol with the prescription pain-killers.

Eamon was through listening to the experts. Especially after last night. He was thinking of the police experts who were fooled by that drunk driver. After he blew in the Breathalyzer, the drunk pretended to pass out. The cops, without bothering to use cuffs, just placed him in the back of the police cruiser. Then they turned their backs to chat with fellow officers from a backup unit, and that was all this so-called drunk needed to make his getaway.

Eamon didn't doubt that the maniac had been drinking. But it was no accident. He'd tried to mow them down with that BMW. They'd already learned that the Beamer was stolen. It seems their guy just kicked the shit out of the car's owner while he was still behind the wheel. Apparently, this happened just minutes before he made his vehicular homicide attempt on Eamon and Mary. Which made Eamon wonder: what if they hadn't just stepped out at that moment for a little night air? Did the guy originally have something else in mind?

Eamon had a hunch it was the same sicko who killed Pinkus. He had no idea what it was all about, but there was too much bang-bang action in one little corner of the world to ignore.

Eamon and Mary's dad had killed the better part of the afternoon drinking beer and watching the soaps and talk shows. Joe Seppala was a heck of a nice guy, really. In fact, if Eamon had been choosing a father-in-law, he could not have done much better. Joe, who had a full head of silver hair and a belly that lapped over his belt some, was an unassuming, easygoing retired cop who reminded Eamon of his own dad. Joe was also a bit of a homebody, preferring to simmer his afternoons on a low flame, cooking gourmet meals and trying his hand at the paper's daily crossword puzzle. But he seemed glad for the company today. He made it quite clear that Eamon and Mary were welcome to stay as long as they needed to.

Eamon could think of worse things. He sipped his

beer in the glow of the TV, as Joe busied himself in the kitchen preparing dinner. The hearty, comforting, wine-fragrant smell of beef bourguignon filled the small house. Joe Seppala owned a modest, two-story brick affair by the old Memorial Stadium. Most of the furnishings were American colonial, sturdy Ethan Allen pieces that probably dated back to the first mortgage payment. What made it nice for Eamon was imagining Mary growing up here. He still couldn't get over his good fortune in marrying the girl whose confirmation and graduation pictures decorated the fireplace mantel. If he weren't all busted up, looking and feeling like hell, he might've really enjoyed this laid-back afternoon. As it was, he washed another codeine down with his beer. Mary would be home shortly from work. Maybe she'd learned the identity of their mystery driver.

Eamon turned up the volume on the TV. Famous Barry, the psychic who talks to dead people, was appearing on somebody's show. Eamon had used Famous Barry on a case about five years ago. It was uncanny, but by the end of their session, Barry had Eamon believing. Not only had the medium made contact with his dead grandfather, but he'd offered up a vital clue in their investigation into a serial killer. Barry was a former mailman who'd had an auto accident and died on the operating table. He went through the whole popular afterlife experience, being greeted by the warm, fuzzy light and the reassuring, loving spirits of dead friends and relatives. Even more amazing was that after the doctors managed to bring him back, the funny light and ghostly figures still remained. From that moment forth, the dead were always around Famous Barry.

He was hitting the talk-show circuit to hawk his latest best-selling book, *Schmoozing with Angels*. "We've sold the rights in fifteen languages," Famous Barry told the unctuous host. "And we've already optioned it to the movies. Tom Hanks is dying to play the lead. In fact, I was lunching with him the other day at Morton's and . . ."

Eamon was disappointed. Here was this guy who could supposedly chat with the dead and he was going the celebrity-bullshit route. What a waste. He had changed a lot since the last time Eamon had seen him. He'd thrown out the open shirts and gold chains in favor of an Armani suit. That wasn't to mention the hair-weave and the sunlamp complexion. Famous Barry had gone totally Hollywood.

The Barry that Eamon remembered was a devout Catholic who'd decorated the walls of his office with dozens of crucifixes and who believed there was only eternal life or eternal damnation, one or the other. There were no in-betweens, no gray areas, no do-overs. God was not interested in excuses or explanations. The gospel according to Barry had frightened Eamon. His God was a harsh disciplinarian, not nearly the merciful, loving presence that others carried in their hearts.

After Famous Barry got done telling the host about his latest venture, which was a series of heavenly theme restaurants, he announced the stops on his upcoming book tour, beginning with Baltimore. Eamon wondered if he should take that as some kind of sign; it was hard to explain, but he needed something to reaffirm his lagging faith, to stoke his desire to believe again, even if it was in the person of some Hollywood phony. All this death and mayhem had taken its toll. When the BMW had come at him last night, he sure hadn't had a sense that eternal life was his.

When Mary came home, she came bearing gifts. "How's my hero?" she said, giving him a kiss and dropping a beautiful, old-fashioned felt fedora into his lap. "I think you're going to need to wear a hat for a while."

"Are you saying that I'm no longer beautiful?"

"Let's put it this way," she said, "you're lucky I didn't marry you for your looks."

"It fits perfectly," he said, adjusting the brim.

"You look like Humphrey Bogart with two black eyes."

"And I feel as good as I look."

"I had some trouble finding that hat," she said. "The haberdashery business isn't what it used to be. Thank God for thrift shops."

"What've you got there?" he asked, noticing the canvas police bag Mary was holding. "More presents?"

She reached into the bag and took out a rather odd-looking nylon contraption, something like a strait-jacket. "This one's for you, and I also have one for my dad. One size fits all. They're bulletproof vests. I'm afraid we're all going to need them for the moment. At least until we pick up one David Deke Branson. It would probably be a good idea to holster down, too. They don't come any more dangerous than this sociopath."

"I gather this is the fellow who nudged me with his car last night."

"They lifted his prints out of the police cruiser and ran them through the crime computer. Branson has spent pretty much the last thirty years in prison. For rape and armed robbery, mostly. Unfortunately, they finally had to release him last month. The prison authorities suspect him of killing several of his fellow inmates. Nobody could ever prove it, though. He's a member of the White Supremacists, one of the nastier jailhouse gangs. An inmate would have to be crazy to snitch on a Supremacist."

"Do you think this is the same guy that killed Pinkus?"

"I don't think there's any doubt. The whole deranged crime fits Branson's MO, down to gutting the two cats. He was doing sick stuff like that when he was six years old. Nobody could ever control him. He was in juvie by the time he was fourteen."

"I still don't understand what it's all about. Why's he coming after us?"

"Well, he's probably not coming after you," Mary said. "Even Pinkus was probably incidental to his main cause. He's out for my blood. Somebody has obviously put out a contract on my life from prison. That's the only thing that makes sense. I've never come in contact with Branson before, so it's probably a fellow White Supremacist or former cellmate that's ordered the hit. No doubt it's someone I've arrested and put away in the past. Right now, we're reviewing all of Branson's records to see who his friends and bunkmates were. So far, nothing rings a bell, though. But we'll soon get to the bottom of it. The department is giving it priority. Of course, there's an all-points bulletin out for Branson."

Eamon said, "I don't think I should leave your side until they catch the fuck."

"Don't worry," she said, "they're placing a patrol car outside the house. And I'll be accompanied to and from work until this thing blows over."

"I still think I should be with you."

"And I think your bodyguard days are over for right now," she said. "I don't know if you've taken a good look in the mirror, but you're not exactly in prime physical condition."

"A few scrapes and bruises, that's all."

"You look like you've just come out of brain surgery. Botched brain surgery."

"Flattery will get you everywhere."

"So what do you think of your bulletproof vest?"

"They're much lighter than I thought," he said, taking hold of one of the Baltimore City Police specials.

"Tough, lightweight, unidirectional fibers are layered between sheets of polyethylene. It's a big improvement over the old body armor. This one you can even wear under your shirt. It's twenty times stronger than steel. Developed to withstand all sorts of new, high-velocity projectiles."

"I just love it when you talk like that," Eamon said.

"You want me to repeat that part about projectiles, don't you?"

"No, I want you to tell me about the part when this is all going to be over," he said grumpily.

16

Before they left, Ray smashed the distributor cap on his rental car and then called the company to tell them the car had broken down at the Peaceful Waters trailer park. When the apologetic voice told him he could have a replacement, Ray said don't bother because he was taking his business elsewhere. The putz actually wanted him to wait around for the tow truck.

The rental car was just one more loose end. At this point, there were almost too many details to keep track of. He'd left his mother's Impala at the Baltimore airport in the long-term parking lot; it would probably be there for years before anybody noticed it. Not that it made a difference, really; he had a nice, new Jeep at the cabin. They wouldn't be doing much traveling anyway, except the occasional supply run into town. And even then, he probably wouldn't take Jill. He didn't want to give the local farm boys any ideas. The horny bastards could find their own goddamn pussy.

Taking Jill's car up north was another calculated risk. But, logistically speaking, it seemed the only way to make the trip. She had a fairly new Toyota that was as bland and boring as the rest of her truly sad life. It was like the girl had nothing going for her without

Ray. It was a good thing he gave a shit or else she'd wind up spending the rest of her life working in the post office and living with the old farts in the trailer park. Which reminded him: in the morning, when she snapped out of it, he'd have to get her to call her job and tell them she was quitting. The last thing he needed was for them to report a missing person.

Ray just had way too much shit to orchestrate. He just needed to buy a little more time. Because even if they got wise to him, it didn't matter, so long as he got Jill to the safety of the cabin. Once there, things would just take care of themselves. Nobody would be able to find them. He'd bought the damn place with cash and used a phony name, besides. It was the same phony name he had on his Pennsylvania driver's license: Raymond Smith. Like why should he fuck himself up by making it too complicated? Keep it simple, that was his motto.

Except there was nothing simple about any of it. He was already worried about getting stopped by the cops. He had Jill in the backseat, sleeping it off under some blankets. Of course, he could just say his girlfriend had had too much to drink or some shit like that. But what if somebody got curious and wanted to know why some dude with a Pennsylvania license was driving a Florida-registered vehicle? What if the fuck tried to wake Jill up for some answers? Because no way he'd be able to get a rise out of her.

One nosy highway trooper could spoil everything. The problem was, he had no way to protect himself if push came to shove. He'd had to leave the Glock at his Fells Point apartment—no way he could chance the airport metal detectors—which was just one more loose end in a fucking world of loose ends to think about. He never even had a chance to clean out the place; he was in such a hurry to get down here and see Jill again. But now he didn't think he'd be able to go back to Baltimore. First of all, he didn't want to chance bumping into Deke. That might be a career-ending mistake right there. Second, who knew if anybody else was looking for him at this point?

But if anybody was searching out his apartment for clues, they were out of luck. Ray had seen to that, all right. In fact, just to throw off the scent, he'd placed a few false clues about, some odds and ends that would have the bloodhounds yelping in circles.

As far as he knew, that girl postal inspector was still in a coma. So he still didn't see how anyone could be looking for him anyway.

Now he needed a gun, though. In case he was stopped, in case of a lot of things. He was following the speed limit and all, but that still didn't do anything for his nerves. He was only one broken taillight away from life without parole.

He'd traveled east, across the belly of the state, to I-95, the big interstate that would take them all the way to the promised land. It was a blaze of cars and diesels under an endless purple sky. Everybody was going at least seventy-five, it seemed, which was ten miles over the limit. And a lot more of them were going eighty-five and ninety, cutting in and out of traffic like suicidal madmen, as if their lives were hardly worth caring about. The world was a bright flash of blue speed and red brake light. Everybody was a blur, just rushing forward into time and space, into a kind of mass oblivion.

Ray stayed in the right lane with the slowpokes and old farts, with all of society's play-it-safe losers. Everybody was blowing by him like he wasn't in the game anymore. Ray realized he couldn't take too much more of this shit. As he neared Daytona Beach, he decided he was going to have to make an unscheduled stop.

America was his kind of town, man. Whatever the fuck you wanted, it was probably for sale. All you had to do was take the off-ramp into that twenty-four-hour, winky-blinky, self-serve world of gasoline and burgers and doughnuts. The whole goddamn country was one big Jiffy Lube: you pulled in and got serviced and then, temporarily satisfied, you just got back on the highway. You just kept going until the next time your fuel gauge bottomed out. Then, no matter where you were, there was that American exit, flashing all those same choices all over again.

It was the same way if you needed a line of coke or a piece of ass. Or even a motherfucking gun. It didn't matter where you were. Because if you had the cash, you could get it. All you had to do was follow the blinking signs.

Ray had little doubt he could get what he wanted in Gooch's Good-Time Bar. It was a cinderblock hole that advertised live dancers and half-priced shots. And there were a dozen or so Harleys parked out front, which was advertisement enough for Ray. Yeah, he had a pretty good idea what kind of place Gooch's was.

He parked away from the cycles. He didn't want any of those boys to get a look at Jill in the backseat. She was still out cold. He must've screwed up the recipe for the Hagerstown Special. Usually it just made a girl all woozy and horny. He'd used it plenty of times on runaways and shit without any problems. It was just a simple mix of benzodiazepine, a sedative and muscle relaxant, with phenobarbital, a no-nonsense barbiturate. Basically all you had to do was crush up some sleeping pills and Valium and maybe add a little Spanish fly. But the trick was knowing what amounts to use. Obviously, that was where he'd made his mistake. He'd made a liquid concoction—something he'd never done before—and used a hypodermic to inject the chocolates.

Ray got into the backseat and felt Jill's pulse. It was slow but otherwise okay. He checked her eyes by pulling the lids back. Total spaced-out dilation. She even had some dried-up vomit hanging from her lips. The girl was a mess. But he knew she'd be okay in the morning. Fuck, shit happens, man.

Before he covered her back up with the blankets, he

stuck his hand down her blouse and felt her boobies. They were nice, plump, and juicy, just like he'd always figured. He got hard just touching them. If Jill was just some other unconscious slut, he would've done her right then and there. But this was Jill, the bitch he was going to marry, and he wanted their first time to be special.

He locked her into the car and then went into Gooch's. It was just what he'd expected. A jukebox blaring Rolling Stones' shit. A bunch of hairy-assed bikers shooting pool. He took a seat at the battle-scarred bar and ordered a shot of tequila. "When's the live dancing?" Ray asked.

"Shelly's taking a break right now," the bartender said. He looked just like everyone else in the place: bearded, ponytailed, big-bellied, tattooed. "That'll be two bucks for the Mex."

Ray planted a twenty on the bar. "Keep the change," he said.

Now the hog looked at him with some interest.

"I got a small problem," Ray said, lowering his voice. "I need some hardware. I've got some jig living next door to me who's eyeing my old lady. I think this fucking jig wants to help himself to some of her sweet white ass. But I got no way to make a statement to him, if you know what I'm saying here."

The bartender nodded thoughtfully. Then he said, "Wait here." Ray watched him go over to one of the pool players and explain the situation. A moment later, the guy had put down his pool stick and joined Ray. It was that easy.

"I don't have much of a selection tonight," the guy said. He was a rawboned redhead with a thick, beer-matted mustache.

"I need something now," Ray said. "I'm in quite a bind."

"I got a couple of twenty-twos. Give 'em to you cheap."

"Those are baby-cunt guns," Ray said disgustedly. "I need a man-sized dick shooter."

"Welp, I got a Colt Anaconda," he said. "That's a .45-caliber, double-action revolver. That ought to keep the jigs away. But she'll cost you. Five hundred with the serial number wiped clean."

Ray took out his fat, bill-bulging Velcro wallet; he wanted to let him know that he was serious.

The guy was suddenly smiling like a greedy fiend. "How do you know I won't jump you for it?"

"And how do you know I won't do the same?" Ray said, staring him down.

"I guess trust is the name of the game," he said, sobering up. "I got the piece in my truck. Let's go."

The guy led him out of the bar to a pickup in the gravel lot. He had it hidden under the passenger seat. "Money first," the guy said, giving him a look at the big, silver-snouted gun in the light of the open door. Ray peeled off five hundred dollars and handed it over. "Looks like it's all there," he said, counting and recounting the cash.

"Is it loaded?" Ray asked, taking possession of the gun.

"Comes with six free shots," he said. "That ought to do you for now."

Ray checked the cylinder. Sure enough, there were six brass-hooded .45s lodged in there. He flipped the safety off. Then he cocked it and took aim at the stranger.

"What the hell you doing?" he blurted, suddenly understanding the way it was going to be.

"I'm testing the borders of reality," Ray said, pumping the trigger twice.

Ray stood there for a moment, feeling the big, bold power of the gun, hearing the big, solid reverberation. Then he quickly scooped up all his money and hurried back to Jill's Toyota.

A minute later, he was back on the highway, disappearing into the mad, racing lights of oblivion.

17

Deke stayed the night at Ray's sorry apartment. He didn't know where else to go. Before this, he'd been flopping down at the homeless shelter on Cathedral. But that big old cement palace was bone-aching cold. He just couldn't seem to generate any body heat. The sheets were soaked with sweat and fever chills.

Deke was thinking about turning himself in. A week in the prison infirmary sure didn't seem like the worst idea he'd ever heard. He could get all fixed up and then just go back to being prison royalty again. One of the untouchables. A duke in the holy order of Supremacists. A cellblock power broker that even the bulls respected. Dang, why, even the African-American niggers knew better than to tango with Deke. Best of all, he could get back to a sensible, orderly way of life. Nothing wrong with three square meals and regulated bedtimes, no sir. Why, it was a fine, healthy way to live, having proper respect for authority and knowing your place in the system. It was damn important to have rules; without them, there was a total breakdown in the social order. That was Deke's problem: nobody was looking after him and keeping him honest.

And, by the looks of things, it was Ray's problem, too. What the heck was that gerbil-brained boy up to? Deke hadn't seen hide nor hair of him in three whole days. But he was sure to be coming back pretty soon. He'd left all his things in the apartment, and Deke wasn't just talking about his weights and his porno videos, either.

No, he'd left a pretty snazzy gun behind, too. Deke had found it last night in the refrigerator, in the vegetable drawer of all places, when he was rummaging around for something to eat. It was one of them slick German semiautomatic pistols. Deke had already taken a real fancy to it. It was sure to come in handy, of that you could be sure.

It was time for the heavy artillery. Because that postal inspector was sure hard to put down. Deke was through with the fun and games now. He was just going to shoot this Wearie fella and get it over with. It was too bad, but he was going to have to just forget about his tasty-looking wife for the time being, on account of the fact that she was being guarded day and night by them blue uniforms. But it didn't seem like her husband was getting equal protection under the law. Deke figured this postal fella wanted to play it cool in front of his wife, like he didn't need no police bodyguards. Big mistake there, brother.

They'd moved themselves into some Marty Moron house up by the old ballpark. But, not to worry, Deke was on the case. It was not a question of money at this point; it was more a matter of honor. Deke had given his word, even if it was to a scumbucket like Ray. And if that boy was trying in any way to double-cross him, he would find himself next on the hit parade, right after the mailman.

Even though Deke had shared a five-foot-by-eight-foot cell with Ray for close to three years, he still had the feeling that he didn't know all there was to know about that boy. Which was highly unusual. Because when you shared living space in the joint, you usually learned everything about your bunkmate, from his earliest childhood memory right down to the regularity of his bowel movements. But Ray didn't like to talk much about his growing-up experiences. Deke gathered that his old man had deserted Ray and his mom for some other bitch. Happened when Ray was just a little sucker, right at one of them there impressionable ages. Deke supposed it was the ultimate rejection, having one of your real parents bail out on you like that. At least Deke had never known that shame. He'd been through his share of foster parents, all right, but since they weren't blood, it didn't really count.

The one thing that hadn't changed was that Ray was still a sorry-assed slob. There were old half-eaten pizzas and half-slurped milkshakes left about. The place was overrun by mice and cockroaches. The toilet had to be one of the most sickening receptacles of filth and disease that Deke had ever come upon. There was practically no furniture. The bed was just this lumpy, stained mattress on the floor. All and all, it was mighty sad.

Why, the homeless shelter offered more commodious accommodations. At least the beds were rock hard over there. Deke had started going to the shelter for the noise. He had enough money for a flophouse or what have you, but those places were too quiet. He needed to hear men snoring and mumbling in their sleep again. The familiar, masculine sounds helped bring him the sweet, heavenly release of sleep.

At Ray's, he spent a shivery, restless night, brother. Part of it, of course, was the way he was feeling. You know, it would not surprise him in the least if those prison quacks were right about his liver, after all. He couldn't even remember the last time he could manage even a little pee-pee. Anyway, he had his trouble falling asleep. He even tried to watch some of Ray's porno movies. But they didn't do anything for him. It just wasn't real enough to titillate. Them movies were all the same. You got these half-undressed office women in their undies and brassieres and their spiky shoes who get snaked by all those Marty Morons. Almost funny, the way they show all these ugly plumbers and TV repairmen getting all this high-class snatch. Of course, Deke understood it was some kind of rape fantasy; that's why the women were always wearing their damn shoes, even in bed. But it just didn't do it for him. Because once you've really taken a woman against her will, everything else pales in comparison.

He probably should've put his John Henry to Ray when he had the chance. Just to show him the unviolable laws of nature. To let the boy know who he was messing with. Because Deke was sure Ray was holding out on him now. Otherwise where the hell was he?

Also, what was he doing with all those guns anyhow? What did he need with a military M-16 anyway? And where was that fat, hairy friend of his? Deke hadn't seen that faggot around, either.

And then there were those maps pinned to the wall. What was that all about? Ray had these maps of Florida and West Virginia tacked up over his bed. He'd circled several towns in each state with red Magic Marker. The boy was probably planning some job without him. Or maybe he was already getting done with it. But what the hell was in Nalcrest, Florida, or Wheeling, West Virginia, for that matter?

If you asked Deke, there were way too many unanswered questions for his liking.

Even though Eamon had plenty of sick time coming to him, he quickly grew bored of sitting around drinking beer and watching soap operas with Joe Seppala. He needed to get back into the thick of things, which meant returning to Dead Letters.

He was still a gruesome sight, a swollen-faced, purple-eyed, stitch-laced baldie in a felt fedora. Just as he expected, he took some ribbing when he entered the command post. "Geeze, take a look at what two weeks of marriage will do to a fellow," Bunko said gleefully.

"She's an absolute animal in bed," said Eamon.

"Are you sure it was a car that hit you?" Bunko asked. "Sure it wasn't a bus? Or maybe a tractor-trailer?"

Eamon smiled wanly at the huge bear of a man who'd been his partner for ten years. Bunko himself was quite a sight. In clear violation of the dress code, he was attired in an old bowling shirt and a loud checked sport coat. He was also puffing away on a cigarette, another violation, right beneath the NO SMOKING sign, in fact. His other hand was wrapped around a large cup of Jack Daniel's–laced coffee, which was easy enough to deduce because he'd left the uncapped bottle in plain view on his gunmetal desk.

"I notice you're not wearing a tie," Eamon said, thinking it was as good a place as any to begin.

"I find them much too constraining," he said, unperturbed.

"I also notice you're smoking even though I recall there's some kind of rule against that, too."

"Want one?" he asked, offering from his pack of Marlboros.

"And what's with the Jack Daniel's?"

"Help yourself, *amigo*," he said hospitably. *"Mi* bottle *est su* bottle."

"Is it your plan to get us fired?"

"Since when do I plan for anything?"

Even though he knew better, Eamon went over to the bottle of Jack and poured some in his own coffee. "Now we're even," he told Bunko, taking a large swallow. "So do you mind telling me what this is all about?"

Bunko said, "Take a look around, pal. What do you see?"

Now Eamon understood. Except for the two of

them, the command post was absolutely deserted. "Where the hell is everybody else?"

"Where do you think?" Bunko said, suddenly getting testy. "The service is giving a week off to anybody who feels he or she needs it. They're also throwing in free psychological counseling. Looks like everybody went for it. Not that I blame them, exactly. I mean, who wants to be around here right now? It feels like a damn morgue."

"Where's Masterson? Now there's a guy who could definitely use some counseling."

"Unfortunately, our beloved boss is still with us. But fear not, he's locked himself in his office with his own little bottle."

Eamon said, "It's another proud day for the Postal Inspection Service."

"I still don't get what you're doing here. You look like you should be on a gurney getting morphine intravenously."

"And you look like you should be home in bed with that special hangover remedy of yours," Eamon said, taking note of Bunko's fleshy red face and puffy eyes. Even his bulbous nose, which was always a cratered and veiny mess, looked worse than usual. "What are you doing? Turning professional on me?"

"I'm in mourning," he said half seriously. "This is my one-man version of an Irish wake."

"I think you're making an asshole of yourself," Eamon said.

"What gives you the right to talk?" Bunko thundered back. "You don't even have feelings like normal people. You probably have no idea what it's like to grieve. When was the last time you shed a tear for anybody other than yourself, Wearie? I saw you at all those funerals. The only dry eye in the house."

"You know that's not fair. I care as much as you do. I just don't show it in the same way."

"You're a fucking sociopath, is what you are."

"I hope that's only the Jack talking," Eamon said evenly.

"Do you even give a damn that your old girlfriend is lying in a coma at Our Sister of Mercy? Or do you stop caring after they're through dispensing sexual favors?"

"Believe it or not, I stopped by the hospital on my way to work. Not that it's any business of yours."

"What's Sanchez's condition?" Bunko asked, the venom drained from his voice.

"No change. Still touch and go."

"It's hard to imagine that it happened right in this very room," Bunko said somberly. "Not that anyone would know. Look how they cleaned everything up. All spick-and-span. Not even a drop a blood. Did you see how they even spackled over the bullet holes?"

It was terrible, really. The command post looked just like it always looked: a functional, fluorescent-lit suite of computer-topped desks, swivel chairs, and gray industrial carpeting. It could have been the city room of a small newspaper or the inside of any modern police precinct. It was a thoroughly bland space that held no hint of the tragedy that had taken place only a few days ago.

"At least we could put a wreath on Shoe's desk," Eamon said, feeling that it shouldn't be business as usual, that they should do something to commemorate their fallen comrades. "Perhaps we should even chip in for a plaque or something."

"How about instead we find out who really shot Frank Shoe and Sanchez and the others? I think solving this crime would be a much more fitting tribute to the dead."

"What the hell do you know that I don't know?"

"I just don't believe Jack McCallum did this. Like I told you before, I knew the guy. He wouldn't have hurt a flea."

"C'mon, Bunk. The guy was a disgruntled ex-postal worker who was being brought up on charges. I read in the paper that he was also a Vietnam vet who suffered flashbacks. This guy was a powder keg just waiting to go off."

"How did McCallum get to Dead Letters?" Bunko asked. "What kind of transportation did he use? His car was parked in the driveway of his house. The cab companies have no record of dropping anybody off at the depot that day. So tell me how did he get here?"

"I don't know—he walked," Eamon said, not buying any of it. "Believe me, this was a classic workplace murder-suicide deal. The police did a thorough investigation, and they're more than satisfied that McCallum did it."

"What about that paperback they found in McCallum's hip pocket? *The Catcher in the Rye.* What do you think of that?"

"Not much," Eamon said. "Except it's interesting to note that several notorious killers have been found with that particular book. Even the guy who shot John Lennon was carrying *Catcher.*"

"Yeah, Mark David Chapman," Bunko said. "But I'll tell you what's really interesting: Jack McCallum didn't read. He was in love with his TV set. In fact, if you went through his entire house, I bet the only book you'd come across would be the phone book."

"Even if that's true, what does it prove?"

"It proves that somebody went out of his way to make it look like McCallum did this."

"I think that the Jack Daniel's has pickled your brain and made you paranoid."

"Then where's the missing gun then? According to the newspapers, Jack bought three guns, an M-16 and two Glocks. But they found only the rifle and one of the Glocks. So where's the other Glock?"

"I'm sure I don't know," Eamon said, shaking his head. "You know, maybe it wouldn't be such a bad idea if you took the service up on that free psychological counseling. I think this thing has really gotten to you, big guy."

"Okay," Bunko said, ignoring him, "then why does Jack get a post office box? He's got a mailbox, a street address, so what does he suddenly need the box for?"

"Maybe he was trying to create a new identity. Maybe at the start of all this, he wasn't thinking about suicide. Maybe he actually thought he'd get away with his rampage."

"Nice try. But the post office box is in his own name. And that's not all. When he buys the guns, he gives the store clerk the wrong address. All the forms have him listed at 417 Division Street. Jack lived at 65 Division. How does he get his own street address wrong?"

"I didn't read about any of this in the newspapers," Eamon said, not so dismissively this time.

"I checked with some friends of mine on the force."

"Don't they think this is all very odd, too?"

"No, they think it's the typical behavior of a deranged serial gunman."

"When did McCallum get his firearm permits?" Eamon asked.

"Well, that's just it," Bunko said. "He'd been licensed by the state for over ten years prior. He had a .38-caliber Taurus. The cops found that gun at his house. Literally had cobwebs on it."

"Why doesn't he bring the Taurus to the party, too?"

"I don't know," Bunko said. "But I'll tell you this: I find it interesting that he paid cash for the other weapons and that he was clever enough to make his purchase just a few days before the strict new gun laws went into effect."

"Okay," Eamon said, wondering that much more, "say Jack McCallum didn't do this. Who did? And why?"

"Got me," Bunko said, letting out a sigh. "It appears that nothing's been taken from the depot. At least as far as we know. So I can't figure what the motive could be."

"Then I'll supply it for you. McCallum was out for revenge. It makes the most sense. The guy had been fired from his job and was probably going to wind up in jail. His life was crashing down around him. The whole thing caused him to go berserk. End of story. Case closed."

"I want to show you something downstairs," Bunko said. "Who knows, it might change your mind."

They took the elevator down into the bowels of the depot, into the migrainous cacophony of sorting machines and conveyor belts. Earplugs were standard issue here at ground zero. Even the massacre had failed to curtail that riot of noise; apparently, there was no time for mourning when you were deluged with over three million pieces of mail a day.

Eamon supposed he would never look at Dead Letters the same way again. He was no longer impressed by that Byzantine network of belts and sorters, that unstoppable crush of movement. So what if it was the biggest postal outpost in the land? So what if thousands of men and women worked from dawn to dusk to dawn to deliver the nation's mail? It was just tons of folded paper in the end. It wasn't worth a single life, as far as he could tell. Even the treasures found at the very heart of Dead Letters didn't intrigue the way they used to. In the old days he used to like to motor back into all that accumulated strangeness, into the hills and valleys of the nation's postal past. But now Dead Letters was just a huge tomb, a charnel house that was true to its very name.

"So do you know anything about M-16s?" Bunko asked Eamon, practically shouting over the din of the machinery. "I didn't think so. I, on the other hand, as a former marine who saw action in Vietnam, am well versed in the pros and cons of this particular automatic assault rifle. In fact, I could take an M-16 apart and put it back together again in my sleep.

"Now, I've got to tell you I was never very keen on

the M-16. Now don't get me wrong, it was lighter than the old M-14 that we had been using and that dated back to Korea. Believe me, that three-pound weight difference was no small consideration in terms of being out in the field. Even the M-16's .223 bullets were lighter than the M-14's .50-caliber. And the M-16 held more ammo than the M-14. And, let me tell you, running out of ammo was not unheard of in 'Nam. . . ."

Eamon put his fingers in his ears and shook his head. It was too hard to hear out by the sorters, and this was getting too complicated for simply shouting back and forth over the automated racket. Bunko got the idea, though, and led the way outside to the loading docks. It wasn't all that quiet out there, either, what with two diesels waiting their turn at the concrete landing. But at least they could hear each other.

"Make it fast," Eamon said, cupping his hands to the wind and lighting a cigarette. It was another cold, dreary, pewter-sky February day. Unfortunately, they had left their overcoats up in the command post.

"Well, as I was saying, I'm a bit of an expert in the workings of the M-16. Not that I ever wanted to be, exactly. But you have to understand that we were one of the first platoons to be outfitted with the new Colts in 'Nam. At first, I loved the gun. Like I said, it was lighter and held more ammo. Me and my platoonmates even liked the sound of the M-16. It took thirty-round magazines, and when all of us were firing at once on full automatic, we made quite a commotion. In fact, I think we scared more of the enemy than we ever killed.

"You've got to understand, war is half psychological. Gaining fire superiority is all important. Loud, rapid-firing weapons like the M-16 help boost your morale, make you feel like you're giving the enemy hell. That's why we loved the M-16 at first."

"Okay, then, what was the downside?" Eamon

asked, twisting in the wind and wanting Bunko to just get to the point already.

"Well, I'm glad you asked that," Bunko said in no particular hurry, seemingly oblivious to the freezing temperature. "The M-16 fires at a very high cyclic rate, ranging from somewhere between seven hundred to one thousand rounds per minute. This is basically an imaginary figure, because the rifle's magazine obviously doesn't carry that many rounds, and even if it did, the barrel would melt before it could fire that many in a row. But even at the lower seven hundred rpm rate, that breaks down to an actual rate of about twelve rounds per second, which means—and I hope you're paying attention here—that a thirty-round magazine will be emptied in less than three seconds if the trigger is kept depressed while the weapon is in full auto mode."

"How the hell do you know all this?" Eamon said, practically shocked by his partner's textbook, by-the-numbers analysis of the M-16.

"I'll get to that in a moment, lad," Bunko said, obviously delighting in this rare display of mental superiority. "Aside from wasting ammo, the high cyclic rate, combined with the M-16's light weight, makes for very inaccurate autofire. Let me tell you, unless the M-16 is fired from a well-braced stance, the gun will tend to jump and shoot high."

"Okay, I think I got it," Eamon said, trying to digest the material. "An inexperienced shooter will waste ammo by keeping the M-16 on full auto. And he'll probably shoot high to boot. That's pretty much the gist of it, right?"

"Those are the two most salient points."

"I gather you learned all of this the hard way."

"The jungle of hard knocks," said Bunko, getting a serious, faraway look in his eyes. "On our first mission with the new guns, we got ambushed by Charlie. It wasn't pretty, believe me. What I remember most is this one suicidal NVA coming at us with a grenade. We couldn't seem to take him out, even though we were blazing away at the son of a bitch. People were shooting high, and even the bullets that were hitting him didn't seem to have knockdown power. He was able to hand-deliver that grenade right into our laps. He took five of my buddies with him."

"But what about the bullets that hit him? Why didn't they stop him?"

"I'm not really sure," Bunko said, his eyes still fogged over with the bad memory. "The M-16's high-velocity bullets are supposed to tumble in flight and generate hydrostatic shock when they hit and tear through human flesh. That means that they're supposed to really rip you apart. But sometimes it doesn't work that way. Sometimes the small .223s don't have the killing power and just punch neat holes through the target. That's probably what happened with our little grenade-toting friend."

"No wonder you know so much about the M-16."

"After that grenade, I took my M-16 and smashed its plastic stock against a tree. Then I demanded my old dependable, predictable M-14 back."

"I still don't understand how all this ties in with Jack McCallum."

"I knew Jack from the local American Legion," Bunko said, still in no hurry, even though his face was red and wind-whipped by now. "He was a marine who saw action a few years after me. In fact, he was a highly decorated combat vet and a member of Marine Force Recon."

"What's that exactly?"

"That's the corps' most elite division. It's sort of the commando equivalent to the army's Special Forces and the navy's SEALs. Doesn't that tell you something?"

"You're saying this guy was no amateur," Eamon said.

"I'm saying that during his stint in the marines,

Jack McCallum was probably a crack shot and a cool customer under pressure," Bunko said. "Although I've got to admit that wasn't the Jack I knew. Over the last few years, he had totally let himself go. He'd become this sad, tubby recluse. In some ways, he actually seemed quite spineless."

"So you don't think he had the guts to commit this massacre?"

"It's not a question of guts," Bunko said. "It's a question of technique. Now I'm going to prove to you why Jack didn't do it."

Eamon followed Bunko back inside the depot like a pupil trailing a respected teacher. They approached the main target site, where six or seven bulk-mail sorters were working the belts and where most of the killing had been done. It was only a small piece of Depot 349's miles of metal conveyor-belt track, a fraction of this specialized postal universe. The rattling conveyor belts were stacked three high and looked like some kind of ridiculous Rube Goldberg contraption. The bulk-mail sorters sifted through the mail that chugged past them on the main belt, which came up to their waists, while doing their best to ignore the constantly moving belts above them.

As they closed in on the bulk-mail sorters, who were concentrated on their work and totally unconscious of the postal inspectors' presence, Bunko said, "Take a look at the higher belts. Do you see the bullet markings and telltale dents? Now take a look up at the ceiling and tell me what you see."

Eamon could make out dozens of small dark holes in the white asbestos ceiling. "I'll be damned. He was shooting high with the M-16. Just like you said."

"The cops found about three thirty-round magazines' worth of shell casings," Bunko told him, talking loud right into his ear because of the noise. "Which is a total waste of ammo and definitely not the work of someone experienced with the M-16. Anybody who knew that gun would have put the rifle's fire-selector switch on either the single-shot or the three-round-burst mode."

"And Jack McCallum knew this gun," Eamon said, understanding perfectly.

"Exactly. He was a Special Ops warrior who would've needed only a single magazine at the most to get the job done. Only an amateur would've had his M-16 jacked all the way up to rock 'n' roll. Believe me, it's a useless bullet hose on full auto."

"But why would someone want to set Jack up? What in the world could the motive possibly be? And why would anyone go to such lengths?"

"I don't know," Bunko admitted. "But at least you're finally starting to ask the right questions now."

18

Ray tired outside of Savannah, Georgia, just as the fucking sun was coming up. It was too bad Jill wasn't sharing the driving responsibilities; otherwise, he wouldn't have bothered with the motel. But as it was, he basically hadn't had any sleep since the night before he and Jack hit Dead Letters. Ever since, he'd been so hot-wired on getting back together with Jill that he hadn't even thought to take a break.

First, though, he cruised up to the drive-through window at McDonald's and ordered up some nourishment for the both of them. Then he stopped at the first motel with day rates that he saw. He negotiated for six hours, and took a room at the end of the puke-green building, away from everybody else. He parked the car three steps from the door.

Their room was called the African Safari Suite, which just meant that besides the king-size waterbed and overhead mirrors, the walls were painted in this spear-chucking jungle motif, with pictures of banana trees and monkeys and shit like that. Jill was still out like a light. But Ray wasn't taking any chances: he tied up her hands and feet so he could go to sleep without thinking about it.

In some ways, she didn't look anything like the girl he remembered. She'd lost weight and she no longer had that nice glowing complexion. That wasn't even to mention that fucking dyke haircut. All her long, beautiful chestnut hair had been hacked off. It was almost like she had made herself ugly on purpose, like she didn't like herself anymore. But who could blame her, seeing how fate had conspired to keep them apart.

Florida had taken its toll on her, that was for shit sure. It was practically diabolical what those postal inspectors had done to her, hiding her in that nowhere, old-people's town and making her toil in the stupid post office, of all places. They had sucked up her will to live and messed with her precious life juices. God knew if she'd ever fully recover from the experience.

At least Lieutenant Wearie was going to get what was coming to him. Deke would apply the hurt like he was the Devil himself. Man, you could order that tombstone in advance.

Ray put the Playboy channel on and wolfed down his two Egg McMuffins. They had some soft-focus bi action going on. Two women slowly caressing and kissing each other. You could hardly even see anything, even though the bitches didn't have any clothes on. It was probably directed by some woman—they always made the worst jack-off films. No close-ups, no raw clits, no hard-ons. This film had to be directed by a bitch—it was going absolutely nowhere. The two lesbos were just massaging oil onto each other's tummies and licking it off. Total snoozeville.

He looked over at Jill, who was laid out on the waterbed, considering it. The problem was, she didn't look so hot. She didn't even smell that good, to tell you the truth. He went over there and removed her blouse. Even her plump, juicy boobies didn't get a rise out of him. It was frustrating. He wondered if he'd have this problem later on, when she was awake for it. He sure didn't want to embarrass himself, not getting wood like that.

Love was confusing. For the last few years, all he ever did was think about Jill. It seemed like if he couldn't have her, he would just rot away and die. She was like that one magic person, the only one who could make it right. When he thought about her, life had some meaning for a change. He'd daydream about them doing stuff together, just walking on a beach, or listening to Hendrix, or smoking a doobie, whatever. She was the part of the picture that made it all bearable. Without her, it was just him and those shitty old feelings.

But now he was having his first doubts about the whole situation. He'd done everything for this girl, put it all on the line. But already he sensed she wasn't all that grateful. All right, it wasn't totally fair, seeing how she'd been spiked with the Hagerstown Special. But when he came through the door of the trailer, he just got the feeling she hadn't missed him the same way he had missed her.

Who knew? Maybe she had some sensitive-as-shit boyfriend in Florida. Like that long-haired singer guy from back home. In some ways, it wouldn't have surprised him. All that time apart. In fact, Ray would not have minded having a few more days down in Nalcrest, just to check up on her lifestyle, to see what he could learn. See if she'd been cheating on him.

He got a little hard now, thinking about her like that, like the bitch whore she probably was underneath it all. What made her so special anyway? She was just mouth, cunt, and ass like all the rest of them. He needed to jerk off now, to get some release. He lay down next to her and squeezed her boobs hard. That was starting to work for him. He kept her face out of it as he concentrated on her boobs and her rope-tied hands. That was good; yes, that was good.

* * *

She felt like she was deep under water and running out of oxygen. She kept pushing herself upward, struggling to reach the light-dappled surface. When she finally emerged from the dark ocean of unconsciousness, she gasped for breath, just as surely as if she'd really escaped from the bottom of the sea.

She could hardly make sense of her surroundings. She saw herself in the overhead mirror, tied up like a prized steer. She was shirtless, but he hadn't bothered to gag her. Super Ray was right beside her, sound asleep and sprawled out in the nude. It seemed they were in a motel room, a strangely painted one at that. A muted television had been left on some sort of sex channel.

She wondered if Ray had forced himself on her while she was out. But then she just as quickly discarded the notion. That wasn't the important thing now. Surviving this was.

She thought about screaming. But she had no idea if anyone would be able to hear her shouts for help. She would have only a few seconds before she woke him up, too. No, she realized that wouldn't work at all. It would just wind up infuriating Super Ray.

She still felt terrible from the drugs. She could taste last night's vomit in her mouth. Not only that, she'd crapped in her pants. All her bodily functions were out of whack—even her breathing was labored and uneven, yet her heart was beating a mile a minute.

She needed to get the hell out of here. The trick was not to wake Ray. It was difficult to move with the ropes but not impossible. The hard part was being quiet about it. Even the waterbed added to her difficulties, as she cautiously maneuvered herself to the edge, careful not to cause too much wave motion. To reach the shag carpeting, though, she had no choice but to roll right off the bed. She landed with a loud thud and was surprised that Ray wasn't startled awake.

With her hands tied behind her back and with her

feet bound together, the only way she could move was by using her knees. She made her way, inch by inch, across the shag, eyeing the locked door like it was a golden mirage. Ray hadn't bothered with the chain lock, thank God, because there was no way for her to rise to her feet. She used her teeth to reposition the lock on the doorknob. Then she put the entire knob in her mouth and twisted it free. Now all she had to do was pull the door open. She couldn't believe it, but she got it done. She could see daylight, freedom . . .

"Don't make a fucking sound," he said from behind her. "I have a gun pointed at you. If you don't back away from that door now, I'll blow your fucking head off."

She was in the open doorway, facing her car in the parking lot. Outside the room next door was a metal cart holding fresh towels and linens. A moment later, the cleaning lady emerged.

"I'm warning you," he said. "Start backing away now."

The gray-haired woman in the hair net and white uniform looked at Jill with an odd mix of curiosity and scorn. As if Jill had somehow tied herself up. As if Jill wanted to be half naked in broad daylight. As if Jill was somehow to blame for her situation. Jill looked up at her with pleading eyes and mouthed the words, "Please help me."

Just then, Ray grabbed her from behind and pulled her back into the darkness of the room. "What's wrong with you, you stupid bitch?" he said, slapping her hard against the face. He was holding a huge silver revolver.

"I'm sorry," she mumbled, just trying to stay alive and hoping that the cleaning lady was hurrying for help.

"You could've wrecked everything," he said, towering before her in all his sick, naked glory. "What do you think?" he asked, preening. "I've been working out. I guess you can tell."

She nodded, anything to appease him.

"I guess you're hungry," he said, pointing to some Styrofoam containers on the table. "I got you some Egg McMuffins."

"I'm a vegetarian," she said meekly.

"No wonder you look like such shit," he said. "You're just skin and bones. You need to fatten up, kitten."

"You're right," she said obediently, trying not to anger him further.

"Okay, I'm going to untie your hands, but you got to promise, no funny business."

He watched as she sat down at the table and took hold of one of the McMuffins. "You're going to like that," he said. "The ham and cheese is what makes it. It's an awesome combo." She took a tentative bite as he kept on talking. "See? What did I tell you? You'll be hooked for life now. It's too bad there ain't a McDonald's close to the cabin. That's one of the few drawbacks . . ."

Even though she'd been a vegetarian for years, she was not about to risk her life over it. Besides, she was so awash in fear, she couldn't even taste the sandwich. She just pretended it was tofu. It was all crazy anyway. She was sitting in her own excrement eating breakfast while a muscle-bound psycho held a gun to her. She just needed to hold out until the cleaning lady brought help. How much longer could it be, anyway?

"See, you needed that meat," he said, as she finished the last of it. "Did those postal inspectors force you to be a vegetarian? Is that how it happened?" She had no idea what he was talking about; she continued to nod like an idiot. "I figured that's what happened. Did they make you cut your hair, too?"

Before she could answer, he said, "Maybe we should be going. We still got a long ways to Pennsylvania."

"I could use a shower," she said, trying to delay him.

"Yeah, no offense, but you do smell like shit."

He checked the bathroom out to satisfy himself that it was escape proof. She didn't know what he was worried about. There was no window in there—and, besides, he was still holding that huge silver gun.

She got out of her stench-ridden clothes and under a hot shower. She wondered if he was going to try anything. But in some ways she was beyond worrying about that. Being raped was plenty horrible, but at the moment it wasn't the most horrible thing she could imagine happening to her. She soaped herself up vigorously, trying to hold out until the damn cavalry arrived. What in the world was taking so long?

She kept seeing that cleaning woman's strangely unsympathetic expression, though. It was as if she thought Jill deserved her fate. As if Jill had brought it on herself. Or was it possible that she thought it was just some kind of bizarre sexual high jinks? No, no, she'd have to have realized that Jill was scared half to death. Jill looked right at her and pleaded for help.

But then why hadn't anyone come yet? Were the police waiting outside? Was that it?

"Hurry up in there!" Ray yelled, banging at the door. "We don't have all day, you know."

As she dried herself off, she suddenly had the terrible feeling that no one was coming to save her. Something told her that that cleaning woman was not going to get involved. Who knew? Maybe she saw sick, twisted things all the time. Maybe a half-naked woman bound in rope wasn't the least bit unusual.

No, that couldn't be, Jill reasoned. How could that possibly be?

"If you don't come out right this second," he threatened, "then I'm coming in after you."

"I'm going to need some clean clothes," she said, wrapping herself in a towel and trying to figure out her next move.

"I got stuff waiting for you out here," he said with less malice in his voice.

She never had a chance. As she stepped out of the bathroom, he brought the gun down hard. Her brain flashed atomic blue. All at once her legs and her mind buckled. All that ringing blue light vanished and she began to plunge into the dark, watery depths again. She was going down, down, down, back down to the bottom of that impossibly black sea.

19

Famous Barry, the psychic who talks to dead people, had generated quite a crowd at the bookstore. Eamon was able to corral Barry on his way in, much to the dismay of his handlers, and get him to agree to a few minutes alone after he finished signing his bestseller, *Schmoozing with Angels*. In the meantime, Eamon had to wait like everybody else to see the great man.

The bookstore was further proof, as if we needed any, that we live in a celebrity-fueled age. It was a giant, spanking-new megastore selling foreign newspapers and esoteric magazines, art postcards and posters, New Age crystals and music CDs, gourmet coffee and buttery croissants, the whole specialized spectrum, including, thank goodness, even a large selection of books. But the books, be it fiction or biography or whatever else, all seemed to be written by celebrity authors, by men and women who were far better known for appearing as guests on Jay Leno or Letterman than for being writers.

Ex-cast members of *The Brady Bunch* and *Baywatch* served up their memoirs. Ivana Trump and Ed Koch were supposedly novelists. Supermodels were philosophical gurus to the masses. Bill Cosby and

Roseanne were the elder statesman and -woman of this new literature. It was enough to make Eamon long for the old days when writers were really writers and bookstores were small, quaint shops with comfy armchairs and shelves of dusty, neglected classics.

But the megastore sure packed them in. Eamon couldn't help but admire the long line for Famous Barry and the constant feed to the electronic cash registers. People who had once been intimidated by the cerebral, highfalutin notion of books were now happily purchasing Howard Stern's latest. It was all part of the democratizing of America. As Eamon watched that conga line snake its way past Famous Barry, he realized that nobody in the country wanted to be left out. It was the death knell for elitism and talent.

Famous Barry's handlers kept the line moving. The two burly men in black, looking like pumped-up Secret Service agents, were brusque with those who tried to engage their boss in conversation, allowing no one more than a signature. Even so, it still took close to two hours to conclude the signing. Eamon had no idea if it would be worth the tedious wait. He had come with one goal in mind: to make contact with the spirit of Frank Shoe. He figured it was the only way to find out what really went down at Dead Letters the night of the massacre. Bunko's M-16 lesson had sown the seeds of doubt.

His private "reading" with Barry took place in the stockroom, a no-frills, box-messy chamber in the back of the bookstore that at least offered some privacy. "So how ya doin', Lieutenant?" Barry said, planting himself down on one of the unopened boxes. "It's been a while, ya know."

"I appreciate your giving me a chunk of your valuable time. I know some people wait more than a year to see you."

"Hey, you forget I used to be a letter carrier before

all this whacked-out shit happened to me. I've always got time for a postal inspector, man. You guys are like the service's top dogs. Don't think I don't know that, man."

Even though Barry had a new hair job and was decked out in a shiny new Italian suit, he still held on to his old, consonant-bruising Philly accent. He was a small, baby-faced man with a bizarre gift that had lifted him overnight from the anonymous shadows into the direct glare of the spotlight. As such, he had yet to make every refinement, which explained why someone sporting an exquisite Patek watch could also wind up sounding like an extra in a Scorsese movie.

Barry said, "Hope you won't take this personally, but you don't look so hot, my friend."

Eamon didn't feel a hell of a lot better. The parade of stitches on his scalp itched something awful. He still hadn't gotten a chance to see a dentist about his two knocked-out teeth. And his face still looked like an ugly, livid sunset. Not to mention the discomfort of being holstered down with a Smith & Wesson and jacketed in a bulletproof vest twenty-four hours a day.

"So you remember how I work?" Barry asked.

It had been five years, but no way he'd forget. Eamon pulled a box alongside and Barry took his hand. The two men sat there quietly for a long, uncomfortable moment, holding hands and waiting for lightning to strike. It wasn't long before Eamon felt the heat, before he was believing again in Barry's strange powers.

"Okay, I'm gettin' somethin' here," Barry said. "I got your grandfather on line. Yeah, Seamus Wearie from the old country. Got a good, clear connection, too. Can hear everything he's saying. First off, he wants to congratulate you on your marriage. Says you couldn't have made a better choice. A babe with brains, that's what he tells me."

Eamon felt almost dizzy from making contact. Talking to his grandfather, dead in the ground twenty years now.

"You know he's your guardian angel, right? Well, the old Irishman wants to tell you that you're a full-time job, all right. Says he needs a good vacation from watching over you. Says you've got to be more careful, that you're being stalked by some kind of evil."

"What can he tell me about that?" Eamon asked.

"Says that you must find your faith again. Says you've lost your way, man, that you're all over the map. Says you must learn to believe in something, and preferably, that something is God. Says that without faith, there is only the nothingness of eternity. Says you are standing on the precipice of a great divide, that you are facing a choice that has consequences for the rest of your life and beyond. Man, this is one serious old Irishman. Oh, shit. I'm starting to lose him. Says he loves you, says . . . Ah, too late. I'm just getting static now. What a shame. We had such a nice, clear connection, too. As good as AT&T, I kid you not."

"Now what?" Eamon asked, still in Barry's hot and sweaty grip.

"Now we wait," he said. "Sometimes it helps if you concentrate on the one you want to reach."

Eamon did his best to picture Shoe, to bring him forth. But after a few minutes of fruitless, concentrated effort, he felt like giving up. "How come it's not working? Isn't Frank Shoe in heaven?"

"Could be anywhere, for all we know. Not everybody goes through them pearly gates, Lieutenant. Besides, that's not always the primary issue. Plenty of people pass over without getting mixed up with that heaven-and-hell stuff."

"What do you mean? Are you referring to purgatory now?"

"You've got to understand you're talking about

only one religion here. What do you think happens to the Muslims and Hindus and Chinese, my friend?"

"To be honest with you, I hadn't given it much thought."

"Hey, listen—the other day I was doing a reading for this American Indian, this Apache guy, and we were able to summon his father from the happy hunting grounds. See, everybody's got a different version of the hereafter. It's basically a question of what you believe in and how much you believe in it. We pretty much control our own destiny, even after we leave this world. Meaning, if you're some kind of atheist, for example, then that's what you're going to be left with. A big, fat nothing."

"You mean some people don't pass over, as you put it?"

"There's plenty that don't make it. Best I can figure it, they're not worthy for some reason or another, or their journey is simply over. Because it's all about what we learn along the way, my friend. It's about being open to stuff and changing ourselves when changing is called for." Suddenly Barry's grip tightened and he said, "Oh, shit, incoming. Bang, boom, we got ourselves a violent death. I can hear the gunshot. Oh, shit, point-blank, man. Terrible way to go. Just a minute. Hold on to your seat; our friend is materializing."

Eamon was sure they'd made contact with Frank Shoe. But then Barry said in a practically awestruck voice, "Oh, man, she's beautiful. She's absolutely glowing. I've hardly ever seen them like that. She's one of the chosen ones, man. She walks in the light of the Virgin Mary. She says she knows you. She says her name is Lita Sanchez."

"Oh, no!" Eamon gasped.

"Yeah, she's a brand-new arrival," Barry said. "Passed over this morning, it looks like. She says not to be sad for her. Says that she feels only love and peace and well-being, man. She wants you to know that she forgives you for everything. She says you're a good man and that it's not your fault."

"Oh, Lita," Eamon said, feeling like he'd been punched in the gut. "I'm so sorry."

"She says there's no time for that. She has only a few seconds before being called away. She says there are things you need to know. Says her killer is still at large. Says she and Frank never had a chance. She doesn't want anyone to blame Frank. Says it's up to you to find this guy. He's a face from your past; that's all she knows."

"So Jack McCallum didn't do it?"

"Says she never heard of this Jack person."

"Then who did it?" Eamon said, talking directly to Sanchez. "Who shot you? I need to know."

"She can't help you, she says. Her memory of the incident has been pretty much wiped clean. The Virgin Mary has purified her. She says she feels only love and forgiveness. Says she doesn't want revenge. It's not about that. But she wants you to know that your life and the life of another are in grave danger. Some woman somewhere. She doesn't know her name. But it's somebody who's connected to you in some important way."

"I need a name," Eamon said. "Something to go on."

"She's leaving us now," Barry said, unlocking hands. "She's being called away by a greater force."

"Is there any way to call her back?"

"Not that I know of," Barry said, getting up from the box and straightening out his fancy suit. "It was something, the way she glowed, man. That's reserved for the very special few. She must've really been something when she was alive."

"Better than I ever knew," Eamon said somberly.

Deke wondered when that boy was coming out. That postal inspector must've been in that damn bookstore for close to two hours. Dang, unless he missed him or something. But he didn't see how that was possible; how could he miss him in that dumb hat of his? He'd been standing out front the whole time, keeping a close eye to all the comings and goings.

God, it was cold out, too. It was another one of them bleak, white, unforgiving days, brother. Deke was past the point of shivering. It was almost like he didn't feel nothing no more, almost like he was having an out-of-body experience. It was a mighty peculiar sensation, not to feel yourself anymore. But it sure was better than a raging fever and all them wildfire chills.

Damn, he needed a real winter coat and some nice leather gloves. He kept watching all them snooty, better-off people going into the bookstore in these fancy-smancy coats that went down to their ankles, for Jesus' sake. He was tired of making do with his old, mangy denim jacket. He wanted what other people had, which was only fitting, when you got down to it. Who did these people think they were anyway, blowing right by him like he was just some bum on the street?

If he wasn't so keen on taking care of that postal fella, he might've taken the time to show these better-offs a thing or two. Why, dang, he wouldn't have minded unloading on them at random, just firing Ray's Glock at anything that moved. Deke could really understand how things could get out of hand, like with that Charles Whitman fella, who just climbed up in that tower in Texas with a rifle and just let everybody have it.

Dang, what was taking that postal inspector so long? He should've been out of that bookstore by now. Maybe Deke really had missed him. What a sorry waste of a morning, if that's the way it turned out. Heck, he should've just followed him in there when he had the chance. Except he hated bookstores. He didn't like places that made him feel like an outsider. And bookstores and libraries were the worst. Made him feel like he was plain stupid or something. Brought back all them school memories of the other kids laughing at him.

Why, he didn't even learn how to read until his second stint in the joint. In those first years, whenever the library cart would come past his cell, he'd always take a book, any old book, just so nobody would be wise to his predicament. If it hadn't been for that old orderly at the Maryland Pen, who kept noticing some of his more unusual choices, he might never have learned to read. Old Bobo helped him to the point where he could manage his way through a newspaper, not much more.

Heck, old Deke's life might've turned out a whole lot different if he'd learned to read early on. Nobody could ever imagine what a hardship that was. In fact, in some very real ways, you almost had to be smarter and cagier to get through life without knowing how to read than if you did know how. Sometimes Deke thought that they invented books and writing just to throw fellas like him. Reading was like a special club that only the special people could belong to. It was the better-offs' way of saying they wouldn't be friends with you.

It must've been that postal inspector's lucky day, picking a bookstore to go in, the one place Deke couldn't follow him. Dang, he surely must've missed him. There was no way anybody, even a smarty-pants mailman, could spend two whole hours in a bookstore. Well, it didn't matter much, Deke reckoned. He'd catch up with him later, and this time, he'd make sure not to lose him.

20

After work, Eamon and Bunko went down to the Blue Marlin, their regular spot. They had always felt at home there, amid the faded, yellowing Colts memorabilia and hardwood floors littered with peanut shells. The Marlin was in Fells Point, one of many such small, undistinguished taverns within winking distance of Eamon's former row house. Now that he was staying at Joe Seppala's place, it was a little strange to be back in the neighborhood, in one of his old haunts.

"I still can't believe it about Sanchez," Bunko said, peering into the gloomy amber of his drink.

Eamon took another swallow of his scotch. He didn't have any words left; this one hurt too much.

"She was a sweetheart of a person," Bunko said. "What a sick, fucked-up world. It just makes me want to cry, for the love of Christ."

Eamon felt the same way, even if his eyes remained dry. It was quiet and doleful in the bar, just them and two ladies engaged in private conversation at the other end. Bunko had loaded up the jukebox with Sinatra, and Frank was singing now about the summer wind, just adding to the overall sense of melancholy.

"You hungry?" Bunko asked. "Maybe we should order something."

"I've got to get home soon," Eamon said. "Mary's father will have dinner waiting."

"I keep forgetting that you're a married guy now. Let's have one for the road. What do you say?"

He should've said no, but what he did was have two more before he realized he'd better call Mary. At the pay phone next to the restrooms in the back, he did his best to apologize. "I'm sorry, Mary, I didn't realize the time. I'm with Bunko at the Marlin."

"That's okay," she said, not sounding angry. "We haven't eaten yet. If you leave right this minute, it'll be just fine."

"I don't know," he said, stalling, "Bunko's a little shook up about Sanchez. I think he could use the company right now."

"Well, how long were you thinking of staying?" she asked, sounding less okay about everything. "Dad's made a really nice dinner. I guess he could hold it a little while longer."

"Look, Mary, just go ahead and eat without me. Trust me, that's the best thing to do."

"Well, when can we expect you?"

"I really don't know. I'll try to keep it short, but I'm not making any promises. It's been a bad week all around. I need a moment to myself here."

"Well, I'll be here when you get home," she said, sounding none too pleased.

He wasn't surprised. After all, he remembered how these things usually played themselves out from his first marriage.

When he returned, Bunko said, "Gave you a hard time, didn't she? Don't deny it. I can see the long, dark look on your face, even with those two shiners."

"What are you talking about?" Eamon said, trying

to shake it off. "I told her what's what, and that's all there is to it."

"You're a lucky man," Bunko said. "Having an understanding wife like that."

"You're right," Eamon said, feeling guilty now. "I should really go now. I don't want to make her life miserable."

"Too late," Bunko said, as their bartender came out from the kitchen with a platter of Buffalo chicken wings and a basket of fries. "I ordered us a little snacking food."

"Now I'm definitely in trouble," Eamon said, realizing that the time and everything else was slipping away from him.

"Ah, what are you worried about?" Bunko said unconcernedly, dipping a wing into the blue cheese dressing. "She'll forgive you in the morning, no problem."

"You don't know Mary. When she gets upset about something, she stays mad for days. I found that out on my honeymoon."

"But I thought you guys were perfect. I thought it was true love and all that."

"Look, don't get me wrong," Eamon said evenly. "I love Mary. She's absolutely terrific. But, believe me, she's not perfect. Just as I'm not anywhere near perfect."

"Yeah, but isn't she the one above all others? You know, isn't she the only one in the world for you?"

"I don't buy that," Eamon said, shaking some Tabasco on the fries. "I'm sure there's plenty of women out there that I could love. Just as I'm sure there's plenty of other guys that Mary could've fallen for. As you get older, you start to realize that there's no one magic person that's going to fulfill your every need. It's finally about getting along and having mutual respect for one another. And to accept that takes a certain emotional maturity."

"Well, now, aren't you the romantic," Bunko sneered. "What about *being in love?* What about all those special tingly feelings?"

"That never lasts. That's just some short-lived chemical high."

"Christ, you're becoming more of a hard-nosed cynic every day."

"So who killed Sanchez and Shoe?" Eamon said, refusing to yield to the question. "If Jack McCallum didn't do it, who did?"

"Maybe he did do it," Bunko said, exasperated by the subject. "Maybe I'm all wet on that M-16 business."

"Bullshit. It was the best bit of detective work you've come up with in a long, long time, partner. Like you said, Jack was in Marine Force Recon. This guy was a sharpshooter. He wouldn't have wasted all that ammo in the ceiling."

"For once, you're right," Bunko said, finishing another glassful of Johnnie Red. "We marines are known for our marksmanship. Even the nut job marines. Look at Whitman, the Texas tower sniper, for example. That crazy son of a bitch had no trouble zoning in on his targets. Or look at Lee Harvey Oswald, another marine psycho. But a hell of a shot, you'd have to admit."

"That's if you believe Oswald was really the Dealy Plaza shooter—"

"Oh, don't give me none of your liberal-commie conspiracy theories. I'm so sick of Oliver Stone and all the rest of you. The Warren Commission did a thorough investigation into—"

"This is where I get off the bus," Eamon said. "I know you, you're going to spend the rest of the night defending the Warren report."

"Earl Warren was an honorable, decent man. And so was everybody else that served on the commission—"

"Take care, Bunko," Eamon said, standing up.

"Not that I don't want to go into the wee hours debating the Kennedy assassination with you. But I think just this one time I'll go home to my lovely, beautiful wife. Call me crazy."

"Believe me, there was no conspiracy. You should do yourself a favor and check out Posner's book. *Cased Closed*—now there's an impeccable job of research."

"You know what's interesting?" Eamon said, as he finished putting on his coat. "You hate every manner of conspiracy theory, and here you are, the one who got the whole ball rolling on McCallum. He's a patsy, just like Oswald was a patsy."

"We're not sure of anything at this point."

"Sanchez herself says that McCallum didn't do it. At least according to Famous Barry."

"Oh, that's just great," Bunko said sarcastically. "Christ, interviewing a dead eyewitness. Is that the best you can come up with?"

Eamon just threw up his hands and headed out the door. He knew he was smart to get out of there. As the night wore down, Bunko would just drain the rest of that bottle of Johnnie and get a whole lot more sarcastic in the process. Not only would he spare himself that, he'd get home in time to make it up to Mary.

He was walking along to his car, in the frozen, peopleless night, thinking these small thoughts to himself, when somebody suddenly appeared a few feet in front of him with a gun. It was the same maniac who'd tried to run him down with the BMW.

"Time to die, mailman!" he shouted, just before opening fire.

Eamon felt the shots like short, quick punches to his rib cage, as the bulletproof vest's myriad unidirectional fibers took the worst of it. The maniac kept firing away with the automatic pistol into the vest, oblivious, fortunately keeping his aim on Eamon's chest. After a moment, the denim-clad gunman seemed to stop firing, as if lulled into sheer wonderment that Eamon hadn't been knocked down by his fusillade. In that odd, momentary lull, Eamon went right after him, tackling him to the sidewalk, overtaking his gun.

"Dang, what are you, Superman or somethin'?" he said, pinned beneath Eamon.

A few seconds later, Bunko came running out of the bar to help. "I heard the shots," he said, coatless and out of breath, kneeling beside Eamon with his snub-nosed Smith & Wesson at the ready. "Who's this creep?"

"Meet David Deke Branson," Eamon said, still straddling him. "This is the same piece of shit that tried to run Mary and me down."

"Hey, watch your language," Branson growled.

"Fuck you, shithead," Bunko snapped.

"Keep it up," Branson said, "and you'll be next on my list. Believe me, I can get you. Even from inside the joint. If I want to mess with you, I will. You better believe it."

He was breathing hard and he didn't look too good. His face was practically blue with frostbite and his thinning blond hair was pasted wet against his bandanna. He was a knotty, bony sort who looked a little like Willie Nelson—that is, if Willie were sweaty sick and had crazy, darting eyes.

"So why are you doing this?" Eamon asked, jabbing Branson's own gun into his face. "Why do you want to kill me? You don't even know me."

"I don't got to tell you nothing," the bonehead said. "Not until I speak to my lawyer."

"Hey, can I see that gun?" Bunko asked Eamon, noticing something.

Eamon duly handed it to him and unholstered his own snub-nosed Smith & Wesson. "Now what the fuck is this all about?" Eamon said, renewing his interrogation. "I don't take kindly to assholes who try to kill my wife."

"Yeah, you sure got a pretty pudding pie, don't you, Mr. Mailman?"

"If you ever even think of my wife again, I'll rip you apart, so help me God."

"What do you know, it's a damn Glock," Bunko said, ignoring them and examining the gun more closely. "Same kind of gun Jack McCallum used. Remember? He bought two of them. Except one is still unaccounted for."

"You know anything about that?" Eamon said, jabbing his gun into Branson again.

"First get off of me," Branson said. "I can hardly breathe down here."

Eamon got up, slowly. "If you try to run, I'll shoot you down. And I'll do it with a smile on my face. Understood?"

"Dang, I ain't running anywhere. I can't wait to get back inside the joint."

Branson seemed positively gleeful at the thought. Eamon said, "Did you know a guy by the name of Jack McCallum?"

"Read me my rights," he said, standing up now.

"You don't got any rights left," Bunko said.

"We're not going to get anywhere with this," Eamon said to Bunko. "I think it's time to dial up the boys in blue."

"Yeah, maybe you're right," he said, sounding thoroughly disgusted. "Keep him covered. I'll go back into the Marlin to make the call."

"You know, you're a lucky fella," Branson said to Eamon, as Bunko started to walk back. "I really wanted to slit your throat something awful. Fact is, I was going to do your pretty wife right in front of you, just so it'd be the last thing you'd ever see. I did that once to a fella; never enjoyed anything more in my life."

The sicko grinned at the memory. "Yeah, my timing was just a little off. Instead, I got to your house and come upon your friend. I never got his name"—

Eamon knew he was talking about Pinkus now—"but I sure had my way with that runt. Yes, sir, I really got off doing that boy up the ass."

It was as if the Smith & Wesson went off by itself. It made a big, unholy sound and seemed to echo for a long time in the frozen, deserted night. Bunko hurried back, but he didn't say a word. He just wiped the Glock off and stuck it back in David Deke Branson's dead hand.

Finally Bunko said, "Don't worry, I saw everything. Why, it was a clear case of self-defense. What else were you going to do? The man was blasting away at you with an automatic. It was just lucky that you were able to get off that shot in time."

They stood around in the flashing blue and red lights, smoking cigarettes and moving in place, just trying to keep warm. It didn't take all that long, though; it was late and it was cold and everybody wanted to get home. Nobody thought to challenge Eamon and Bunko's story.

"Did everyone a favor, that's what I think," one of the detectives said to Eamon. "I wouldn't have minded popping that asshole myself." Detective DiCaprio was a young turk in a leather bomber jacket, trying hard to walk the walk. "Your wife is first-class. We can't let any ex-con go 'round terrorizing one of our own. That's a damn given. Asshole should've known better."

The other detective, a stocky black man with a decidedly low-key approach, was taking a closer look at the bulletproof vest, exhibit one, in the high beams of a patrol car. Eamon got a little nervous watching him at work. Detective Hovis was deliberate and focused, even in the controlled chaos of a crime scene. Cops and EMS workers, along with Bunko, slouched against their vehicles, just wanting to get this over with. Branson's uncovered body lay on the sidewalk right where Eamon had shot him.

After a few minutes, Hovis rejoined them, saying to his young partner, "Let's give everybody a break and close this one up."

"You want to rope it off or anything?" DiCaprio asked.

"I don't see why. Just put the cadaver in a Ziploc bag and send him on his way to potter's field."

"They still got to do an autopsy first," DiCaprio said, before heading over to that cluster of patrolmen and EMS workers.

"I doubt they do a real autopsy on this one," Hovis said, turning his attention back to Eamon. "Nobody gives a rat's ass about a turd like David Deke Branson. A bullet to the head, that's what the ME's going to put down in his report. Yeah, I doubt very much that they'll waste the time to make even one incision in Branson. I mean, who's going to care about one less turd in the world? What do you think, Lieutenant?"

Eamon wondered what he was getting at. "It's not my call," he said, trying to sound nonchalant about it and noticing that Hovis's serious brown eyes were firmly fixed on him.

"Sure, I understand," Hovis said, smiling, of all things. "You know, I was kind of interested in knowing how you felt about our new lightweight vests. I've always wondered how they'd hold up in a barrage of bullets."

"It saved my life; what more can I say?"

"He must've zapped you with that Glock at least a dozen times," Hovis said. "It's amazing that you were able to draw your own gun in the middle of all that and fire off a perfect hole in one."

"What are you getting at?" Eamon asked, tensing.

"Why, nothing at all," Hovis said, scratching his head. "Except about a year ago, I was using that very same kind of vest on an undercover assignment and got blammed by a Sig Sauer P226, which is a German 9 mm very much like the Glock. You know what's strange, Lieutenant? With all those bullets nailing me hard—because even with the vest on, you feel it; am I right?—I didn't have a chance to go for my gun. I guess you're just a better man than me, Lieutenant."

"If you think I did anything improper—"

"We're done with our inquiry here," Hovis said, cutting him off. "Did you know that Branson was one of the original members of the White Supremacists?" Here, Hovis flashed a broad smile. "Yeah, it was suspected that he killed several black corrections officers during his long prison career. Ain't that something?"

It was right at that moment that Mary pulled up in her car, trapping the two men in her headlights. "Good evening, Detective Seppala," Hovis said in a courtly way, tipping his hat to her as she went to embrace Eamon. "Well, I'll leave you two alone now. We're through for the time being."

"What are you doing here?" Eamon asked, holding on to her hard.

"I got a call from the desk sergeant. Are you all right? Did Branson hurt you at all?"

"I don't know yet," Eamon answered strangely.

"Let's go home," she said, not hearing him. "I'll drive. We'll pick up your car in the morning. Let's just get out of the cold now."

In the car, Mary had all sorts of questions, but Eamon had very little patience for them. "What's the matter?" she said. "You can tell me. You need to talk it out. You just killed a man. That's got to be difficult to deal with."

"It was self-defense, Mary," he said tersely.

"Who said it wasn't? Talk to me. You're all wound up."

"I'm fine. That piece of shit deserved to die. It was about time somebody took care of him."

"I know you don't mean that—"

"Would you rather it be me lying back there?"

"Of course not. I just think maybe you should talk

to my priest. I've told you about Father Joseph. He's—"

"Just drop it," he said, turning on the radio.

They listened in steely silence as Casey Kasem counted down the week's top hits. When they got to Joe Seppala's house, Mary slammed the car door extra hard and stormed into the house, all before Eamon could unbuckle his seat belt.

Once inside, Eamon had only one thing on his mind: he needed to know who Branson had bunked down with in the joint. He found Mary in the kitchen, boiling water for tea. "I need that list," he said. "I need to know who Branson's cellmates were."

"You mean he was after you, not me?"

"Just where is it?" he said gruffly, not having the time for it.

"I don't have it on me, but I can remember the most recent names. There was a Phil Benton and a Digger Hecht. Does that help? And then there was a Ray somebody or other. Ray Duffy, that was it."

"Ray Duffy," Eamon repeated, unbelieving. "Jesus, that explains it."

"Explains what?"

"I'm sorry, Mary, but I can't go into it now. I've got to get a move on it."

"But it's so late. Can't this wait until the morning?"

Eamon tried to think who to call first. First thing was probably to tell Bunko and get an all-points bulletin out for Duffy. They would probably need the FBI's help in tracking him down, so he'd have to inform Montrez. Then there was the matter of Jill Winters in Nalcrest, Florida. He'd have to check on her. But he couldn't see how Duffy would be able to locate her. It was hard to believe that all this havoc had been wrought in the name of revenge. But Duffy had to be behind the Dead Letters massacre. And that meant he was still on the loose, up to God knows what now.

"Can't you tell me what this is all about?" Mary asked again.

"Ray Duffy," he said, shaking his head. "No wonder."

The teakettle started to whistle. Neither one of them made a move to stop it.

21

It was two in the morning and Ray was right outside D.C. on I-95, right on the heels of a couple of fast-moving big rigs, making good time now. He knew all the truck drivers were hopped up on speed at this hour; shit, he'd been popping bennies with his Coke Classics since South Carolina himself. At this point, he was pretty tired, but he was so close there was no way he was going to stop for a rest. Anyway, it wouldn't be long at this rate.

He probably should've merged into I-270, which was the quickest possible route to the cabin, but 270 would've taken him right past Hagerstown, and that was something he didn't need to be reminded of at the moment. Now he'd have to shoot up to Baltimore and use I-83 as his alternate route, which would still get him up to Harrisburg and parts beyond.

The key now was staying alert and focused for this last leg of the journey. He needed to think of good things, of the kind of stuff that helped sustain him over all the long, hard years that Jill and him were kept apart. The problem was, he was coming up empty. For some reason, every time he'd bring back one of his special memories of him and Jill, he'd start to see the holes in it, like the reality wasn't anything like he remembered it to be. Like every time he'd think of Jill and him hanging out in Moe's Tobacco Shop, having one of their heavy-duty conversations together, he'd start to see how she was always trying to cut him off short, trying to find some excuse to get out of there quick. Like she didn't want to be bothered. Like he was just some goofball clerk or something.

Or take, for example, the time they went to the movies, which Ray had always considered to be the all-time most magical night of his life. He was going to take her to see some women's shit, some Meryl Streep or Glenn Close weeper, but she wanted to see that new Oliver Stone movie that everyone was making such a fuss about. So they saw *JFK*, which was all right, no big deal. It was a bit talky for Ray's tastes, just not enough action, even if they did give you a good slow-mo look at Kennedy getting it in the limo. But as far as Jill was concerned, this was some movie, a real work of art. The girl kept going on about the look of the film and the editing and all that shit. After all, she did used to have some kind of job out there in Hollywood. Not that Ray could tell you what it was, exactly.

But anyway, Jill was just going on a mile a minute about the stupid movie, getting into the whole conspiracy angle, thinking that it was amazing that all these high-level fudgeheads were involved in it. That's when they had their first real argument. Because Ray basically had to set her straight and tell her that it was all a pack of lies and that you had to look no further than Oswald to figure out who whacked the president. For some weird reason, she just couldn't believe that a deranged lone gunman could come up with such a brilliant plan. She thought there were just way too many coincidences and all that. Ray, on the other hand, had no problem believing that one creep with a lot of time on his hands could do all sorts of shit. But Jill just didn't want to hear it.

Anyway, now that he was remembering it, after their little argument, she got real weird and quiet in the car. He didn't know what the big deal was. Who cared about politics and history anyway? Ray told her that that shit just got in the way and prevented people from thinking about the things that really mattered. He was trying to get at the fact that they should be concentrating on each other, on their newfound love. But she wasn't showing any interest now. And then when they pulled up to her parents' house, she just hopped out of the car and rushed inside. No kiss, no thank-you, not even a fucking handshake.

At first Ray was pretty pissed off with the bitch, as you can well imagine. But then he noticed that she'd left her sweater behind in the car, this little white cashmere number with buttons that smelled real heavily of her. That's when he realized it was intentional on her part. The poor girl just couldn't handle how strong her feelings were for Ray. She was dizzy from everything happening so fast. It was weird, but Ray often knew what Jill was feeling even better than she herself did.

They were coming up on Baltimore now and he could see in the rearview that the bitch was still passed out in the backseat. She'd been out some time. He thought he would've had to give her some more drugged food by now. But she wasn't stirring, so he guessed it was all right. Maybe she'd wake up just as they pulled up to the cabin. Man, that would be just excellent.

Still, he wasn't all that sure how he felt about her anymore. He kept seeing things that he hadn't seen before. He'd been blocking a lot of the unpleasant stuff out. Like what happened with that white cashmere sweater, even. At first, he was grateful for such an unforeseen gift, putting his face into that sucker for hours, just inhaling her intoxicating female aroma. But then when she started refusing his phone calls, he got angry, understandably enough, and by the time he was through with that fucking sweater, it wasn't recognizable. In some ways, it was real good he had that thing to rip into; otherwise, who knows what he might've done.

That was what he was starting to realize about their relationship: that they weren't good at talking things through. For example, the bitch kept returning his letters without even bothering to offer up an explanation. So instead of confronting her with his complaints, he just took an ax to her mailbox, which just seemed to make things worse. But what was he supposed to do? The bitch just wouldn't give him a chance to express his feelings to her. Like he never wanted to hurt that old dog of theirs. But she left him no choice, really. At first he just kept old Fido hostage for a couple of days. But when even that failed to get Jill's attention, he was forced to play hardball.

Actually, if Jill didn't undergo a big change of attitude real soon, he might just have to get tough again. Only this time, he wouldn't be taking out his frustrations on the mailbox or the family pet, that was for shit sure.

Ray followed the Nite-Glo exit signs for I-83, getting all at once nervous and excited about starting their new life at the cabin. They were only about two hours away now. It was going to be great living in nature and doing all that outdoors shit. He was going to fish for trout and chop wood for the fireplace, and Jill was going to stay home and wash clothes and cook dinner and wait for him. It was going to be like a dream come true. He didn't know much about fishing, but he'd already bought a pole and some flies at the local sporting goods store. Had to put up with some nosy oldtimer who asked a lot of questions and talked about fly casting like it was some kind of holy

religion. But Ray didn't make any snide remarks.
Because fishing was one of his good memories. Him
and his dad up at Blue Springs. Catching all them
rainbows and frying them up over that campfire. If his
dumb whore of a mother hadn't screwed everything
up, he would never have run off on them. She just
nagged him to death, that's what it was.

It hadn't been easy growing up without a dad
around. Couldn't do none of them father-son things,
like joining the scouts or Little League. And he never
learned how to do any of that basement-woodshop
shit, either, like hammering away and drilling stuff
and doing whatever the fuck it is the average moron
does. But big deal—so what—so he missed out on
some things. Man, you had to put that shit behind
you. You couldn't waste your life feeling sorry for
yourself. So fuck his father and fuck his mother and
fuck everybody else while he was at it. He didn't need
nothing from anybody.

He didn't even know why he started thinking about
this shit in the first place. He just had to get to the
cabin now with Jill and everything would take care of
itself. At least he was going to have a better life than
his stupid asshole parents. He'd taken some real bold
chances to be reunited with Jill. He'd risked everything for love, which was a hell of a lot more than
most people could say. At least there was something
meaningful about all that.

Ray checked the rearview again to see if Jilly was
still in dreamland. She looked so sweet and cute all
bunched up like that with her eyes closed. What was
he thinking before? This girl was no bitch whore; she
was his little angel princess.

Suddenly, the rearview filled with red lights and he
heard the police sirens. Shit, he hadn't been paying
attention to the speed limit. He debated trying to
outrun the cops for just a second. Yeah, right, like
Jilly's little four-cylinder was going to outrace a

cruiser. As he eased over to the side of the highway, he reached for the Anaconda.

She'd come out of it several hours earlier. Except she didn't dare open her eyes—didn't dare let Ray catch on. From the familiar hum of the engine, she knew she was in the backseat of her car, flying along some highway, probably I-95 northbound, if it was true about going to Pennsylvania. The one good thing was he hadn't bothered tying her up.

Even though her hands and feet were free, she kept herself in a fetal position, praying for an opportunity. Sooner or later, she figured, he'd have to pull in for gas or food, and that's when she'd try to break free, in a public place, with other people around, with at least a fighting chance. She didn't want to tangle with him in the car. He'd probably just club her again with that big, silver gun of his. Or else they'd just wind up getting killed in a car wreck.

In the movies or on TV shows, it always looked so easy to get away when they'd take someone hostage. In a situation like this, she'd probably be thinking, *Just go for it, baby. Grab the driver from behind. What are you waiting for? Start choking him and cause the accident on purpose.* But when you were really speeding along at sixty-five or seventy-five miles per hour, it was another story. Because when you were watching TV, the fear factor never entered into it; you'd better believe everything looked a whole lot different when you yourself were the hostage.

Jill was in scared little knots at the thought of making her big break. Her hands and her feet felt numb with dread, and she didn't even know if she had it in her to scream out when the time came. When she was a little girl, that was a recurrent nightmare, the one where some strange man was coming through her bedroom window and she was too scared to even cry out. It was a childhood nightmare that had returned to her in the last few years while living in Florida.

She couldn't afford one of those long, silent screams now. Her life was on the line. No one had to remind her what Ray was capable of. This was a guy who cut up her beloved dog, leaving his ear and tail at the front door when she refused to take his phone calls. A person who could do that could do just about anything.

It was weird when you met a really, truly insane person. You never expected it. You always expected people to be more or less like yourself, or at least to act halfway normal. But when you met someone like Ray, it totally threw you off course. It was like working without a compass, without knowing where you were and where you were headed. The thing was, Ray had no such problem; he knew exactly where he was. You, on the other hand, were left to guess wildly. His power seemed to live in that vast, dark unknowingness.

Jill had always been a very nonconfrontational person. She was one of those people who really didn't know how to say no to others. That was why when Ray kept pestering her to go to the movies with him, she finally relented, having run out of believable excuses. She should have told him to get lost, to just fuck off, but that wasn't in her nature, just as it wasn't in Ray's nature to take a hint. His strange, unyielding persistence should've been her first warning. It was in his predatory blue eyes, like the eyes of a crocodile half submerged, waiting, biding its time.

In some very important ways, Jill had no one to blame but herself. Yes, Ray was the sick psycho nutjob who'd abducted her, but somehow she had played a part in all of this, too, albeit an unwilling and unwitting one. When she thought about the course of her entire life, she became aware of how often she just went along with the crowd, how rare it was for her to exercise her own free will. She absolutely hated to cause problems or to draw any attention to herself. It seemed like she had made most of the major decisions of her life out of a kind of unconscious fear, as if she were secretly afraid of what might happen if she didn't conform to everyone else's expectations of herself.

Thinking about it, she realized it was the same thing with all the men she'd been with. They were always picking her, not the other way around. She never seemed to go after what she wanted, never seemed to make that choice for herself. It was always that way. In high school and college, she just seemed to say yes to the first guys who came along, getting involved in long relationships with people who weren't right for her because she just didn't have the heart to break it off with them. Her relationships never seemed to end with a bang; they just seemed to peter out, dying of their own inertia.

Even after college, out in the bright party swirl of L.A., it was the same old song. She just let things happen to her. She couldn't seem to say no to the bad-boy actors and self-aggrandizing directors who temporarily set their sights on her. In the company of these men, she found herself marking time, holding her expectations down. She grew bored and they grew tired and inevitably they sat her down for the breaking-up-is-hard-to-do speech. Sometimes in the distracted air of their soliloquies, as these actors spoke seriously and soulfully about remaining friends, she would allow her mind to wander, to consider the newfound possibilities, as if this, at last, was her chance to break the interminable cycle. But she never seemed to stay free for long. Always there would be someone new, someone else that she couldn't very well say no to.

It was the same with Maria, even. It was Maria who asked Jill to dance in that club in Tampa; it was Maria who asked for her number and followed it up with a call. And it was Maria who decided when to call it quits. Jill's whole life seemed capricious and arbitrary, as if she hadn't thought enough of herself to take charge of her own destiny. Even her career in set design was totally unplanned; one of her fine-arts professors at Berkeley just happened to mention that her talents might lend themselves to Hollywood and that, if she was interested, he had a friend in the business. Winding up at Berkeley was also part of the careless, practically accidental trajectory of her life; her high-school guidance counselor had merely suggested that it might be something she should check into.

Somehow she had not held herself accountable, and that's why she was rolled up like a ball in the backseat of her little Toyota Tercel with her eyes shut tight, pleading to a God she no longer believed in for a second chance. She had not asserted herself with Ray, had not told the creep to get lost from the get-go. And then, to exacerbate everything, she had tried to hide from him and the rest of the world in a witness protection program that had seen fit to place her in the swampy boondocks of central Florida. Which was just what she deserved. There she'd been, licking stamps in the Nalcrest post office and living in a sad, dilapidated trailer park, watching her life trickle away like the hoary cliché of sands in an hourglass.

She should've known better than to try to run away and hide. Instead of solving her problem, she'd managed only to avoid it for a short while. But now she was getting another chance to show her mettle. And still she was scared, feeling the terrible queasiness in her stomach as the car started to slow down now. With her eyes still squeezed shut, she could feel the car easing over to the side of the highway, coming to a complete stop. She braced herself, trying to be ready for anything.

A long, helpless minute passed without anything happening. She kept waiting for Ray to open the door, to get out, something. But nothing, just the heavy silence. She had no idea where she was, but when Ray cranked down the window she could feel the cold northern air flood into the car. She wondered if he'd pulled over for a smoke or something. She didn't hear any other cars whizzing by, which made her guess that it was either very late at night or that maybe they weren't on a well-traveled road.

Ray didn't make a move, though. She could hear his labored breathing, almost as if he were nervous. Suddenly, she heard the crunching of steps outside the car, of someone making their way toward them. In a flash, she understood what was happening: Ray must've been pulled over by a cop. A shot of adrenalized hope rushed through her.

"May I see your driver's license, sir?" she heard the no-nonsense voice say.

"Why, of course, Officer," Ray said in an overly polite way.

Jill opened her eyes and, seeing the green-uniformed trooper, said in a voice much weaker than she wanted to, "Please help me. He's kidnapped me."

"What's that, little lady?" he asked, bending down to get a look at her.

Before she could say another word, she heard the gun go off, one powerful explosion followed by another. The trooper was no longer framed by the driver's-side window.

Ray turned back to her and snarled, "You little fucking bitch. You were faking all this time, weren't you?" She could hardly hear him with the gun's deafening shots still ringing in her ears. "You no-good bitch whore. I ought to waste you right here. Serve you right if I did."

She couldn't help the tears that were filling her eyes. It was all so unreal, too much for her five senses to absorb.

Ray said, "You think I'm kidding, bitch? I mean it. Try anything and you'll wind up just like your little friend here."

Ray opened his door and got out to take a look at the trooper. "Yeah, your boyfriend's plenty dead," he said through the open window, stepping over him. "I'll show you what I think about you and this piece of shit."

Ray unzipped his fly and began to urinate on the dead trooper. Jill had stopped crying; somehow this had gone way beyond tears now. Strangely, she wasn't even scared anymore. At this point, she was just wishing that he'd turn the gun on her and be done with it. She didn't want to be a part of his world anymore.

22

Eamon wasn't sure he'd find the church doors un-
locked early on a weekday morning, so he was somewhat surprised to find Father Joseph up by the altar,
preaching to an empty house. The young, red-bearded
priest in jeans and clerical collar was standing in front
of a lectern practicing his Sunday sermon. He didn't
seem to notice Eamon's arrival.

"We are living in a secular world that seems to grow
more impolite, more unruly with each passing day,"
he announced to the vacant pews. "It falls on each of
us to bring as much civility as we can into our daily
lives. In these angry, alienated times, we must find the
love in our hearts to be charitable and tolerant of
others less fortunate, who may not be so lucky to feel
God's divine touch."

Father Joseph stopped to scribble something down,
mumbling out, "Better scratch 'divine touch.' I've
used that one a lot lately."

Eamon cleared his throat to get the priest's attention, and then made his way to the lectern.

"Can I help you?" Father Joseph asked, appearing
just a little disconcerted by the presence of a stranger,
especially at this uncharitable hour. It was just after

eight A.M., and the weak February light didn't do much for the ornate stained glass windows. The Last Supper and other usually radiant scenes were reduced to a pallid blue, as their deep, religious reds and ambers had yet to materialize.

"You look troubled," Father Joseph said.

"My wife thought I should talk to you," Eamon said. "She seems to think you have all the answers."

"Your wife is a fine judge of character," the young, bearded priest said, offering Eamon a kindly smile. "Is she one of my parishioners?"

"Look, I'm sorry, but for the time being, the less you know about me, the better."

"Well, don't worry, my son, God knows who you are," Father Joseph said, affecting a paternal air that didn't quite come off. "Have you been in an accident or some kind of fight?" he asked, examining Eamon's battered face. "You look like you've been through quite an ordeal."

"It's not anywhere near over yet; that's the problem."

"Why don't you tell me about it? That's what I'm here for."

"Maybe I shouldn't have come. I'm not so sure this was such a good idea. I don't know what I was thinking, really."

"You look like you're in a lot of pain. Would it make it easier if we spoke through the walls of the confessional booth? Maybe it would free you to unburden your soul."

"Anything's worth a try," Eamon said, feeling the overbearing sanctity of the church weighing down on him. It made him think of when he was just a kid and was convinced he was going to burn in the eternal flames of damnation for his licentious thoughts and for what was then the biggest no-no, the unforgivable sin of self-pleasure. In those days, the old, whiskey-nosed priest would just tell him to say a few Hail

Marys, Our Fathers, and that would be the extent of it. Today he didn't think he'd get off so easily.

Eamon followed Father Joseph to one side of the gloomy church, where there were two vintage, dark-wood confessional booths, almost side by side. "In the old days we really packed them in," he said. "Nowadays there's not much demand for it. I man it just a couple of hours a week. Mainly for the Social Security set. I guess it brings back good memories for them, as odd as that sounds."

With that, he disappeared into the nearest booth and Eamon took his place outside on a hard, bare stool. "Now, my son," he said through the small voice opening, "how long has it been since your last confession?"

"Too long ago to care about," Eamon said, wishing he'd never agreed to this foolishness. "Father, let's just get down to it. I've committed a mortal sin. I killed a man last night."

"No wonder you're in such turmoil, my son."

"Believe me, the man was human garbage."

"That's for God to decide."

"Well, maybe He used me to carry out His will."

"Are you a police officer?" Father Joseph asked.

"Something like that."

"So it was in an official capacity——"

"It was revenge," Eamon said. "I didn't have to shoot him. It was eye for an eye, tooth for a tooth, just like the Bible says."

"It also says, 'Thou shall not kill.' Don't you feel any remorse at all?"

"I feel anything but that."

"Then I don't know how I can help you, my son."

"Didn't you ever experience doubts?" Eamon blurted. "Didn't you ever wonder if it was all a giant setup? What if there isn't a God? What if we're all wasting our time here?"

"No one is immune to doubts, my son, not even the best of us."

"Then what brings you back? What makes you believe again?"

"Everyone has to find the answer within themselves," the young priest said. "But for me, I've always come back to God for the most simple reason. And that is: I find the alternative too horrible to contemplate."

Ray Duffy's Fells Point apartment was overrun by mice, cockroaches, and FBI agents. Tony Montrez, their chief liaison at the Bureau, had brought in his top lieutenants, Bob Matthews and Hal Linse. Eamon respected and had worked with all three men before. The dark-suited Bureau boys all looked like they left a barbershop five minutes ago, clipped and shorn to perfection, smelling of cheap, bracing American cologne, ready for some early-morning action. On the other hand, the three representatives of the Postal Inspection Service, which included Eamon and Bunko and Del Masterson, all looked like they could do with a shave, a clothing allowance, and a good night's sleep.

"What do you think, Agent Wearie?" Montrez asked, addressing Eamon in his familiar FBI mode. "Do you think Duffy's holed up in Wheeling?"

"I think it's a ruse, sir," Eamon said, referring to the gas-station maps tacked up over Duffy's bed—with the cities of Wheeling, West Virginia, and Nalcrest, Florida, highlighted in Magic Marker—and the library-issued guide to Wheeling left open on the coffee table. "It's too simple, too pat. Think about how complicated and organized the Dead Letters massacre was. Why does Duffy go to all that trouble, then screw up by handing us a map of his whereabouts? That's not his MO. This guy likes to leave behind a whole lot of confusion in his wake."

Montrez, a dead ringer for the actor Harrison Ford, just rubbed his chin, mulling it over. The others said nothing, unfailingly deferential and respectful as they were of the gray man. He was a legendary FBI figure, as well known for cracking cases as for his unwavering calm and his head of slate-gray hair. He was at the end of a long and glorious career now, spending most of his time in the concrete depths of Quantico, in the Investigative Support Unit, passing along his accumulated wisdom to a whole new generation of recruits.

"It's possible this is like the Donald Carmichael case," Matthews said. He was a tall, handsome, square-jawed carbon copy of his boss, another one, Eamon thought, to make you feel like you weren't measuring up. "Remember that one, up in Ohio? Went to some elaborate pains to kidnap his next-door neighbor, that thirteen-year-old girl? All very organized. But then the moment he had little Sue Cassidy in the car, he got real sloppy, like he'd used up all his mental resources for the planning of it and hadn't considered what was going to happen after he pulled it off."

"That's right," Linse said, nodding vigorously. "Wound up butchering her after only a couple of hours. When we interviewed him, Carmichael said he couldn't handle her kicking and screaming. Just made him snap. Had never intended to kill her initially."

"No, this guy's not situational at all," Eamon protested. "He's not reacting to things as they happen; he's got it all in his head beforehand."

"I hate to disagree," Linse said politely, "but when you put Duffy away, he was diagnosed with a paranoid personality disorder. He was a classic stalker. He was totally situational. If you didn't answer Duffy's phone calls, he cut up your dog. He wasn't thinking things through at all."

Eamon had to admit he had a point. Linse, a slender, button-down sort with a high forehead and thinning blond hair, bared a slight smile of triumph. They were silent again in the shabby confines of Duffy's studio apartment. It wasn't much: a mattress on the floor, a TV-VCR combination, a selection of porno tapes and magazines. The worse thing was all the mice. Duffy didn't use those simple, old-fashioned traps that snapped a mouse dead; no, he put out these dishes of sticky, flypaper-like goop that just kept the poor critters glued in place. Eamon noticed that some of the mice had even tried chewing off their own feet in a futile effort to escape.

"The guy's a sicko. What else do we need to know?" Del Masterson said, making his usual charmless entrance into the discussion. "This Jill Winters is dead meat if we don't get a move on it."

"I'm afraid Del's right," Montrez said with a tired, unwelcoming expression; it was no secret the two men hated each other. "She just has a couple of days at most, or maybe we're talking about hours. Who knows for sure? It's all about power and control, though. And Duffy won't wait long to exert his ultimate control over her."

"Yeah," Bunko said, his first words in ages, "these guys are great at dominating the dead. Then they can get all the love they missed out on. All the love their stinking mothers didn't give them. They cut up the poor girl, pretending it's dear old Mom, getting off on it the whole time."

"I don't think that's what we have here," Eamon said. "Ray Duffy's mother died of cancer."

"She died at home with no witnesses around," Agent Matthews said.

"This isn't one of those Edmund Kemper cases," Eamon said, referring to the infamous serial killer who cut off his mother's head. "We have no evidence to suggest that he's killed girls before."

"What about the evidence of paraphilia we've found here today?" Agent Matthews said. "What about all those different pairs of women's panties in his bureau drawers? This is more than just some kinky case of transvestism we're talking about. The underwear is in too many different sizes. How did Duffy come to have these things in his possession?"

"What's the big deal?" Del Masterson said. "Maybe he just took the panties as remembrances."

"That's just it," Matthews said, "remembrances of what exactly? Nights of passion or nights of murder?"

Just then, Montrez's cellular phone bleeped. "Yeah, roger that," he said, taking the call and sounding like a pilot. "Check. Copy that." Then he turned to everybody else and said, "They found Duffy's mother's car at the Baltimore airport. A 1978 Impala. There's blood stains in the trunk. We've also found out that someone used Jack McCallum's American Express card to rent a car at the Tampa airport on Saturday the fourteenth, the day after the massacre. The rental car was picked up at the Peaceful Waters trailer park that same night with a broken distributor cap."

"And Jack was lying in the morgue with his brains blown out," Matthews said, "so he sure as hell didn't rent that baby."

"The fourteenth was Valentine's Day," Linse noted. "I forgot to get my wife anything and she gave me heck about it."

"Duffy was obviously paying attention to that particular date," Montrez said. "The fact that the massacre happened on Friday the thirteenth is probably no coincidence, either."

Matthews said, "According to the local postmaster, the last time anyone saw Winters was late Saturday afternoon, at the end of her shift. But he also hastened to add that she called in sick Monday morning. Said she didn't sound like herself at all."

"No wonder," Montrez said. "Duffy probably had a gun to her head when she called."

"So Duffy definitely used Jill's car in the abduction," Linse said. "That's no longer speculation, as far as I'm concerned."

"Of course we've got an all-points out for it," Montrez said. "And Agents Smite and Burgess from our Tampa office are at the trailer park now, going through Winters's place with the forensic technicians.

They'll be faxing us pictures of the crime scene later this afternoon. We already know, though, that the trailer's a wreck. It looks like somebody was sure in a hurry to get out of there."

"Duffy's got quite a jump on us," Matthews noted. "He grabbed the girl on Saturday night—and now it's already Thursday. That's not good news."

Eamon was impressed by what they were already able to piece together in a single night. It was hard to get away from the long arm of the Bureau. He knew sooner or later they'd catch up to Duffy. But it was anyone's guess if Jill Winters would still be alive by then. And he couldn't help feeling more than a little bit responsible for her fate. After all, he was the one who'd personally guaranteed her safety in postal's newly established witness protection program.

"Let's go through the apartment one more time," Montrez said. "It's all we have, so let's be doubly thorough."

Masterson said, "I say we stop sucking on our thumbs and get down to Wheeling and set up a command center."

Montrez looked at him with stony contempt. "Del, it may interest you to know that I'm leaning in that direction. I've got the Gulfstream gassed up and waiting for us on the tarmac. But first things first. Let's finish up here. You never know, it's possible that even an old pro like yourself might've missed something."

Montrez and Masterson were complete opposites. Del, a former FBI special agent, was a meaty-faced drinker who'd never chosen a word carefully in his life. He was a loud, uncouth, trigger-happy veteran in a finicky PC age and, after twenty-five years of insubordinate service, was given the choice of retirement or going over to postal. Tony Montrez, though, had no vices. He was subdued and meticulous, wary of the spotlight. He liked Italian food and collected duck decoys and listened to old jazz records. Eamon had known him thirteen years, and that was as thick as the personal file got on the gray man.

But today, oddly enough, Eamon had to take Del Masterson's side. He had a good idea what his boss with the sagging gut and ketchup-spattered tie was going through right about now. Hell, Eamon was feeling it, too; the Bureau's starchy best always brought out those keen, sharp feelings of inferiority, that sense that postal was a ne'er-do-well brother in the law-enforcement family.

What was the use in denying it? Eamon had once dreamed of being a G-man himself. After an unhappy, mundane year on Long Island's Suffolk County police force—which mainly involved pulling over drunks and breaking up domestic disputes—he took the FBI's written and physical exams and was invited to go through their four-month training program at Quantico, the modern fortress in the green hills of Virginia. It turned out he was a natural, scoring high on the firing range and in the classroom. Unfortunately, it was a lean recruiting year, and instead of waiting around for the Bureau to chip away at its hiring freeze, he opted for the Postal Inspection Service, which seemed eager for Quantico's fresh blood.

"Not exactly posh," Montrez said, surveying Duffy's digs. "What did he do with all the money from the sale of his mother's house?"

"Maybe he bought another place," Eamon suggested. The two of them stood by the stove in the kitchenette, which was covered with mouse droppings, as the others went through the paces again, checking and rechecking every square inch of the bare, dingy apartment. "This just doesn't look like home base. I mean, there's practically no furniture to speak of. But it's more than that. Besides the pornography, there's nothing that tells you who he is. I mean, where's *his stuff?*"

"Yes, I see your point," Montrez said. "There's not

even a set of glasses or a coffeepot in the kitchen. There's no toiletries in the bathroom. So where's he keeping all of his things, then?"

"Someplace remote," Eamon said. "Someplace where nobody can get to him too easily. He's gone to a lot of trouble to get to Jill Winters. Now he wants some time with her alone, someplace where he can put out the Do Not Disturb sign."

"Why not Wheeling, then? You know, his mother's family is from Wheeling. He probably has an attachment to the area."

"Naah, he never liked his mother," Eamon said. "Those feelings of resentment and hostility came out over and over again in his letters to Jill Winters. He called his mother a nag and a bitch. He couldn't wait to be rid of her. Have you seen those crazy letters yet?"

"No, I haven't had a chance. Though I can tell you I've had the privilege of reading our coverage and the psycholinguistic analysis. All of which seemed to support the findings of the court-ordered psychiatric evaluation. Duffy, I gather from the report, is a classic antisocial loner. Feelings of inadequacy brought on by a dysfunctional home environment. His father ran off when he was five. His mother was an alcoholic. Even had some mental problems of her own—was institutionalized on two occasions."

Eamon said, "Yeah, Ray's father never divorced his mother. He just started a new family somewhere else, like Ray and his mom never existed. He died in his forties of a heart attack, when Ray was still in high school."

Montrez said, "It explains everything and it explains nothing, all at the same time."

The gray man had seen it all with his tenure with the Bureau, and yet even he didn't know the answer to the age-old question of nature versus nurture. Eamon had taken a refresher course with him at the National Academy this past summer in criminal profiling.

Montrez told the class that he believed that some criminals were born and some criminals were made and that that was the best he could come up with after all these years. Then he told them not to spend too much time worrying about it because, as he put it, their job was to catch criminals, not explain them.

"I don't know where Duffy's headed," Eamon said, "but believe me, he's not going anywhere near Wheeling. He wants to start out fresh with the girl. He went somewhere where nobody knows him and where he can act out his fantasies with Jill Winters."

"And what are his particular dark fantasies?"

"Oh, to be married and in love with the girl of his dreams. That's what his letters to her were all about. You see, at the heart of everything, he wants something fairly normal, even if he's going about it in the sickest and nastiest of ways."

"You may be on to something here, Agent Wearie. I could use a good man like yourself on my task force. Have you given any more thought to joining us?"

It was an offer that Montrez always seemed to make to Eamon and one that was seemingly always open to him. "What, and leave the glamour of the Postal Inspection Service?" Eamon said, grinning. "For your rinky-dink outfit? You've got to be kidding me."

"Hey, check this out!" Del Masterson yelled across the room. He was playing one of Duffy's porno tapes on the VCR. "Take a look. These are homemade, boys. Not your store-bought kind."

They gathered around the lurid glow of the television and watched as Duffy had sex with a barely conscious young woman. He was taking her from behind, but she seemed really out of it, like she was drugged or something, like she had absolutely no idea what was happening to her. She was just a kid, from the looks of things, maybe sixteen or seventeen at the most. Even though the quality of the video was poor, Eamon couldn't make out any bruises or ligature marks on the girl.

"What do you make of this, men?" Montrez asked, looking not embarrassed, exactly, but maybe a trifle sad at the sight of this unwholesome coupling.

"Christ, Duffy's a regular sledgehammer," Masterson said with his custom inappropriateness. "The boy's got some stamina, I'll say."

"I'll wager this is just a sex thing," Linse said. "I don't expect these are videos of kills."

"I think Hal's right," Matthews said somberly, keeping his eyes on the screen. "If this were a kill, Duffy would never leave the video behind. Same with the women's undergarments. These trophies would be way too precious to him. Instead, he's just treating them the same way he treats his skin magazines, like they're useful for short-term pleasure but otherwise easily replaceable."

They stopped off at his old place on Sycamore, only ten blocks from Duffy's pigsty. Eamon needed some fresh clothes and Bunko didn't mind tagging along. It was a still, cold, sickly yellow day, with heavy, voluminous cloud cover.

"Looks like snow," Bunko remarked.

"The weatherman said we might get a bunch of it."

"Anything to cover over this dirty, ugly world of ours."

"It's hard to believe I never ran into the creep before," Eamon said, unlocking the front door of his small row house, "considering how close he lived from me."

"You know, he's even the same age as you," Bunko said, stepping inside. "You're both thirty-five. Just shows you how the breaks go. Duffy's a piece of shit, all right, but he hasn't had much of a life. I'll say that much in his defense."

"I couldn't care less," Eamon said. "This is the same shithead who killed Shoe and Sanchez and the others."

"We don't know that for sure yet. All we have is

confirmation on the Glock that Deke Branson had on him. Same one that Jack McCallum supposedly purchased in Dixie's Guns & Ammo. For the moment, that seems to be the only thing connecting Duffy to the fiasco at Dead Letters."

"It's enough for me."

"The place feels different," Bunko said, taking notice of the house now. "Looks the same, but feels different somehow. Maybe it's just not having that funny tenant of yours around anymore. That Pinko fellow never seemed to leave the place, you know. I remember the way those two cats were always following him around, too, like he was Little Bo Peep or something. Not a bad guy, really. Once you got to know him and once you got past the fact that he was nutty as a fruitcake."

The house did feel different, and Eamon knew it would never feel the same again, not after what happened there. The yellow police tape was gone now and the real estate company had already had someone in to repaint the living room. But, still, you could feel the emptiness, the godforsakenness. It was cold in here, too; the thermostat must've been set down around fifty and the feeble winter light only added to the desolation. It was hard to believe he'd lived here for the past ten years.

"You know, I've been meaning to tell you something," Bunko said. "I had some rough moments last night after the police got through questioning me. I have never lied like that before to save someone else's ass."

"I owe you big time," Eamon said. "But, believe me, Branson had it coming to him. He murdered Pinkus and he took away my home. And that's not counting that he tried to kill me and my wife. I hope he rots in hell."

"You've changed," Bunko said. "You've turned hard. I never thought I'd see the day."

"Yeah, you're right. I have changed. And, let me tell you something, old friend: there ain't no going back now."

"Well, I'm not so sure I agree with your methods. But the world is a little safer today, there's no arguing that."

"Now we've got to figure out a way to save the girl."

"She's probably dead by now," Bunko said, with a wan little shake of his head.

"I don't know about that. She's smart and resilient. She might find a way to hold him off for a few days."

"Well, it looks like we're going to jet down to Wheeling later this afternoon with the glamour boys."

"Duffy's playing us for suckers," Eamon said. "He wants us to waste our time down in coal country. For Christ's sake, he knew we'd find his apartment. He left those fake clues like bread crumbs for us to follow. It's the same place he's been living in for the past six months. The address was right in his probation report. It doesn't get any more convenient than that."

"I hear you, brother," Bunko said. "What I don't get is how come they didn't pick him up for violating his parole. The guy hadn't reported in with his PO in months."

"You know the cops are too busy for that shit. The guy was small potatoes. Unless you're a rapist or a murderer, they can't waste the time with it. How were they supposed to know that Ray Duffy fit the double bill?"

"Hey, we'd better get a move on. Montrez's liable to leave at any time. Be sure to pack lots of extra underwear and socks. No telling how long we'll be gone for."

Eamon went into his old bedroom and quickly went about the task of filling a travel bag. He tried not to notice the pictures and other keepsakes on the top of his dresser, the little reminders of his former life.

Then he went into the bathroom and swallowed back some more painkillers. He still hadn't had the chance to see a dentist about his two broken teeth. He looked in the vanity and was surprised again to see his banged-up, angry face. For the first time that he could remember, his outer self perfectly mirrored his inner self.

23

Things were definitely not going as planned, that was for shit sure. No way he wanted to take out that cop so close to home. Well, there was nothing Ray could do about it now, except to make sure there weren't any more unforeseen accidents.

All because of that bitch. Well, he'd deal with Jilly soon enough. He had her in the basement, which would keep her out of trouble for the time being. There were no windows down there and he had the door double-bolted, so there was no way out. Later, if she was a good girl—that is, if she ever proved she could be trusted again—he'd move her upstairs with him. Right now, she was on probation.

The thing was, he could watch her every move. He had a security camera mounted down there, which was connected to the TV in the living room, so he could check on her whenever the fuck he felt like it. It was amazing the shit you could buy today; the whole setup cost him only four hundred bucks. He warned the bitch that if she tried to screw with the camera, her ass was grass. So far, she wasn't doing too much; basically, she was just sitting on the couch with this all-depressed look on her face; oh, she'd done some crying, all right, but she was pretty much through with that shit. The girl could be real emotional, he'd give you that. If he knew Jill, she was probably just feeling bad about their rocky start together.

She didn't even seem to notice how nice Ray had made her part of the house. He'd gotten all this modern crap from Ikea, this big Swedish furniture store, that he was totally positive Jill would go nuts for. There was this wild, foamy red couch that doubled as a bed. He also bought this glass breakfast table with two futuristic-looking chairs so they could take their meals together. Then he got a couple of funky, handwoven Indian rugs. And he threw in some of these framed museum posters and potted plants to make it seem even more homey. Okay, the plants were dying. But what could he do about that? It wasn't like there was a lot of sunlight down there.

Upstairs, it was a whole lot more traditional. He bought the place furnished from this old widower who was moving in with his daughter somewhere. It just seemed easier not to have to deal with buying everything new. So he had the guy's rose-patterned dinner plates and scratchy silverware, besides all his worn-down, dog hair–covered colonial furniture. The house was a steal at thirty-eight thousand, but it was pretty decrepit and stuff was starting to fall apart. Like, for instance, the roof leaked big time, man. He'd set some buckets up in the attic as a temporary solution, but he knew sooner or later he'd have to have someone in to attend to it.

Because he sure couldn't do it himself. It all went back to not having his father around to teach him all that men's shit—you know, plumbing, electrical, what have you. And all that handyman stuff was always coming up. Like this morning, for example, he had one hell of a time just getting Jill's car up his snowy drive, which was almost a half mile long, for shit's sake. Anyway, they got stuck at the very bottom by the mailbox. The damn car just wouldn't budge. It was bad news, because he couldn't just leave that sucker down there with the Florida plates, getting all sorts of unwelcome attention.

So he and Jill walked up to the house together, which was just one more thing he hadn't counted on. Unfortunately, she got a real good look at the layout of the place before he was able to shove her downstairs. Anyway, he had to get her fucking car in the garage, which was this old, falling-apart barn where he'd been keeping the Jeep. So he figured he'd just tie the Toyota's bumper to his expensive new all-terrain, four-wheel-drive Jeep and just haul ass. But it turned out to be a lot harder than it sounded. Even his Jeep had trouble in that deep snow and it took forever to finally get Jill's car in the garage. It really pissed him off. You know, here he was all tired and shit from that long drive up from Florida and he had to spend his first morning back getting all aggravated like that, like he knew the first thing about pulling cars in that sloggy shit.

That's what he meant. Everything that was so easy for most guys was a big pain-in-the-ass learning experience for him. Even removing Jill's Florida plates turned out to be no picnic. Finding the right wrench, looking everywhere for it—just more stinking aggravation, man.

There was no way to enjoy the mind-boggling scenery and that tasty, fresh country air, even. Usually he'd get all in awe about the Tuscarora Mountains in the distance, all those snow-dusted evergreens and shit. It was God's country up there. Not too far away you had the Juniata River pouring into the Susquehanna, the real deal. Oh, yeah, there was also all those crappy, seen-better-days mill towns with all the laundry hanging outside, not to mention them rusted heaps in people's yards. But still, he was right near Blue Springs, the place where him and his dad went fishing that one time, the place where it all began, man.

But by the time he got in the house, he just couldn't settle back; he was overtired from everything. And he had all sorts of new worries. Like how was he going to get that dumb driveway plowed now? He hated having strangers on his property, even if he needed them to do stuff. Then he noticed that he was running low on oil. He'd forgot to turn down the heat the last time he was up. Shit, nothing was going his way.

Except he remembered that he'd hidden some weed in a coffee can in the kitchen. So he put Jimi's "Purple Haze" on and rolled himself a fat one and started to finally mellow out.

After all, he had managed to pull the impossible off. He was back home with the woman he loved and all that shit. And, as far as he could tell, nobody was the wiser.

It felt awfully sweet sitting there in his house, in an ancient Betsy Ross rocker, taking those deep, calming tokes while watching Jill on the closed-circuit television. Though, if you wanted to know the truth, he was a little disappointed by the action. The girl just sat there on that foamy red couch with this empty, dipshit expression. Not only that, she didn't do anything interesting. He thought maybe he'd get lucky and catch her fingering herself or something. But no such luck. Although it was kind of neat watching her go to the bathroom right in a pail, right in the open like that. The girl took a dump same as everybody else, squatting and squeezing.

Obviously, the pail was not the long-term answer here. Man, keeping her in the basement was a lot trickier than he ever anticipated. He hadn't even figured out how to handle her showering-hygiene needs yet. He was starting to seriously wonder if the bitch was more trouble than she was worth. Shit, he was probably going about it all wrong. He read this book once on taking people hostage—not that he was keeping Jilly hostage or anything like it, understand—

and it was full of interesting advice on how to go about it. The key was to keep people in the dark, so to speak.

You didn't want your captive to know too much about what was happening to them. You wanted to blindfold them and keep them in the closet and shit like that. And you didn't want to feed them too often, or even really talk to them too much. In the book, they called it sensory deprivation. It was maybe something worth considering.

Because Jill sure didn't seem too grateful for all of Ray's efforts. She hardly even noticed the new furniture or anything. And that whole depressed, woe-is-me routine was getting a little stale by now. The girl just sat there like a big lump of meat, not doing much of nothing, really. He'd probably have to get her some books or some shit to occupy her time. Maybe she liked to knit sweaters; a lot of women did.

There he went again, always thinking about her needs. What about his needs? He wasn't exactly having the time of his life, though he had to admit he was in a better position to enjoy Jimi's awesome riffs. And, of course, he had the added benefit of a nice, fat doobie to help him relax. And, as usually happened, when he smoked weed, he started getting horny. So there he was watching the TV, kind of concentrating on her vacant face and feeling into his own pants, when it dawned on him: why the hell should he be wasting his time jerking off now?

The time had come to make himself known. And if she didn't like it, too bad. The bitch could spend all her time blindfolded in the closet, for all he cared.

At first, she just cried hot, unabated tears of pain and anger, demanding to know why God had it in for her. *Why me, Lord? What have I ever done to deserve this? Am I so terrible? Why, then? Why are you punishing me like this? Answer me, damn it!*

But she knew God couldn't hear her where she was. It was up to her now. She needed to pull herself together, to just snap out of it, girl. This was no time for teary regret and finger-pointing. She knew the sicko was watching her through the eye of that camera. No doubt he was getting off on the show, thinking he had her right where he wanted her.

She wanted to live; she needed to live. That was the only thing worth remembering now.

There were too many beautiful, fantastic things in the world that she wanted to experience again. She wanted to catch snowflakes with her tongue again. She wanted to eat a mushroom pizza one more time. She made herself think now of those many little things that made life worth living. She wanted to view a Matisse again, any painting of his at all. She wanted to see the fall foliage in the Shenandoah Valley, to be overwhelmed by that panorama of dying gold and crimson one more time in her life. There were just so many things, more than most of us ever really, truly realized.

Sometimes, hearing a cool new song on the radio, she would just get up and dance like crazy in her tiny trailer. It was amazing to feel that kind of spontaneous joy.

Or how nice it was to lie in bed on a blue summer's night, listening to the chirp of crickets.

The tart, explosive sweetness of a really good orange.

Sharing a bottle of wine with a great old friend and losing track of the time and just talking all night.

Seeing the sun come up and being reminded of the awesome wonder of it all.

Or what about going to the ocean and becoming a kid again in the big waves, bobbing up and down and just forgetting all about being an adult for a little while?

There were just so many things. She wanted to be

kissed again—not by just anyone, but by someone really, really special. Just to be lost in a kiss, to feel that the whole world was just background music to that moment.

So many things.

Most of all, though, Jill wanted to see her mother again and to tell her how much she loved her. That was the biggest mistake of all, going into that witness protection program and promising not to have any contact with her mother or anyone else who meant anything to her. Three years and counting now, without hearing her mom's unbelievably reassuring voice. Three whole, wasted years.

No, there were no two ways about it: she had to get out of this thing alive. Jill owed her mother that much.

Survive, girl, survive. Whatever it takes.

She couldn't let these horrible, dreadful feelings of powerless rage overtake her. Not now, not with everything at stake. She needed to be alert, focused, resourceful. Later, with any luck, there would be plenty of time to be angry and scared and vengeful and all the rest of it.

Now, though, she had to think as rationally as possible. A pretty tall order, considering her circumstances.

The only way out was by taking the stairs up. There were no windows. The floor was concrete. Ray had warned her that if she so much as went up the stairs, he'd kill her. He had made the same threat about touching his little security camera, too.

Maybe she could simply outrun him. Maybe she could divert him for a second and just run the hell by him. But what if he'd locked the front door? He'd be right on top of her before she knew it. Even if she made it to the road, there might not be anyone there to help her. Last night, when they got stuck in the driveway, she saw that it was just a lonely, icy country road. Who knew how close the nearest town was? No, what was the use? Super Ray would track her down, and he'd be more enraged than ever.

She needed him out of the house somehow, so that she could plan and scheme. She would have to give him a list of things that she needed, things that would take him into town. She could tell him she needed tampons, something that he wasn't likely to have lying around.

Once she got him out of the house, maybe she could break that glass breakfast table and fashion some kind of weapon out of the shards. With a little time, why not? All those years in set design had taught her how to improvise.

Or maybe she could tamper with the oil burner—break it somehow, so he'd have to bring in a repairman. No, that wouldn't work. That would only serve to infuriate him further. Hell, if things didn't pan out, she could always blow the place to kingdom come, taking the sicko out with her. At least then he would never get the chance to hurt anybody else.

Right now, the key was to play along with him, to buy herself some time. The last thing she wanted to do was get him all riled up. She had to start acting more like what he wanted her to be, more in keeping with his warped vision of her. She had to be *his little Jilly*—nothing less would do.

She knew from his letters that he had some weird ideas about her purity. He kept calling her his virgin angel. He was under the impression that she was somehow different from other girls. That she was sweeter, nicer, more wholesome. Now she had to *be* that. It was the role of a lifetime—the role that could keep her alive.

First, she had to stop hating him. That was the hardest part. Then she had to make believe that she wasn't being held against her will. How difficult could it be? After all, Ray didn't seem to think she was a hostage. In his mind, they were being reunited—they were starting out on a new life together.

She needed to understand him, to find the logic at the core of all that chaos. In some perverse, strange way, he actually loved her. Or at least he had loved her at one time. She had to represent *something* to him. But what? Was she the unattainable high-school cheerleader who would never think to look twice at him? Or was it something more? Did she represent a life that he could never have? Was that it?

They used to talk a lot in the tobacco shop where he worked. Or at least he would talk and she would just sort of nod and smile, too polite to make a dash for it. But he seemed to steer clear of personal matters; his family never once came up. He always seemed more comfortable talking about some story in that morning's newspaper or who David Letterman had had on his show last night.

One day, out of curiosity, she looked up Ray's picture in the high-school yearbook. For the life of her, she couldn't remember him, even though she must've been in classes of his and seen him all the time in the hallway and whatnot. He wasn't exactly a toad or anything, but he was exceedingly average looking. A pimply, square-headed kid with smirky eyes and a big-time cowlick, a person she must've walked by a million times. It just made her wonder, that's all. What if everybody walked by you all the time without ever bothering to notice? What would that do to you?

That was a lot of loneliness to consider. He obviously missed out on a lot of normal growing-up experiences. In some ways, it explained his emotional immaturity. He probably never got to go on dates and so he never got to *experience* a healthy relationship, so he didn't know anything about love and sharing intimacy. All his notions about these things probably came from television and movies and God knows where else. Ray was like some great big emotionally stunted adolescent.

Jill was just starting to feel like she was getting some insight into him when she heard the basement door being unbolted. Even though she was queasy with dread, she told herself to act calm, to play along with whatever was sent her way.

It didn't help her frazzled nerves, though, when Ray came barging down the stairs, appearing ornery and not a little high. "What the fuck are you staring at?" he said, his eyes glazed over with pot or something.

"Nothing, Ray," she said meekly, unable to keep the fear out of her voice.

"Shit, it smells in here," he said, spying the pail she'd used to take a crap in earlier.

"I'm sorry, Ray. I didn't know where else to go."

"Yeah, I guess," he said sheepishly, averting his eyes.

He was shirtless, wearing only a pair of drawstring sweats. He rubbed distractedly at his crotch; she could see the beginnings of an erection. He was probably going to rape her now. She reminded herself that as bad as that was, it wasn't the worst thing that could happen to her. She once had a friend who was raped—Debra Ellway. It was bad at first for Debra, but she worked her way through it, and in the end she was alive and able to get on with the rest of her life. A couple of years later, Debra even married some nice guy and they started a family together.

"Ray, I like what you've done to the basement," Jill said, trying to personalize everything. "Really, you have good taste, Ray."

"You think so?" he asked, sounding somewhat suspicious and still grabbing at his crotch.

"Oh, I know so, Ray," she said brightly, pushing her fear to one side. "You're a natural. I couldn't have done it better myself."

"I'm kind of glad you noticed," he said, as he let go

of himself for the moment. "I thought maybe you didn't appreciate my efforts here."

"To the contrary, Ray. I feel you've already done so much to make me feel at home."

"This is nothing, kitten. Wait'll you see the upstairs. There's a lot of work still to be done. But we'll turn it into something special, you'll see."

"I just can't believe I'm here," she said.

"It took some doin', believe me," he said, coming over to join her on the red couch now. "You wouldn't believe the shit I had to put up with and all the sad fucks who tried to stand in my way. But we don't have to worry about that shit no more, do we?" he said, sitting down right next to her. "I got to tell ya, Jilly, you look awfully juicy."

"You've got some muscles," she said, checking out his massive arms and preparing for the worst. "You must really work out a lot now."

"You noticed, huh? Yeah, well, I guess I look pretty good these days. I started in with the weights on the farm." Suddenly, his face flashed with red heat. "Hey, that's another thing we got to talk about. I mean, you're the bitch who testified against me, remember? I never woulda wound up at Hagerstown in the first place if it weren't for you."

"They made me, Ray. The cops told me they would hurt me if I didn't. They were very convincing."

"Yeah, well, I guess anything's possible," he said, cupping her breasts with his large hands. "I waited a long time for this, let me tell ya." Now he forced her to feel his hard-on. "How do you like that, kitten? That's the real salami."

She had only one other card to play now. "Oh, Ray, I'm just a little nervous because this is my first time. I just ask that you be gentle with me."

"I keep forgetting," he said, suddenly feeling a little less hard now. "I hadn't really taken that into consideration."

"I'm so worried I'm going to disappoint you, Ray. I know you're an experienced man of the world and I'm just this naive, small-town girl. I just hope I can live up to your expectations. I know you've waited a long time for this."

"Don't you worry about that, Jilly," he said, as he stopped groping her breasts. "I ain't going to hold that against you."

"Oh, Ray, you're so sweet and kind," she said, feeling him soften in her hands now. "You know, I wanted to wait until we were married. But you've already waited so long, and I know it's different for the man that way."

"Yeah, well, you got that right, Jilly. Men's needs is different, that's for shit sure."

"I trust you, Ray. I know an experienced lover like you will know just how to handle my first time. I'm sorry to be so worried. But my mother told me there could be a good deal of pain and blood associated with losing your virginity."

He was totally limp now. "Yeah, maybe your mother's right," he said, looking and sounding embarrassed now. "Maybe we should wait on this." He got up from the couch, not even having the nerve to look at her now. "I think I'll go fix us something to eat. You hungry? I got a good selection of canned soups and frozen shit. I'll be back down a little while later."

She had bought herself a little bit more time, that was all. She knew he'd be back for her, and the next time, he probably wouldn't suffer from performance anxiety. But in the meantime, she had learned something important about herself. When push came to shove, when she needed to pull off a nervy acting assignment, she herself suffered no such performance anxiety.

24

Back at their gunmetal desks in the raw fluorescence of the command post, Eamon and Bunko tried to decipher the most important clue in the case so far, which had just been faxed in along with a dozen other crime-scene photos. That this clue was written in lipstick on a roll of toilet paper and found in the victim's Nalcrest, Florida, trailer home only added to their sense of urgency:

SAVE ME
RAY 171

There was no doubt in the inspectors' minds that this cryptic message came directly from the hand of Jill Winters and was not some ploy of Ray Duffy's to throw them off the scent. Lipstick on toilet paper was too desperate an SOS to be the work of Duffy. What the hell 171 meant was an entirely different matter.

"Maybe it's a telephone area code," Bunko suggested.

"No such code exists," Eamon said. "I've already put it through the computer."

"Maybe it's a partial of his license plate or something."

"No, I've checked and it doesn't match the plate on his rental car. Which is just as well. Because then it would be useless to us. I get the feeling she wasn't through writing, just by the way her script trails off. My guess is that she was about to add another numeral or more."

"Yeah, I agree," Bunko said. "Looks like she was cut off suddenly. Christ knows what she was getting at here."

Tony Montrez and his top lieutenants were in another corner of the command post sorting through the same photos. The Bureau boys thought it might be helpful to see what the two teams could come up with independently of each other. The competition was on, no doubt about it. As usual, postal was the heavy underdog.

"Just once I'd like to show up those blue suits," Del Masterson said, joining them and eyeing Montrez's posse. "Smug bastards."

"Whatever happened to teamwork and shared information?" Bunko asked.

"I hate sharing," Masterson said. "It's for losers."

Eamon said, "What a great attitude to have, with a young woman's life on the line."

"Forget about her," Masterson said. "She's dog food by now. Duffy's cutting her up into little pieces as we talk."

"Del, until we learn otherwise, I think we'd better consider Jill Winters alive and kicking. It'll keep us that much more focused on the job before us."

"Wearie, get with the program. Duffy's full of unarticulated anger and rage. He's not going to wait around forever before he acts on it."

As much as Eamon didn't like what Masterson was saying, he thought there was something to it. Time was running out. That was the only thing they could be sure of. He knew Montrez was still debating whether to head down to Wheeling this afternoon. He had the company jet parked next door at Patton Field, where the service's stripped-down DC-8s took off and touched down. Snow was complicating his decision; there was a blizzard warning for the area. Snow had already started to fall, and the weather seers were predicting record accumulations tonight and into tomorrow. If they were going to go, they'd have to leave pretty damn soon.

"When's that fuck going to make up his mind?" Masterson said, still eyeing Montrez. "We don't got all day. That snow is already coming down pretty heavy. Another hour or so and they'll close the field."

"It's just as well," Eamon said. "Wheeling's a wild-goose chase."

"Well, I'm glad you feel that way, Lieutenant," Masterson said, an evil little smile beginning to form. "Because you're not going along for the ride. I want you to stay behind and take care of things from this end."

"You've got to be kidding me," Bunko said, jumping in. "He's the only reason we're in the hunt at all."

Eamon said, "Don't sweat it, Bunk. I'd rather stay here anyway. It's where I can do the most good. But thanks for coming to my defense, old buddy."

"I wasn't doing you any favors, believe me," Bunko said, sighing. "I just don't want to be stuck with Del all by myself."

Before Masterson could respond in kind, Agent Matthews came over to tell them they were leaving momentarily. "We have confirmation now that Duffy was renting out a post office box in his own name in Wheeling's main delivery branch," Matthews said. "That's more than enough for us. Grab your bags and let's make haste."

Several minutes later, Eamon was sitting by his lonesome in the unfamiliar quietude of the command post. He went over to the minifridge by the coffee maker and cracked some ice into a paper cup, then returned to Bunko's desk for the bottle of Jack Daniel's. It seemed like this was the first moment he'd had to himself since he got back from his Hawaiian honeymoon. He lit up a cigarette and remembered his bride in the aquamarine pools of Kauai; it was just over a week ago that they'd been cavorting in paradise.

He poured himself another stiff one, just as the first one was easing its way into his bloodstream and beginning to dissipate some of that full-throttle, brain-overloading intensity. As enjoyable as these mind-dulling sensations were, he realized he couldn't continue to the bottom of the bottle. Jill Winters was still out there somewhere, and if she had any hopes left, they were resting with him.

He needed to clear his mind and to begin all over again. Since he wasn't getting anywhere with that damn number—171, what the hell could it mean?— he needed to leave it behind for a little while. He laid out the other crime-scene glossies on his desk. Jill's trailer looked like someone had left in a hurry. But other than a bunch of upended bureau drawers, there didn't seem to be much of a sign of a struggle. Oh, there were clothes strewn all over the place. But there weren't knocked-down chairs or broken mirrors or bloodstains. It was Eamon's guess that Duffy did the packing, which explained the mess and suggested that he intended to keep Jill alive for a while. It also meant that she was in no condition to pack herself, which probably meant that he drugged her—which was also in keeping with Duffy's MO.

He liked to drug women and then he liked to have sex with them. If the homemade videos found in Duffy's apartment weren't proof enough of this, they'd also learned that in the past several months, two anonymous young women had telephoned the police to complain that Duffy had drugged them and raped them. But because neither one of them was willing to come forward, the police were unable to follow through. Eamon assumed that the girls were underage runaways, accounting for their reluctance to press charges.

They should've stopped this guy dead in his tracks months ago; he should've been picked up the moment he'd violated his parole. It never ceased to amaze Eamon how the Ray Duffys of the world were continually falling through the cracks of the system, as if nobody cared to follow through on anything. No, no, that was bullshit, he realized. It wasn't that nobody cared, it was just that there weren't enough staff or hours to keep track of all the Ray Duffys out there. He took another slug of the Jack, seeing how he was just as culpable as the police in this mess. When Ray Duffy was paroled from prison, he should've checked up on him himself, done his best to put the fear of God into him.

After all, this was his case. He was the stupid son of a bitch who had guaranteed Jill's safety. What was he thinking when he convinced her to enter their version of the Justice Department's witness protection program? It was just that they knew Duffy was never going to let go. He was a classic stalker. They had worked cases like this before, mostly with celebrities, with the kind of famous actresses and singers who could afford the electric fencing and around-the-clock bodyguards. But what about someone like Jill? What in the world was she going to do to protect herself?

Dr. Alan Stavis, the Bureau's resident stalking expert in the Behavioral Science Unit, agreed with their assessment of Duffy. Stavis told them that Duffy was an inadequate personality who fed off his fantasies about Jill. These elaborate fantasies nourished him, kept him alive, and offered hope. Without her, Duffy was empty, exposed, bereft. For whatever reasons, be it a dysfunctional home environment or an absence of love and imagination, Duffy had no adequate means of his own to sustain himself. His intelligence was purely crafty and predatory. His interior life was practically nonexistent. That's why he latched on to the former Jill Summers. She was lively, vivacious, attractive—in short, everything he wasn't. Duffy needed her for survival, as a way to compensate for his own shortcomings. Dr. Stavis concluded that this inadequate personality would rather self-destruct than ever let go of its dark fixation.

If Eamon was ever going to find this inadequate individual, he was going to have to learn to think like him. He needed to push his hatred and contempt for Duffy out of the way for the moment—not an easy thing to do from the perspective of the silent, funereal command post. Only a week ago, Frank Shoe and Lita Sanchez were at their desks, working their own cases. But he needed to somehow get beyond that. He needed to get into Duffy's head in order to understand him. He thought maybe the best place to start was by rereading the letters. Nothing documented the way his mind worked better.

There were over a hundred of them. More than a hundred letters in Duffy's childish chicken-clawed print. The spelling and punctuation were equally atrocious. Indeed, it was hard to get away from his inadequacies; they stared you right in the face.

> Dear Jilly,
> I am not going away so just get used to that fact. We have a lot to talk about. Jilly I hope you get this leter. Did you get the other ones??? Jilly its late at nite and I just got out of bed and needed to write you. A lot of things have been going through my mind. I wanted to tell you about them. Im

so afraid that I won't hear from you again. Jilly, why dont you return my phone calls??? Jilly I wish we could start all over again. I wish I could even start this leter over again. I keep looking at the paper and thinking I should tear it up and go back to sleep. Like whats the use??? Jilly Im really <u>PISSED</u> at you. I cant help it. You should really anser me man. I told you this shit means a lot to me. Jilly Im not some crazy jerkoff, thats out to hasel you. But Im telling you Im really really, MAD AT YOU NOW. Id knock your head off if you were here right now. Listen Jilly this is my last unresponded to letter. I mean Ive been thinking about it very sereosly and I realize that you havant been too cool with me. The way I look at it is that your the one whose going to be missing out. That is for shit sure. Dont you know that Ray is one great dude??? You should be able to see that. He LOVES Jilly. He would do anything for Jilly. He needs her. Cant you see that man? Jilly fuck it to hell. I know you too well and youv seen me at my worse so there shouldt be any thing left unsaid. I guess you allways knew all this but it makes me feel better to put it down. I gotta go for know. Love your friend, <u>RAY</u>

Dear Jilly,

I know I promised that I wouldt write you no more but, I just have to get this out and I got no one else to tell. Im listning to Jimi and taking hits and its all so fucked up. Jilly I wanted to write you a rippin happy leter and to tell you that its alright. But that aint the way its playing out for me.

I miss <u>YOU</u> Jilly. I think you know that now. Lots of times I look at things, and wonder how youd look at them. I THINK of YOU a lot. I have an unresolved conflict with U that I want to resolve some day. You shoulda kissed me that night after the movies in the car. I know now as I knew than that I love you and that I was a prick to let you get away from me. Instead of thinking it out I shoulda just grabbed you and made you love me. Man what makes me mad and sad all at the same time, is that it isnt all my falt. I wanted you to love me like the angel virgin you are. I gess I still want that. And now youve made me scared of wanting that. Like I have no right wanting that and that I cant have it any way. Do U understand where Im cuming from??? Some times I dont even understand my self. Ill write you again in the morning when Im feeling better. TAKE CARE AND KNOW THAT RAY LOVES YOU JILLY. Its a fact so dont bother changing it.

Dear Jilly,

O Jill Jill Jill. O buteful princess girl. O Im trying to see your face but I cant seem to see you now. My head is hurting to find a piture of you. Jilly whats running through your mind right this very second??? Jilly are you okay??? Jilly do you know how much I miss your smile??? Thats a reason to live right there my little virgin princess. Your so diffrent from all the other bitchs Ive known. You have <u>FEELINGS</u>. Dont ever lose that Jilly. Its what makes you speciel. Its raining outside today and Im waiting around for some thing to happen in this grey rainy day void. I need US to be back together again. I mean I put a lot into our RELATION-SHIP. I dont know if you really know that, I mean you maybe sort of know it. But you better beleive I put all of me into it. And it took a lot of ME out of it. Man I needed you but, I gess you really didt need me. I dont know. You jest want to shake my hand now like it never happened and tell me to be freinds. But I cant do that. A hug wont do it now. We got to go the distantse. Cant you see that you were ment for me and that God wants us to be one??? Jilly do you know what I would do to be with you right now??? Jilly just give me one more chance. If your reading this now think of what we once had. I cant beleive just because I said a few words out of place that its all over. Or has this been building all along??? Maybe I jest didnt see it BE-CAUSE im so in love with U. You should really call me Jilly. Theres so much we need to get to the bottom of. Jilly I know that it hasant allways been EZ and I know that weve had our tenchens and that its been hard on us and that there are no EZ ansers. I gess weve hurt each other without realizing it. But weve also inspired each other and have had conversations that have left us changed. Jilly I just need explaining man. I feel we both deserve at leest that. I dont want to have to remind you of all the years weve known each other going back to high school and everything else. Believe me Jilly I am still your freind even if you dont want me to be. RAY LOVES YOU FOR-EVER. Thats not just talk Jilly, my word is my bond as you will one day see for sure.

Dear Jilly,

I cant go on like this forever you know. Our break up is causing a lot of pain. Beleive it. I didnt want to menten it before but, I hope this has nothing to do with that longhaired loser friend of yours. This Keith guy is <u>BAD NEWS</u> Jilly. Ive been around so I know how these leechs operate. I know this Keith guy is singing these sensitveasshit songs that you girls like. But dont fall for his act man. He just wants one thing jest like every other fucking animal out there. If he has done anything to you at all my little virgin angel than I will have to take abbrobriate mesures. Jilly dont let this turd intafere with our relationship. I know you are very vulnerble right now but we have to stay true to each other until this is resolved to our mutual satisfattion. This is not like when we were in high school and you were seeing that hairyass football player. I can no longer stand to the side if you know what Im saying here. You know I used to wait for you by your locker everyday just to see your amazing face. I dont even know if I would have gratuated if it wasant for you Jilly. You are my reason going all the way back. We have just got to work this out between us. Im not kiding. I just want to love you and have you love me back. Is that so wierd??? I went past your house last night and I noticed that you were up late, the light in your bedroom was still on. I gess this is got you pretty upset too. Please call me Jilly. There is still time. Ray is a good man with lots of patence. That is no bullshit Jilly. Why dont you trust me any more??? This is just killing

me. PLEASE TAKE CARE OF YOUR-
SELF AND TRY NOT TO THINK
BADLY OF ME.

Dear Slutface,

I can not help myself any more. Your jest
a fucking bitch Im telling you. Not ans-
ering my calls and leters. Dont you see
what this is doing to me you bitch? Your
like all the rest of them. Just another slut
whore. As bad as my own fucking mother
who is a total cunt in her own right. I hope
you understand the consequances of your
actions. Ray is plenty fucking pissed. This
not a thret but I may have to just come over
to your house and get you. You leave me no
alterative you cunt. Ray has tried to be
civel about everything but, there is only so
much that one person can handal. At this
point Im not sure you can hold me accountable for my actions. Ray has been
tested. Now maybe its your turn to be
tested you fucking fucking, fucking cunt.
Id like to see how you think it feels. Im
cuming for you and now it wont be nice
like before. You had your chance dildo
breth. Now I have to just treat you like all
the other cunt whores out there. Its too
bad. Because maybe we coulda made something cool hapen together. Its your own
fucking falt beleive me. Ray has had
enough. Have you bitch??? Have you had
enough??? Now its your turn to suck dick.
This is not a joke. You better take me
sereosly.

Eamon put the stack of letters down for the moment and lit up another cigarette. One could read
only so much of this at one time. Still, this last missive

stood out from the others in a number of important
ways. To begin with, its language was more profane
and brutal than the others, its threats more overt than
implied. It seemed that even on paper, Duffy couldn't
completely rein in his violent temper. Not that
Eamon had ever needed any reminding to take Ray
Duffy seriously.

25

The supermarket was totally packed on account of the big snow they were supposed to be getting. Everybody was stocking up on flashlights, batteries, cat litter, and bottled water like they were nuclear survivalists or something. Bunch of assholes was what Ray thought, the way they got so excited about a few fucking little snowflakes.

He was doing some stocking up himself but not on account of no wimpy snow. It was just that the Stop N Shop in Green Ridge was pretty far from home and he didn't want to have to make the trip again anytime soon. Must've taken him a good forty-five minutes to get here. Of course, he could've taken his chances in Blue Springs, but he didn't want to run into any nosy locals, especially because he had to buy some of them Maxipads for Jill's feminine needs. The dumb bitch had actually asked for tampons, which instantly made him suspicious about her claim to being a virgin.

He knew she probably wasn't really. He figured she probably lost it to Bill Bartell, that big-dicked football god she was going with in high school. Not to mention all that unwatched time out in Hollyweird. Ray wasn't a total moron here; he knew she wasn't the

Virgin Mary or anything. But he still thought of Jill as pure-hearted, as the beautiful, angelic, unaffected girl that she always would be. You just had to look into her amazing green eyes to see all that poetic beauty and shit.

Actually, it bothered him that she probably lost her cherry to a stud like Bill Bartell. Ray just didn't know how he was going to measure up to those kind of high sexual expectations. And after that sorry performance this afternoon, he had plenty of reason to be concerned here. His dick just shriveled up into a little California prune when she started talking about it being the first time and whether there was going to be blood like her mother had said. Shit—blood and motherhood, that'll do it every time.

But Ray had a funny feeling that the bitch was playing him for a sucker. Yeah, she had him going, all right, with that little virgin routine. But the next time she tried it, he didn't care what line of crap she was selling, because he was going to introduce her to the Woodman, no two ways about it, man.

Actually, he was kind of enjoying his little shopping excursion. He had filled up one cart and now he was halfway through his second. He wasn't just stocking up on munchies, either. Sure, he went on his usual cookie-and-chip binge, clearing the shelves of Oreos, Chips Ahoy, Pringles, Tostitos, all the usual garbage he craved when he was sucking his bong off. But the thing was, today he was, like, being a regular shopper, too, getting paper towels and detergent and toilet-cleaning shit, all the crap you saw in the commercials that made your house all lemony and spotless. It was a good adult feeling to buy Brillo pads and napkins and air freshener; it said something about a person, like you were ready to take on all sorts of other responsibilities, too.

He was even picking up a lot of specialty items for Jill. He knew she was one of them veggie freaks, so he got some jars of artichoke hearts and hot peppers and Spanish olives, the works. Then he grabbed a couple of meaty T-bones for later on; it was like he was thinking of everything.

He had to wait awhile on the checkout line, but it was worth it. He got this total spunk queen punching up the register. The girl had a luscious strawberry-blond do and a juicy pair of grapefruit. Couldn't have been more than high-school age. Even had some teenage acne, which turned him on that much more. Her name tag said Alysia.

"That's a nice first name you got there," Ray said, just trying to be friendly. "What's your last name?"

"Buckley," she said without thinking. "Why do you want to know, anyway?"

"I'm new to the area," Ray said. "Just trying to be neighborly."

"Uh-huh," she said, pausing to look him over and looking just a little bit suspicious about the whole thing.

"You work here all the time?"

"Just after school during the week," she said, biting her lip in a nervous kind of way.

"I'll keep it in mind," he said, putting the info away for later.

"You do that," she said a little too sarcastically for Ray's liking.

He thought it was a pretty good sign that he could be attracted to someone new like this. It seemed like he'd been preoccupied with Jill for way too long, like years and years of pissing into the wind without anything coming back his way. Finding this new girl was definitely a ray of sunshine on an otherwise gray and snowy day, just the way it seemed to open up possibilities, as it were. It made him feel young and shit. The thing with Jill felt old and tired all of a sudden.

He led one of the kids who did the bagging outside with the other cart to his Jeep. It was coming down pretty good now, these big, heavy floaters that were really sticking to the ground.

"So what's that Alysia Buckley like?" Ray asked the bagger.

"Sticks to herself—you know," the kid said, sounding unhappy about it. "Like the rest of us ain't good enough or something."

As far as Ray was concerned, that was sweet music to his ears.

Jill had no idea how long he'd be gone. All she knew was that she had to work fast. There was no telling if she'd get another opportunity like this.

She realized that she was going to have to kill him, because if she didn't finish the job, he surely would. There weren't going to be any second chances. She was going to have to stab him; she couldn't think of any other way. At first, she thought maybe she'd try to crown him with that metal pail she'd been using to pee in. But Ray was way too big and strong; he'd just overpower her.

Of course she gave the basement door her best try; in fact, she'd hurled herself into it so hard that she thought she might have dislocated her shoulder. Sore and frustrated, she had to resort to plan B, which wasn't much of a plan, really. All she did was take down one of his art posters—Picasso's *Two Faces of a Woman*—and remove the glass frame. This she broke into several large shards, the best of which she hid next to her in a crease of that foamy red couch. Then she waited.

If she'd known just how long she was going to sit there waiting for him to come back, she would've taken the time to work on her crude weapon. Maybe she would've tried shaping it and smoothing it down against one of the oil burner's metal parts. Or maybe she would've even come up with a more complicated and winning plan, something more befitting a former set designer. Maybe she would've tried to fashion some kind of dummy to put on the couch, covered it in a blanket or something so it would look like she was sleeping, so she could sneak up behind Ray as he went to check on her.

As it was, though, she waited and she waited—for close to three interminable hours, she waited. It took a lot out of her to sit there like that, feeling all her emotional strength and resolve drain away with each passing minute. She needed to keep herself focused and motivated on her ultimate mission. She needed to hate him like she'd never hated before. She dredged up every sick thing Ray had ever done to her and played it over and over. Her life was on the line, that simple.

Except . . . except Jill had never hurt another human being in her entire overly conscientious life. She couldn't even step on an ant; why, every time an insect got into her trailer, she would just put it in a jar and release it outside. That was even why she was a vegetarian. It wasn't for health reasons; it was for philosophical reasons. She just didn't know if she could really do it—tear into him like that with a piece of jagged glass. It went against her entire nature.

Maybe she just should've accepted her fate, trusted in God and the great ineffable. Maybe that's why she was here in the first place, to recover her faith and to make amends with her maker.

No, that was all bullshit. There was only the here and now. That was why she couldn't kill anything. Because she really believed that there was no heaven or reincarnation or any of the other bogus concepts that were always foisted on the ignorant, unquestioning masses. It was absolutely amazing what the world bought into. All these religions that told us how to live and die on the basis of some higher power that never had the guts to show Himself. Where was God if He really existed?

If God existed, He surely would show Himself now. This was the time, no doubt about it. She would gladly become a convert. All she wanted was a sign, anything at all that could help point the way. No, it was just as she thought all along: God was not going to show Himself in the basement of Ray's house, or in any other place, for that matter. There was just the damp, musty smell of forgotten death down here. This was her tomb. Ray was going to rape her until he got tired of that and then he was going to mutilate her and kill her and bury her bones in his yard. That was not the kind of thing that would happen in a world watched over by God.

Ray knew no one was watching over him. Jeeze, Louise, he had to be pretty sure of it to be doing the things he was doing. He was like that creepy character in that book she once read. What was the name of it? Oh, right, *The Collector*. It was about this sicko who collects butterflies and then mounts them under glass. But eventually he gets tired of butterflies and decides to start collecting bigger specimens—human specimens.

Ray was just like that character, operating in the same kind of heavy-duty trance, refusing to let the world intrude on his own disturbed reality. Really, it was like he could hardly hear you. You were just this butterfly, this pretty pair of wings. It didn't matter how much you kicked and screamed. He just went on about his business regardless, hearing only the strange, disconnected voice inside his own myopic head.

Suddenly, she heard sounds upstairs; the monster was home. He kept going in and out of the house; she heard the door slam open and shut a number of times. Then there were all sorts of clanking noises, as if he were rummaging in the kitchen, taking out his anger on the pots and pans. But then it got quiet again; she couldn't even begin to guess why.

An hour later, the basement door was being unbolted. "I made you some din-din," he trumpeted from the top of the stairs, holding a tray of steaming food.

She remained on the couch, immobilized by a clammy combination of fear and dread, as he came down and started laying out the table. His back was to her. This was her golden opportunity. She grabbed hold of the broken piece of glass, but she couldn't seem to do it. Her body just wouldn't budge in spite of her brain's insistent commands.

Damn, girl, this is it, your last chance. There won't be any others.

"Come and get it, kitten," he said. "Believe me, I went to a lot of fucking trouble."

He sounded quite pleased with himself. Damn, his good mood was only adding to her difficulty.

"There's more," he said, starting back up the stairs. "I'll be back in a jiff."

Then he was back, laying out more goodies. Again, his back was turned to her. She clenched the glass hard, letting it cut into her own skin. She had to do it, she had to do it. *Now, girl, now.* She got up and ran toward him. She had to take that shard and rip into him with it.

She grabbed him from behind, by the head, with every intention of slitting his throat in one clean stroke. She managed to stick the glass under his chin, but before she could really get at him, he cried out in startled wonder and agony. It was enough to stop her cold.

"What the fuck?" he said, putting a hand to his bleeding neck. "You cut me. You bitch, you fucking bitch, you."

She dropped the bloodied shard.

He still seemed too stunned to retaliate. "I can't believe it. After all I've done for you. You fucking cunt. Look at what you've done to me. I'm bleeding, for shit's sake. Look, there's blood everywhere. Fuck. I trusted you. I . . ."

His voice trailed off. She waited for him to attack, but then he did a strange thing: he began to cry.

"Shit, I loved you, you fucking bitch," he said, sobbing all the while. "I loved you, but you're like all the rest of them, everybody else in my life. Nobody ever loved me. I was never good enough—the shit I had to take. Everybody always laughing. Not like you. Not like Miss Pretty Popular Cheerleader. What the fuck would you know about it?"

His face was red with blood and tears. He brought her into sharp focus now. "I'm going to make it hurt," he said, moving in for the kill. "Just the way I was hurt."

She didn't make a move to stop him. He slapped her hard across the face. "Like that, you cunt?" She didn't even blink. Then he grabbed her by the throat and began to choke the life out of her. "This is the last thing you're ever going to see, bitch!"

She felt like her eyeballs were going to explode. She couldn't breathe and her whole body was seared by heat, but still she didn't try to push him away. *Finish it,* she thought in the burning haze, *just finish it already.*

"You're going to pay for everything that's happened to me!"

She was just an apathetic bystander to her own death. It was only too bad that the last thing she would see on this earth was the retarded madness in Ray's face.

See, there's no God, she thought, just before losing consciousness. *I knew it. I just knew it.*

26

It took over an hour to get to his father-in-law's place. Usually, it would take Eamon a mere fifteen minutes to navigate his way across town, but the evening's rush had stalled in a snowy squall of fender benders and near-whiteout conditions.

The radio weathermen, usually an excitable lot anyway, were orgasmically predicting that the blizzard of '96 was already a good bet to topple the blizzard of '46 as the all-time chart topper, which was certainly interesting, considering the fact that that oldie but goodie had packed a walloping twenty-nine inches of the white stuff. It had been some time since their temperate little town had seen anything bearing down on them like this. And, of course, Baltimore seemed spectacularly unprepared for the onslaught.

Driving home, Eamon was struck by the absence of sanders and salters. Snow was already drifting on the side streets, making them virtually impassable. To make matters worse, stuck cars were being abandoned in place, right in the middle of the road, which of course would just hinder plowing efforts later on.

He was relieved that his car, a five-year-old Pontiac without the benefit of snow tires or four-wheel drive, had handled the treacherous conditions without incident, although he was just a mite jealous of all those city cowboys in their sport utilities, those Grand Cherokees and Pathfinders and Explorers that seemed to plow on without a second's hesitation. Eamon suspected that more than a few of these hardy vehicles were on the road for no better reason than to show off their stuff. *Heck,* Eamon thought, *I guess if I'd spent thirty thousand dollars for a truck, I'd be out there having a good ol' time, too.*

As it was, he was just happy to get home in one piece without any new misadventures. Stepping into Joe Seppala's house, he was greeted by the hearty, intoxicating aroma of another one of Joe's gourmet dinners and by the heart-lifting sight of his wife curled up on the couch in front of the TV. Just seeing her there like that, his raven-haired, violet-eyed girl in domestic repose, filled him with blissful warmth. In a way it was rather amazing how this simple, infinitely ordinary scene pulled at him; it was better than sex and money put together. Sometimes it took so very little to please a man.

"I'm so glad you're back," Mary said, looking up. "With this weather, I was getting worried."

"A little snow, that's all it is," he said, grinning and brushing the flakes off his overcoat. "It's nothing after you've escaped helicopter crashes and hit-and-run drivers and deranged gunmen."

"I guess," she said. "Still, they're saying it's the blizzard of the century. It's coming down at over two inches an hour and it's blanketing five states and—"

"The only problem is we've still got to go to school tomorrow. It's not like when we were kids, is it?"

"I know," she said, losing the schoolgirlish excitement in her voice. "I'm on call tonight, even. Just in case we come up short. That's the problem with living so close to the precinct."

"Oh, great. Another romantic night alone with your dad."

"It's not for certain. But I have to answer the call if it comes. Anyway, I think my dad has been just great to us."

"Oh, he has, he has," Eamon said, agreeing, hanging up his coat, scarf, and hat in the entryway closet. "What's on the menu tonight?"

"He's making his famous veal Marsala with—"

"—Oven-roasted herbed potatoes," their genial chef said, entering the room with a tray of appetizers. "My secret is fresh rosemary and garlic—one of nature's most delectable combinations. In the meantime, to keep your palates modestly entertained, I've put together a little antipasto. Nothing too fancy. Nothing that wouldn't be served in Palermo's finest trattorias."

He put the tray down on the coffee table, in the same manner that Picasso might've unveiled a new work. It was the bold, colorful presentation of a master artist, a robust combination of roasted red peppers and fresh mozzarella, marinated mushrooms, and olive oil–drizzled bruschetta.

"You, sir," Eamon said in the throes of adulation, "are nothing short of a genius. When that sad day comes to leave your wanton hospitality, I hope we will find the courage to go on. Returning to our pathetic former culinary ways will not be easy."

Joe Seppala laughed. "Well, my boy, I think you've earned yourself a beer. In fact, I've just come into a case of a rather tasty, richly flavored English ale on which I would like your expert opinion."

"I'm at your service, sir. Though I should warn you that beer tasting is not to be taken lightly. It may take many samplings of this new ale before I can render my verdict."

"Well, son, if you're up to the challenge, then so am I."

After Mr. Seppala returned to the fragrant simmerings of his kitchen, Eamon turned to Mary and said, "How in the world did I get so lucky?"

She was looking at him funnily, almost as if she didn't recognize him. "I still can't get used to it," she said, eyeing the line of stitches going up his shaved scalp. "When do they come out?"

"A few days. I still haven't seen the dentist, either."

"God, this has been such a nightmare."

"Whatever we've been through, it's been worse for Jill Winters."

"What was she like?" Mary asked.

"What's with this past-tense stuff?" He bristled. "She's still alive, as far as we know."

"I'm sorry; I didn't mean anything by it."

"No, I'm sorry, Mary," he said, letting out a deep sigh. "This thing has been eating me up inside. But to answer your question, she's probably still the same shy, quiet person she was before all this happened. That's the shame of it."

"What do you mean?"

"I mean I don't think she's got the inner grit to help herself in this situation. Not that too many people have. But I remember Jill as a woman who wasn't very aggressive or confident on the surface. Don't get me wrong, she's smart, but she's no risk taker. There's something at the very heart of her that's scared. Scared of life, maybe. I don't know. It's probably a lost cause anyway."

"But you just insisted she's alive."

"Yeah, you're right," he said, pausing to take a long draft of the English ale. "It's just that I was thinking about who she's up against. Duffy's not playing by anyone's rules but his own. He's got nothing to lose here. And he sure as hell isn't scared. I don't know what he's scared of, but it ain't dying, that much I can tell you."

It was time to get back to work. Talking to Mary about Jill Winters had made him feel doubly guilty to be sitting there in the cozy comfort of Joe Seppala's house nibbling bruschetta and sipping a fine, imported brew. It was anyone's guess where Jill was at the moment, but it was a sure bet that her surroundings weren't nearly so amiable. Eamon had brought home Duffy's letters; he thought it was as good a place to begin again as any. So as Joe finished his lavish dinner preparations and Mary went back to watching the TV news, Eamon pushed himself back into Ray Duffy's angry, distorted mind.

Dear Jilly,
    I would jest like to here your voice again. U owe me some kind of <u>EXPLANATION</u> man. Life without you is not worth living. Its like Im jest here you know. Do you know what I mean??? Jilly do you??? This is one more leter that your not going to get I gess. I still got to write it anyway. I dont know what to tell you any more. Im so tired of it. I know you cant be having the greatest time in the world eether. I dont think Im wrong about that. Cant you see how much I care about you??? Why do you think I was always looking after you for??? Why else would I waste my time like that following you and shit??? I did it all becuse I love you. Some times, I think it is all one big dream. Like it almost never happened or something. There is so much sadness in the dream Jilly. Yeah even I can get sad if you want to know the fucking truth here. Some times even I am lonley. That is no joke Jilly. And some times even I am sorry for the way things have worked out. Yeah Im sorry for a lot of things. But thats a hole other story. Take care for now. Allways, your old freind Ray.

Dear Jilly,
    Ray misses you. He cant help him self. It

is so sad. Him and Jill should be toogether. But now that they dont see each other no more how can they be??? Its all becuse life is confuseing and complikated. Ray tryed every thing it seemed to him but it was to no avale. He offered his body and his mind to Jill but she needed more time. It seemed like there was nothing left to offer. Maybe there wasant. But Ray never got the chance to find out becuse he never saw Jill agan. Now would that not be a sad story if it came to pass??? Jilly we mustant let this happen. You see yuve got this great freind named Ray. He cares about you so much that it hurts. It hurts him so much that he thinks some time that he would be better off without Jilly, the girl who is hopefully reading this leter. Its so messed up. Its driving Ray nuts. He does not know what to think no more. He cant figure out whats going on in Jillys head. HE HOPES, really really hopes that Jilly isant crazy fucked up like every body else on the earth. Ray loves Jilly. First as a person and than next in the regular sence. He allways has. When he was younger and did not know the way things worked he thought he had a chance. When heed see Jilly he would almost trembul with all the feelings that he felt. It sounds stupid now but it is totally true Jilly. He was young and in love and thats a dangeross combo. Thats why he had to get out of bed one nite and write this leter to Jilly any way. He jest needed to tell her some things. Things that had been there for so long and that would have been there even longer if he did not tell her. REMEMBER ME JILLY. I wont be around for ever you know.

Dear Jilly,

You proably do not know this but I have some speceil memerys. You are in most of them. I remember when we were in high school and you would be doing cheerleader practise and I would be there too watching you. Some times it was awsome the way the sun would jest hit your hair. It was like heaven or some thing Im telling you. Or some times I would just see you getting on the bus and than see you thru the window. Jest that would be enuff some times. I coud live off those pitures for days and thats no joke. Those are not the only memerys that I have thou. My dad used to take me to Blue Springs to go fishing when I was jest a little little boy. Once we cought all these trout. It was really some thing I am telling you. We fried them up and had the best time ever. That was before all the things went bad on us. My mother never liked Pensilvania thou. But I think about Blue Springs a lot I can tell you. But mostly my memerys are of you Jilly. I do not even remember too much about my growing up. I dont know why but I jest dont recall that much of every thing. But I remember the green green in your eyes. And that white dress you some times used to ware. That was always nice. I looked forward to it. That is no joke. You can not realy imagen how many times I have thougt of you over all these years. I remember every thing. Do you???

Eamon put down the letters and pondered for a moment the significance of Blue Springs, Pennsylvania. Duffy didn't often make a geographical reference. Not only that, it was a town that had a special association for him, a place where he and his dad had bonded. That was not something to take lightly, considering that Duffy hardly knew his father; he'd run off on them when Ray was about five years old or so. Still, Blue Springs had never come up before; it wasn't in any biographical data they had or in any of the police or parole reports. It would have to be checked out of course, but . . .

"Absolutely outrageous," Mary said, interrupting his speculations. "I hope they give whoever did it the chair."

"What's that, darling?" he said, turning his attention to the TV news. "What's got you so excited?"

"Didn't you hear about this incident? Happened the other night. Just one of the most despicable things I've ever heard," Mary said, shaking her head with real disgust. "Well, this trooper was shot in cold blood after he stopped a motorist on a routine speeding violation. And as sick as that is, that's not the sickest part. After he blew away the officer, the degenerate got out of the car and took a leak. Urinated right on the dead man, like he was so much roadkill."

Eamon reached for the remote control and clicked the volume up. A TV reporter was standing in the driving snow alongside I-83, the interstate that ran from Maryland into Pennsylvania.

"A dashboard videocam in the trooper's cruiser caught very little of the incident," the reporter said. "Used for recording drivers in a series of drunk-driving tests, it did not capture the shooting at all. However, the videocam managed to reveal the make of the suspect's car. The police are looking for a fairly recent Toyota Tercel. Unfortunately, they don't have a plate number to go along with that.

"The police have set up a toll-free hotline—1-800-555-4200—in hopes that someone might've seen something. They are looking to talk to anyone who may've been traveling on the interstate between York and Middletown in the early hours of yesterday morning. This is Chad Curtis reporting for WQRX."

"Jill Winters drove a Toyota Tercel," Eamon said excitedly. "That's the car Duffy left Florida in. I'll bet you anything that he took out the trooper. It matches his screwed-up MO, all right. Does your dad have a map anywhere about?"

Moments later, Eamon's fingers were tracing up I-83 on one of Joe Seppala's road maps. He saw that I-83 ended in Harrisburg, Pennsylvania, which was within shouting distance of Blue Springs—just another twenty miles or so north.

"Duffy's in Blue Springs," Eamon announced. "No doubt about it."

"How can you be so sure?"

"I've got to go," he said. "I've got to leave right this minute."

"But there's a blizzard."

"Exactly. Montrez and his men will never be able to fly in. I'm the only one who can get there in time."

"Get where?"

"Blue Springs, of course. Where do you think?"

"But where in Blue Springs? How will you find him tonight?"

"It's a small town. I'll think of something."

"But you could get killed if you go alone," she said, dizzied by the speed of events. "And it's snowing like crazy outside. You'll never get through. They've closed portions of all the major highways. You're absolutely out of your mind."

"That's what it is," he said, not hearing her at all. "Of course," he said, slapping his hands together as it all seemed to jell at once. "That's what 171 is. It's a ZIP code. The first three numerals of a ZIP. Jill Winters worked in the damn post office, for Christ's sake. She was trying to leave a small clue. I'll just bet it's for that general area of Pennsylvania. In fact, I'd wager anything on it."

"I don't have any idea of what you're talking about at this point," Mary said, looking bewildered. "You need to eat something. You need to think a little bit more on this. You're not making sense."

"I've got no time for making sense," he said, going into the closet for his coat.

"What if you're wrong?" she said, imploring him to stay.

"What if I'm right? Did you ever think of that?"

27

Ray had never felt so much fucking pain, man. It was just like kind of flooding through him all at once. It happened right after Jilly attacked him with the glass. And he wasn't talking about the physical sensation of getting cut, either. Hey, he was choking that bitch and she was turning blue, and suddenly he was seeing all sorts of things that he really didn't want to remember. It was like he couldn't stop the bad memories from devouring him. He was like crying and shit, and suddenly he was seeing his dad and mom and the way things used to be when everybody was younger and shit. He just let Jilly drop to the floor; she was no longer in the picture anymore.

There was so much that he wanted to forget, so much that he had blocked out. Everybody was always rejecting him. Jilly, that fucking bitch, was just one more in a long, long line of tormenters and rejecters.

He saw his dad giving him a good swat and telling him he was just a little fairy boy for crying. "I got no respect for pussies," he said, towering over little Ray.

Then he flashed on how his dad would drink himself into oblivion and take it out on him and his mom. "C'mere, you two. What the fuck are you looking at? Where do you think you're going? I ain't through with either one of you."

Then that day when he finally left: making a point of taking Ray aside and saying to him, "It's because you're just a little fairy boy, that's why I'm leaving. You'll never amount to nothing. I'm ashamed that I could father such a girlie boy. What, you going to cry again? Is that it? Well, suit yourself. Cry your little fairy-boy eyes out. It won't do you no good anyhow."

Then it was just him and his mom. Nobody coming to see them or nothing anymore. She would just suck on her cigarettes and sip her jug wine and gobble them sleeping pills at night. He'd try to make her laugh or try to get her attention or just pull on her sleeve the way little kids do, but she would just say, "Later, honey; your mama's tired right now."

Ray cried, remembering it all now, remembering every last fucking thing that ever happened to him. The way his poor mother got so old and weird so fast, and the fact that they had to lock her up those couple of times. Then one night, when he was like eleven or something, she crawled into his bed. That was bad news, man. She kept on doing it, too, night after night, even though he still wet his bed, even though it was all wrong and perverted and everything.

He smashed his fists into the basement walls, screaming, "No, no, no!" over and over again. He just smashed his knuckles bloody. The blue bitch was just lying there with this warped face, like she was laughing at him or something. Or maybe she was just dead. Who cared anymore? There was nothing left of him anyway.

It was always the same. The way everybody used to make fun of him in school. The way he was always in the special dumb people's classes. The way he was dumpy, fat, and ugly and the way everybody used to beat up on him. The other boys would grab his bagged lunches and play keep-away with them until they were all crushed up. Calling him "tubbo" and "fart breath" and "faggot." They were always waiting for him, in the hallway and at the bus stop, taunting him, taking his books and money, giving him wedgies and flats, beating the shit out of him, leaving him crying for his mommy. It never seemed to stop. Every day was more humiliation, more abuse, more tears. They never let go, never gave him a break.

Those fucking, fucking, fucking bastards.

Lou Farley forcing Ray's head in the urinal that one time in the tenth grade. Guys pissing on him, actually pissing on him. The girls coming into the boys' room to get a good look at the show.

They could all fucking die, for all he cared.

Man, the pain was unbelievable. The way these memories were just like punching him in the gut, knocking the freaking wind out of him. He didn't even know how it got so whacked out like this. How'd he even wind up here? In this basement of this dumb old house in the middle of nowhere, with the blue bitch lying on the floor beside him. He thought she might be really dead. But when he went to check, he could hear her breathing still, making these soft little moans.

Good, he thought, *I don't want you dead yet. Somebody's got to pay for what happened to me. It might as well be you. We'll go out together. It'll be a blast; you'll see.*

He worked to put the pain aside, to get control of himself again. He was a bloody, emotional mess. His neck was still bleeding. He didn't think it was serious, though. The bitch just didn't have the balls to follow through on it. But he would. Oh, yeah—you could count on that. There was going to be some follow-through now.

He went upstairs and got some rope and then came back for the bitch. He took off her clothes, tied her up, taped her fucking mouth shut, and carried her back up.

Yeah, now things were starting to fall in place.

He'd leave this world just like he came in, wrapped

in blood and mucus. He'd make it look good, leave those homicide dicks with something to think about when they finally found the bodies, which would probably be sometime in the spring. Yeah, he'd haunt their little cop dreams for a long, long time to come, that was for shit sure.

He got his nastiest magazines and spread them open all around the living room. And then he put a classic of the genre—one of his very first purchases, in fact—on the VCR: *Behind the Green Door*.

Then he went into the kitchen and got some of the cutlery out. Yeah, all the big steak knives. That would give them homicide dicks some more to think about.

Knives and porno and a naked dead girl—or at least a soon-to-be naked dead girl. *Yeah, feast on that, boys.*

It was time to go get the guns now. He had the Anaconda and this .357 Magnum and this regular old Smith & Wesson, all of them bought off the street. They were all okay, but he was saving the best for last. Because his favorite was the rifle, this fancy old Winchester hunting rifle that the old widower who owned the place before him had just left behind. It was mighty sweet, though, this blast from the past, with its laminated cherry stock and with these little duckies etched over the trigger.

Yeah, Jill looked up when she saw that little beauty. It was nice to see that kind of fright in her green eyes again. Yeah, he was going to stick that Winchester into every orifice in her body.

"So what's your pleasure, kitten?" he said, sitting down next to her on that ratty, dog-haired couch. "I can't begin to tell you what a shitty mood I'm in," he said, thinking he'd start in with the knives. "Shit, I know what you're thinking: *It don't look like anybody's taken the trouble to sharpen or even clean these blades in a while.*" She closed her eyes real tight. "Don't make it harder on yourself," he said, taking hold of one of the bigger mothers. "I really want you to look at me, kitten, when I'm talking to you." She just kept them closed anyway, like she was trying to keep all the big, bad monsters out. "This ain't like when you were a little girl, bitch. I said open them."

Now he had her attention again. "Good, that's better," he said, getting some fucking control over the situation again. "You know, I got to tell you, you bitches have never made life easy on me. That's a whole other can of rejection. I mean, the guys were always beating the shit out of me and stuff. But you bitches hurt me in other ways. I remember this one puss in the seventh grade that I liked. Little Mary Ann Hood. Yeah, there was this kiddie dance, and I got the stupid fucking idea—don't ask me how—that I might ask her to go with me. Are you following this so far, bitch?

"That's good. Because Mary Ann Hood was not exactly like this pretty girl like you, you see. No, she was a bit of a bow-wow, really. This was like before I started setting my sights so high. No, I just figured I had a chance with this one. She seemed kind of nice, too. Did I mention that? Yeah, well, she didn't seem so hurtful like so many of the other junior-high priss queens out there. Anyway, you're probably wondering what Mary Ann said when I asked her to the big dance.

"Yeah, Mary Ann basically said she would never ever go out with a gross, disgusting faggot like myself. I can't remember her exact words, but they were something to that effect. Yeah, it was only the beginning of a long line of rejection from you whore-bitch cunts."

He took the knife and made his first cut: a nice, authoritative stroke down her cheek. It was interesting, the way the blood didn't flow all at once, the way there was this kind of hesitant, stunned moment before the body reacted and supplied it. Once it started flowing, though, it just kept on doing so.

Just then the lights began to flicker. "Oh, I forgot

about that storm out there," he said. "I think I got some candles somewhere. Now don't you go anywhere, kitten. I'll be back in a jiff."

Luckily, that old widower guy had left a bunch of candles in one of the kitchen drawers. By the time he got them, the lights had gone all the way out. He came back into the living room and lit up about ten of the damn things, giving the whole place a nice, spooky glow.

"Now isn't that cozy," he said, sitting back down. "Now where were we exactly?"

28

The wipers and headlights on Eamon's car seemed absolutely useless. It was a hard, grainy, wind-whipped snow that swirled and lashed, as blinding as a cyclone of dust. He plodded on, at twenty miles per hour, squinting into the white-blue whirling, unable to make heads or tails of where he was. Just staying on the road was no small feat.

He was starting to think that Mary and her father were right, that he should've just stayed home and waited until the storm blew over. Every other minute or so, he considered aborting his mission. But then he'd get a picture of Jill Winters in his mind and he'd think better of it; what if a few extra hours turned out to be the difference between life and death?

If he wasn't going to make it, it was going to be because he *couldn't* make it, not because he didn't make the effort. He'd probably run into a tree, anyway, or another snow-blinded car; so what was the point of debating it? The problem was, he needed radar: he *really* couldn't make out a damn thing. It was like piloting a submarine or something; in the unseeing comfort of his capsule, he moved slowly, cautiously forward, anticipating that jarring moment of impact as if it were only a matter of bell-ringing time.

He was thrilled and relieved to make it as far as the interstate. There was only one lane open, but it was still a vast improvement over the cluttered, one-way streets of the city grid. All he had to do now was keep his eyes pasted to the red taillights ahead of him, to follow the poor bastard in front of him. There were dozens of abandoned cars to the side of the highway, snow-buried remnants of some lost civilization. He prayed that he wouldn't wind up like that tonight. *Give me a break, God,* he prayed. *I need this. And Jill Winters needs this. Don't let us down now.*

He put the radio on and lit up a cigarette as he tried somewhat unsuccessfully to calm himself. He knew he was out of his league, but he also knew he was right about Duffy's being holed up in Blue Springs. It was a small, small town, and if Eamon didn't miss his bet, there was somebody somewhere who'd seen something. To that end, Sheriff Earl T. Vose, the law in Blue Springs, was already making inquiries. Eamon had had the good sense to make some telephone calls before he exited Joe Seppala's house. The first one he made was to Montrez and the boys to let them know the score. Within minutes, Montrez had contacted Vose and filled him in on the situation.

Montrez was also able to find out the ZIP code for Blue Springs and the outlying area: 17204. It wasn't an exact match, but it was sure close enough, especially considering that it was right above Harrisburg, whose own ZIP began with 171, the lipstick numerals found on the toilet paper inside Jill's trailer. Now, it was entirely possible that Jill was being held in the city of Harrisburg—except Eamon wasn't biting.

Guys like Duffy needed unwatched space, a remote locale, to pull off their sociopathic plans. And if they did choose a city for their playground, they usually went for something big and anonymous, not some dinky town like Harrisburg, which had too many of the drawbacks of a small burg and too few of the benefits. Besides, it stood to reason that Jill, as a full-time postal clerk, might know the ZIP for Harrisburg. But it would take a much bigger leap of logic and faith to insist that she knew the ZIP for Blue Springs, so odds were, she didn't. She probably didn't even know exactly where she was being taken. She was just trying to leave some little crumb behind, something that the investigators could work with later.

Eamon felt like he was being pulled into Duffy's unholy vortex, as surely as the way his car was being sucked into the swirling snows. It was hard to explain, and harder still to rationalize, but it was almost as if he didn't have a choice, as if he were somehow being swept along with the bad weather, on the angry winds of fate.

It just felt so unreal, this magic-carpet ride into the unknown. He felt nothing, not even the road, and he saw nothing except for the red taillights ahead of him. He'd get there, though, somehow, because . . . because it was his destiny. Don't laugh; it was out there, before him, in the wild, dancing snow, in that mad blurring of crystals and night. He just kept lighting the cigarettes and prowling the radio dial in search of favorite old songs—anything to quell the jitters.

At least he was warm; the Pontiac's heater was purring nicely, thank you very much, and he had plenty of gas. Normally, from Baltimore, it took less than two hours to get to Harrisburg, and then it would be another thirty minutes or so to Blue Springs, except this was anything but a normal night. Still, he was moving, and there weren't too many other people out on the road; hell, he was starting to think he might make good time after all.

He even had some veal Marsala sandwiches, in case he got hungry; of course, he had his father-in-law to thank for that. Mary also stuck a snow shovel and a bag of cat litter in the backseat, in case he lost his traction somewhere. Eamon knew he was a lucky fellow to have so many people watching out for him like that. It was a nice, cozy feeling to belong like that, to have love in your life, to know that people gave a damn about you.

He figured that was what separated him from Ray Duffy in the end. Duffy was a sicko, all right, but he didn't wind up that way all on his own. People weren't born monsters, Eamon was sure of that. Why, just take a look into the eyes of any infant; it wasn't likely that you were about to see evidence of an evil seed. Naah, it was never like that. The truth was far more normal, far more unsettling. Eamon knew that all of these inadequate personalities—America's stalkers and serial killers and serial rapists—didn't just come out of the anonymous woodwork for no reason. The root causes were much more understandable than anyone ever wanted to believe, always pointing to an absence of familial love and supervision.

Now, Eamon was not some liberal pushover who thought we should go soft on criminals—far from it. That was why he believed in the death penalty. He knew better than most that there were people who were just plain unredeemable, who had crossed over a line that you could never return from. Of course, there was also the little matter of justice, too—justice for the victims and their families.

Eamon had seen too much in his fourteen years of law enforcement to want to coddle criminals. But that didn't mean he didn't want to help people before they went egregiously wrong, because there were plenty of people worth saving out there. Mostly, they were kids, though, kids who were just starting to go wrong. Kids who could still be reached, if anyone cared to give a damn.

Who knew if an unredeemable like Duffy had ever once been a savable human being? It was hard to say. But it was a safe guess that nobody ever did much caring and watching over him when he was growing up. By the time he was in high school, he was probably exhibiting all the classic signs of antisocial behavior. Some of it, the teachers would see; some of it, they wouldn't. But his grades were probably terrible and he probably cut most of his classes. He probably didn't have many friends, and the ones he did have would be of an equally low caliber. Probably routinely came to school high on drugs. Probably into pornography in a big way. Probably cruel to little animals. Probably a fire starter too, or a bed wetter. But he was probably also allowed to squeak through. Why? Because it was easier to do that than to deal with him. It was that simple.

Not that Eamon was entirely blaming the school system. It was a place of learning, not a correctional facility. Besides, all learning began in the home, with the parents. But his point was that all the signs would have been there from the beginning, from kindergarten, most likely. No matter how secretive Ray Duffy tried to be, there would have been some very odd things about him, some things that you almost couldn't fail to pick up on. It was just that the whole country was good at looking the other way.

Suddenly, the red taillights in front of him became bright-red brake lights. Eamon slowed down, seeing as he did that traffic was being diverted by a state trooper. The poor bastard was standing out in the deluge, in front of his flashing blue cruiser, which was positioned sideways across the only clear lane, waving motorists off the interstate.

As he pulled alongside him, Eamon rolled down his window. "Is there an alternate route to Harrisburg?" he shouted into the howling.

"Mother Nature's taken care of them, too," the trooper answered brusquely. His face was a sore, frostbitten red and his mustache was plastered with ice. "We're recommending that people stop for the night right here in Manchester. You'll see a motel and a service area when you come off the exit."

"I've got to get to Harrisburg and points beyond tonight," Eamon said.

"Make new plans, then."

Eamon took out his inspector's shield and held it up for the trooper's inspection. "I'm a federal agent working in conjunction with the FBI on a breaking case. I'm going to have to ask you to let me through now."

"I'm sorry, I still can't do that," the trooper said, shaking his head. "You'll never make it. There's drifts of up to four feet in places, covering the entire road. You don't even have snow tires on your vehicle, let alone chains."

"Look, you've got to let me through," Eamon said, the desperation all too apparent. "I've come too far to turn back now."

"Believe me, they won't find you until morning. You'll be a block of ice by then."

"You know that trooper who got killed on this road the other night?" Eamon said, down to his last playing card.

"Know him?" the trooper blurted. "Stevie and me were in the same class at the academy. We were practically brothers."

"I'm on the heels of his killer," Eamon said. "But time is fast running out. I need you to let me pass, or we might lose our man altogether."

The trooper finally acquiesced. "Now I've got no choice but to let you through," he said, still shaking his head. "Not that I think you got a prayer in hell." Then he went back into the cruiser and moved it up a notch, allowing Eamon just enough room to pass.

The first few miles came and went just like the ones before it. Oh, to be sure, the visibility was just a little worse without the red taillights to follow; nonetheless, Eamon thought the road was more than adequately passable, that it was just another case of overzealous authorities exercising too much caution. He went on thinking that right until the moment he slammed into the snowbank.

Well, it wasn't a snowbank, exactly. It was more like one giant drift staggering across three lanes. He tried backing up, he tried going forward, he tried shifting gears, he tried everything to no avail. He just couldn't get any traction. He kept at it, with his car squealing like a stuck pig. Finally, he got out to take a look.

His immediate assessment: hopeless.

Jesus, how could he have been so stupid? All his frantic maneuverings had only made matters worse: he was totally wedged in now. Well, he would just have to dig himself out, that's all there was to it. Thank God for Mary and her snow shovel.

Except shoveling wasn't all that easy, either. Not with that hellish wind that kept whipping the snow back in place. Even if he managed to get himself out, which was looking more and more doubtful, he certainly wouldn't be able to continue on. The road ahead disappeared into a billowing sea of white, a desolate no-man's-land. The best he could do at this point was to put the car in reverse and hope to somehow find the strength to push her out.

The only way he'd get to Blue Springs tonight would be by some kind of miracle.

She kept thinking of what Gileo Robbins had once told her about the nature of pain and suffering. Jill had gone out with Gileo for a few months way back when. He was a tall, bean-thin Buddhist who taught megarich, hyperstressed Hollywood producers how to meditate. He was also a very patient, very sensitive lover. Jill smiled in her mind's eye at the memory of Gileo's endless, lolling hours of foreplay.

Gileo had grown up on Long Island, one of six children in a traditional, middle-class family. His father was a Grumman engineer and his mother was a full-time homemaker, so they were pretty surprised, to say the least, when their oldest son decided to renounce their petty, bourgeois ways to go off to Nepal in search of spiritual enlightenment on some mountaintop with a bunch of orange-robed monks. But Gileo had his reasons.

Gileo told Jill that he had spent his whole life feeling cursed. He said he felt truly damned, that there was something or someone out there that wanted harm to come to him. He felt it even when he slept, as if some evil spirit were hovering over him. It caused nothing but pain and torment to him. He tried telling his parents and the church rector about this curse on his life, but of course they told him that he was being silly and that there were no such things. Finally, his parents paid for sessions with a psychologist, but nothing came of that, either.

As he got older, Gileo turned to drink and drugs to assuage the pain. But that only sent him plummeting to new lows as he stumbled in and out of treatment centers. And soon his spiritual agony turned into a terrible physical ordeal. He was diagnosed with multiple sclerosis, which meant he couldn't walk anymore, and he began shooting up heroin again.

Gileo told Jill that he still thought that all of it—the drugs, the perpetual agony, even the MS—was the result of some curse that had been put on his life. He was sure that someone in the spirit world had it in for him.

It was then, at this lowly point, that Gileo set out for Kathmandu, Nepal. He figured he had nothing to lose. He arrived at the Buddhist monastery in a wheelchair, dizzy-eyed with smack.

Gileo's teacher, an esteemed lama, began by telling him that the nature of all life is suffering. Gileo told the lama that he did not need to travel how many thousands of miles to hear that. Then he told the lama that there was a curse on his life and that the evil spirits wouldn't leave him alone. The lama did not laugh at him; instead, he said to Gileo that these spirits must be in much pain themselves. The simplicity of this stunned Gileo. The lama further instructed that it was going to be necessary to make amends with these spirits, to actually embrace their suffering and to let them know that Gileo forgave them for everything. *Their suffering is your suffering,* the lama explained to Gileo.

Gileo told Jill that that night as he lay on a cot in the monastery, he felt the familiar enveloping dread as the spirits appeared, somehow finding him all the way on the other side of the world. But he was prepared for them. He was scared but he did just as the lama had said, reaching out to the spirits, telling them out loud that he knew of their great pain and that he loved them, even after all that had happened to him. He said he could truly understand their suffering because he had suffered much himself.

Seconds later, the dark room filled with a brilliant white light. It lasted only a moment, but as the radiance went away, he felt a great lifting, as if a lifetime's accumulated burden had disappeared with the light, as if he were free now, finally free of the curse. Gileo told Jill that from that moment on, he loved everyone and every living thing. He no longer needed the heroin or anything else to get him through the day. Not long after, feeling returned to his legs and he was soon walking again.

When Gileo told Jill this story, he kept asking if she believed him. And she said, *I guess,* thinking it was a pretty cool yarn, even if he was making it up.

Now, though, she was sure it was all true. She thanked Gileo for his wisdom, for sharing such a strange and private saga. Who knew that she would one day be making such use of it?

All life was suffering, Jill now knew. And some suffered more than others. She forgave Ray now, because he was obviously in terrible agony, whether he knew it or not. Forgiving him was essential, though, because it allowed Jill to forgive herself. Yes, she forgave Ray and she forgave herself for not living the life she had wanted to live. She had not loved enough during her brief time on the planet, but now in her final minutes, she was filled with love for, as Gileo had said, everyone and every living thing.

Her eyes were awash in tears but not for the reasons Ray probably believed. He continued to stick her with his knives; he made little nicks into her breasts now as he recalled the abusive women who made up his rejection-tormented past.

But she no longer felt the sharp, stinging physical sensation of being cut anymore. All pain was behind her, emptied into the vastness of time itself. She was all accepting, all loving, all ready to die.

Everything was ceasing to be now. Even her memories were vanishing, melting away like so many reverse Polaroids. Everything that she once held dear was leaving her. But she let go, she just let go, because the letting go was called for.

Ray jabbed at her with the rifle now. She really couldn't even make out what he was saying anymore. It was just words anyway, frightened, lonely words. Poor, poor Ray. He was suffering so.

Jill felt almost a mystical sense of control and mastery. She was like one of those all-knowing, orange-robed monks on the mountaintop. Gileo would have been proud of her.

29

Eamon took a break from his futile exertions to free the car from the grip of that monster snowdrift. He leaned on the shovel, on the verge of giving up. It was still coming down something fierce, blowing about like a warning from God. It was hopeless, and it was typical, too—typical of his stubborn-headed ways, winding up stuck in the middle of nowhere on a night from hell. When was he going to learn to think before he acted? What was it going to take for him to finally get it? Did he have to freeze to death before he got a clue?

He would have gone on berating himself except he was suddenly nearly blinded by headlights. Two huge, roaring plow beasts were bearing down on him, showing no signs of stopping. They gave him several blasts of their horns as he frantically waved his hands at them to spare him. They came to a halt just a few feet from his car. Moments later, one of the drivers opened his door and climbed down from the cab of his snorting yellow beast.

"Having a little trouble, are we?" the unlikely hero said, giving him a good-natured wink. "The trooper said we might find you like this. I'll tell you what:

you get back in your car and I'll try to push you
out."

Before Eamon could explain that he'd already tried
that, the guy had positioned himself in front of the car
and was digging himself in for some traction. He was
a beefy, ruddy-faced sort, the type of man normally
featured in cigarette ads, riding a horse in the shadow
of the Rockies. He was also coatless, which might
have accounted for the burst of color in his cheeks.
That said, it took this green-uniformed municipal
worker all of ten seconds to free the car.

Eamon was in awe. "Jesus," he said through his
rolled-down window, just beginning to thank him.

"Don't mention it," he said, giving him the
thumbs-up. "Now all you got to do is fall in line and
we'll take you as far as Harrisburg. How does that
sound, pardner?"

Nothing had ever sounded better. Things were
starting to look up in a big, big way. He was traveling
with angels now: these plows were like a winged
escort, shoving aside the mountains of snow like they
were just so much weightless powder. It was hard now
not to believe in divine intervention, hard not to
think that God had interceded in such a hopeless,
helpless situation. As he followed in the path of the
plows, which were churning up the real estate at a
good pace now, a sense of newly born confidence
surged through him.

Of course he was going to make it in time. Of course
he was going to save Jill Winters. What was he
worrying about? Everything was for a reason—
everything. He felt practically untouchable, cloaked
in the goodness and the righteousness of his cause.
After all, he was on the side of the angels—fleet, fast,
invincible.

He rode into Harrisburg with his window open, just
wanting to feel that cold, bracing air, to be wide awake
for whatever came his way now. He was gladdened by
the sight of civilization, by the snow-blurring, com-

peting neon of gas stations and motels, by all that impervious glass and granite and light in the near distance. But he felt a tinge of disappointment at highway's end when the two plows exited in the opposite direction of his destination. His winged escort was officially over. They turned right; he turned left. It was up to him from here on in.

Route 111 was slick and messy, but it had also been plowed and sanded in the not-too-long-ago past. He was sliding around a bit, but fortunately, there wasn't anybody else stupid enough to be on the road. The storm still hadn't let up. It was a lonely, ghostly tantrum, full of howling pathos. It was kind of scary, really, the way you felt it in the marrow of your bones—a cold, wet fear that was the same for our earliest ancestors. It was strange and humbling, amidst the glitter of the technoworld, to be reminded of human vulnerability.

Eamon was starting to feel a lot less confident now in the face of such swirling, menacing havoc. He noticed the downed trees and power lines in places. Still, he pressed on, relentless. And he was almost there, just a couple of miles outside of the town of Blue Springs, when he hit a slick patch and went into a violent skid. He pumped the brakes and turned his wheel right into it, just as he'd always been told to do in such a circumstance, and went sliding off the road, right into a snowy ditch.

He wasn't hurt, but he was derailed. He'd need a tow truck to get his car back on the road, but it wasn't the end of the world. He'd just have to walk into town. Of course, he didn't have boots; he was wearing dress shoes. Of course, his feet felt like they should be amputated after going only a few yards. Of course, it was dark, too. Usually, snow provided all the blue refraction you needed. But this storm just seemed to suck all the light and goodness out of the universe.

He stayed to the main road, though, and it wasn't long before he was trudging into town. He wouldn't have been able to drive in anyway, seeing as nobody had even attempted to plow yet. Right away, he saw that all the lights were out. Oh, great, added adventure. Sheriff Earl T. Vose had a little house right off Main Street, a narrow, dreary clapboard that had been replicated multiple times on both sides of the street. Its chimney was serenely smoking, though, and the windows were softly aglow with candles.

As he rapped on the door, Eamon felt only exhaustion and frostbite. He could only hope that Vose was up to the job.

The door opened to reveal an older gentleman who happened to look just like a walrus. He was bald and of large girth and had a mustache reminiscent of tusks. "Yup, what can I do for you?"

"Lieutenant Eamon Wearie at your service. United States Postal Inspection Service."

"Well, don't that beat all," the flannel-shirted walrus said, slapping his knees in surprise. "I know you fellas called earlier, but I never supposed you'd be able to make it up here in this weather. Well, I'll be."

"Aren't you going to invite me in?" Eamon said, in no mood for pleasantries.

"Sure, sure, son. Don't mind my manners. Like I said, just plenty surprised, that's all."

It was dark but warm in there with that crackling fire in the brick fireplace. It was nice to walk into a living room without the TV going, for once. He immediately noticed the open bottle of scotch on the coffee table, reflecting those log-licking flames.

"Can I get you a drink?" Vose asked, noticing where Eamon's attention was at.

"So what have you learned so far, Sheriff?" Eamon said, ignoring his hospitality. "Do we know where he is?"

"I really didn't think you'd show up tonight," he repeated apologetically.

"Christ," Eamon said, already exasperated with the

old man. "Didn't you make any calls to check around some?"

"This weather is mighty churlish—"

"Screw the weather. Aren't the phones working?"

"Well, yes, but—"

"You got any dry socks?" Eamon asked, realizing he wasn't going to get anywhere with Vose. "I need a moment to think here."

"We're not going to be able to do much till morning, young fellow. I think it's best you settle in for the night. I got a spare bedroom and—"

"Just get me those socks," Eamon said, not wanting to give in to common sense now.

With the old man gone, Eamon reached for the scotch and took a nice, healthy swallow from the bottle. He'd earned that much. Then he took another, for good luck.

When Vose returned with the socks, Eamon said, "Who does all the real estate in town?"

"Well, as you might guess, there ain't too much selling and buying in Blue Springs. This is a small town where houses can stay on the market for years sometimes."

"Exactly," Eamon said, slamming his hand on the coffee table. "Now who's our local real estate agent?"

"That would be Doris Humphrey—"

"Get her on the phone."

"Well, it's awfully late—"

"Sheriff, I really don't think you understand what's at stake here. Just get Doris on the fucking phone."

"Well, you don't have to be so surly about it."

"Look, I'm sorry, but I don't have any patience left," Eamon said, removing his frozen shoes and ice-crunched socks in front of the fire. "Just do what I tell you, understand?"

Vose, looking all childishly petulant, punched her up on the portable phone. "Yup, Doris? Sheriff Earl T. Vose here. Yup, I know it's late. But I got a little problem. Yup, you ever happen to run into a fellow by the name of Ray Duffy? Yup, a stranger to these parts. Never heard of him? Well, I didn't think you did. Look, Doris, I'm sorry that we had to disturb you—"

Eamon grabbed the phone out of Vose's hands. "Hello, Doris, this is Lieutenant Wearie. I'm a federal agent working on a high-priority case. I need to know if you've had any unusual transactions in the last six months or so. What I mean is, has any one buyer stood out? Exactly, someone paying all cash for their house certainly fits the bill. I see, and how old would you say this man was? In his mid-thirties or thereabout. A Raymond Smith, you say? Paid thirty-eight thousand dollars in cash for Bob Dedham's old place. The sheriff knows where it is, you say? Okay, thank you, Doris. You've been a big help. You can go back to bed now."

"Well, I guess you cracked the case, then," Vose said, looking like his feelings were hurt. "Awfully rude about it, but I guess when you're a big-time big-city fellow, it don't matter whose feelings you go and step on. Not that I care, mind you—"

"Sheriff, where's Bob Dedham's place?" Eamon said, ignoring his daftness.

"I'm not so sure I'm in the mind to tell you now."

Eamon was about to let him have it when he suddenly got an idea about what was ailing the sheriff. His eyes having adjusted to the flickering, burnished room, he took note of all the gold-framed photographs of Mr. and Mrs. Vose. They seemed to occupy every square inch of wall space. Just the two of them. Snapped on their wedding day and on all their subsequent anniversaries. Pictured on the decks of cruise ships and in the lobbies of grand hotels. On film, they appeared a totally loving and devoted couple. Eamon just had a hunch, that's all.

"Your wife die recently?" he asked Vose, draining the toughness from his voice.

"Things sure are different around here," the old walrus said wistfully. "How did you know, anyway?"

"I'm sure sorry for your loss, sir," Eamon said, trying another tack now. "I hope you'll forgive my manners. The way I just barged in here like that. It must've been very upsetting."

"Happened only two months ago, you know," Vose said. "Weren't lucky enough to have children, but we always felt blessed anyway. Betsy had the big C. It was rough sailing there for a while . . ."

His voice just trailed off. "I think I should be on my way," Eamon said. "Let you get some rest. Again, I'm sorry I was so rude earlier."

"Oh, that's okay, young feller," Vose said, starting to view Eamon more kindly now. "You had a job to do. I can understand that. I used to be a pretty good officer of the law myself. At least until this thing happened with Betsy."

"If it's not too much trouble, sir, I was hoping you could point me in the direction of Bob Dedham's place."

"Sure, sure," he said. "You're going to need your car. The Dedham place is just on the fringes of town."

"Oh, that might be a problem. My car's disabled."

"Well, I could loan you mine," Vose said, looking slightly pensive. "But she ain't so good in this kind of weather."

"She'll have to do."

"Hey, young feller, I got a better idea. Do you know how to use a snowmobile?"

"Absolutely," Eamon lied.

"That's just dandy," the walrus said. "I got one by the side of the house. Let me just go find the key. Now where did I put that thing? It's been a while since I used it."

It took Vose about fifteen minutes to come up with that key, fifteen terrible, antsy, cage-climbing minutes. It was at the bottom of some coffee can. Eamon tried to remain polite as Vose explained the secret of making a perfect cup of coffee. "The secret is mixing the beans," he said, as if they had all the chat time in the world. "What I do is get me a bag of that gourmet mocha mocha java and mix that with some regular Chock Full o' Nuts and . . ."

Just get on with it, Eamon thought. *Just give me a fucking break, already.*

Finally, Vose gave him the key and the directions to Bob Dedham's old place. "Shouldn't have too much trouble finding it," he said, leading him out the door and back into the howling night. "You got something to protect yourself with?"

"Yeah, I'm fine," Eamon said, knowing he wasn't talking about a pack of condoms. "Standard police issue," he added, patting the Smith & Wesson that was holstered under his overcoat.

"You know, young feller, that Mr. Montrez urged some caution on this end. He told me to tell you not to do anything until we had some backup. Said you might think about waiting till tomorrow when the cavalry gets here."

"*I am* the damn cavalry," Eamon said, taking his leave.

The snowmobile was on a trailer covered with a snow-heavy tarp. Like a maniac, he set about clearing it off and getting it down. That done, he looked the little machine over: it had skis for runners up front and tanklike treads in back; it had mileage and gas gauges and a simple starter; basically, it was like a motorcycle in that you operated the speed and braking from the handles.

Satisfied, he hopped on and turned the key. She started up with an ugly jolt, making a cantankerous, sputtering racket that you might notice on another night. He took it slow at first, until he got the hang of it. There was nothing to it, really. Except when he started building speed, it became real hard to see. He needed goggles, the way the snow was whipping into his face, and he needed fresh, warm clothes, anything but the things he had on, which were cold, wet, and cutting.

He got the little vehicle up to its maximum speed of thirty-five miles per hour and sailed through the tiny village of Blue Springs, which was no more than a silent, mournful snowdrift at the moment. It would be pretty in the morning, though, after the storm was over, in the sparkling sunlight, putting those first footprints down. People would wander about with their cameras and their dopey, wonder-eyed expressions. Then the shopkeepers would begin the hard business of clearing their sidewalks—and, soon, one by one, they would open for business. First to unlock its doors would be the small, rustic hardware store, which would make a bold display of its snow-removal equipment. The cabooselike diner would surely open, too, bringing to the street the strong, pleasing smells of coffee and bacon. The bank, with its imposing Greek pillars, would do a half day's business, just to prove the resiliency of money. By late afternoon, the pizza joint and the video store would also be open, and there would be the profound sense of a world returning to normal in the little town of Blue Springs.

Eamon definitely liked thinking about how it was going to be after the storm tomorrow. It was easier to think of that sunny, renewed place than to imagine where he was gunning off to right now.

Bob Dedham's old place was a mile back from his mailbox, which was posted at the bottom of Route 111. Eamon debated taking the snowmobile up any farther, worrying that Duffy might hear his encroachment; the element of surprise was crucial. He abandoned the vehicle down at the mailbox and made his way up to the house, which looked as dark and quiet as the rest of town. There was a buried Jeep in the drive, so obviously somebody was home.

Eamon decided to check out the ramshackle old shed next to the old-fashioned farmhouse first. He drew his gun and unhinged the wooden barn door, which made a terrible creaking noise when he pulled it open. Well, now at least he knew for sure that he was on the right track. There, under an assortment of old gardening tools hooked into the walls, was Jill's Toyota, without the plates.

He wasn't sure what to do next. The smart thing was probably to look around some more, see what else he could learn. But he was getting dumber and more impatient by the minute. He decided that he was just going to burst in the front door of the house and come in blazing bullets.

He figured all subtlety was lost on Ray Duffy.

He came out of the shed and fearlessly made his way to the farmhouse. Now he could make out the candlelight coming from the smudgy, darkened windows. He thought to make the sign of the cross before he made his mad charge. Eamon rushed up the porch steps, with gun in hand, and then used his body like a battering ram into the front door, collapsing it all at once.

It took a second to right himself. And it took at least that long for him to register the scene. It was a scene from hell, an absolute obscenity. It would be difficult to say what he noticed first, if it was that collection of big, gleaming kitchen knives or that floor-slick of open porno magazines. Or if it was the naked, blood-scarred girl hog-tied on the couch. Or if it was Duffy himself, wheeling at him with the long barrel of a rifle before he had the chance to consider anything.

It was just bang, bang—that fast—and it was over.

Eamon knew he got one shot off before he was hit in the chest. He couldn't be sure if he nailed Duffy, but he sure hoped so, because he knew he wasn't going to get off another round.

Lying in his own blood, he watched it all leak away from him. His ears rang like crazy; his eyes were full of red flash. That was some gun Duffy had, like a hunting rifle or something. Just dumb luck that Duffy had it in his hands when Eamon crashed through the door.

At least he didn't feel any pain—at least that. It was just hot and cold all at the same time, tingling and numbing, like July and February merging into one month.

He was mortally wounded, but his whole life wasn't playing out before him—nothing like that. He just found himself wondering the same things he always seemed to be wondering: Is there a God? Is there a heaven? Is there any sense to all of this? Or is it finally just the blackness of eternity?

At least he'd get to find out now—at least that.

There was that time where she went with Gileo to Boulder, Colorado. It was just a few days, a few days that lingered now in the final minutes of her life, for some unexplained reason. Gileo had wanted to check out the American Buddhist program at the Naropa Institute. Jill just tagged along, not out of any real interest in Buddhism, really. Her interest was in Gileo. She liked his hard, bean-thin body and his dark, wounded, deep-socketed eyes. She was such a slut for beautiful, long-haired, groovy-eyed, tortured souls.

Jill realized that she had always been a little superficial. She never took the chance to dig a little deeper, not with herself, not with others, not ever. She was just afraid, afraid of being real, afraid of feelings, afraid of disappointment. She thought she was protecting herself; little did she know that she was killing herself, slowly but surely. Life was meant to be lived. How easy, how simple, how simply ignored.

Not only had she not challenged herself to do more and better in this life, but she had so often failed to take advantage of the many wonderful opportunities that were forever landing in her lap. Their trip to the Naropa Institute in Colorado was just such a blown opportunity. Instead of using her time to find out more about this eclectic religion and its wildly different and interesting adherents, she played it like a real spoiled child. She yawned loudly during meditation sessions and kept up a steady stream of rude, cynical comments about their soybean food, Birkenstock sandals, and free-love antics. Gileo was not amused.

After they got back to California, Gileo told Jill that he didn't think they were cut out to be with each other. She really liked Gileo, maybe even really loved him, but all she did was shrug her shoulders and say something like *I guess, if that's the way you want it.* She pretended to herself that it was no big deal. After all, there were plenty of other men in the sea and all that. Besides, she told herself, Gileo was just some stupid Buddhist. And so what of it, anyway?

She wasn't just scared; she was a liar, too, a liar to herself.

Well, in the next life, she was going to do it all differently. *You'll see,* she promised, *you'll see.*

That was when she heard the first big noise. She was all safe and lost in her Gileo trance when there was this crazy, out-of-the-blue crash at the door and all this winter air came whooshing in. It startled her out of her murky, lost depths. Suddenly everything was real again, all here and now. There was this man with a gun, standing there with this horrified, unbelieving expression on his face. Ray pulled the rifle from her vagina and turned it on him in a split second. Then there were two loud booms, one right after the other.

Then the unbelieving stranger was lying there in the open doorway, clutching his chest, making terrible gurgling sounds.

Ray hadn't got out of this unscathed, either; he'd been wounded in the shoulder. "The fuck shot me," he was sobbing. "Did you see that? Did you see how he shot me. Look, I'm all bleeding. *Fuck, that just sucks.*" Ray went over to the dying man. "Shit, can you believe it? It's that fucking Eamon Wearie asshole. How the fuck did he find me? That guy is such a pain in the ass. He never leaves me alone. I can't believe it. It's just like him to do this."

Ray was standing over Wearie's body, with his back to her. It hurt to know that it was that nice postal inspector lying there. She wondered, just like Ray, how he'd ever tracked them down. He was still alive, just barely. Ray put his foot on the inspector's chest and took aim at him again with the rifle. He pressed the barrel right into his face. Jill waited for the terrible, inevitable explosion. For some reason, Ray didn't pull the trigger.

"Fuck you," he said, pulling the rifle away. "Why should I do you any favors? Better to let you bleed to death. You piece of shit. Do you see what you did to me? Do you? Shot me right in the shoulder. I've never been shot before. Doesn't hurt as bad as I thought it would. I guess you just grazed me or some shit."

Ray had completely forgotten about her on the couch. She was going to make the most of her opportunity; she wasn't waiting around for the next lifetime anymore. Even though her hands were tied behind her back, she was able to position herself closer to the coffee table, closer to the burning candles. . . .

It was working: she was burning through the cords. The candle flame was indiscriminate, though, as it failed to distinguish between rope and flesh. Jill didn't even flinch.

It suddenly dawned on Ray that the inspector might not be alone. "I wonder if he brought anyone with him," Ray said dubiously, taking a tentative step outside. "Come out, come out, wherever you are!" he hollered now into the snow-driven winds.

By now, Jill had successfully freed her hands. She couldn't be sure she'd have the time to do her feet. Instead, she grabbed one of the kitchen knives and brought it behind her back, so it would look like she was still his little tied-up hostage. Then she waited for him to come back inside. She was anything but afraid now.

In fact, if she could've, if her mouth weren't bandaged in duct tape, she might've actually smiled. She was getting yet another chance. Few people were ever luckier.

Ray came back in, spewing his normal venom and hate and self-loathing. "Fucking assholes," he said. "Can't a man enjoy a nice evening at home with his girlfriend without some nut kicking down his door? What kind of fucking country is this, anyway?"

And then he remembered Jill again.

"Jilly," he said, on her like a laser now. "I guess you thought I forgot about you. Not fucking likely," he said, stepping over the inspector and making his way over. "We've got so much still to discuss. I feel we could go on talking all night. Isn't that the best? When you have a friend like that?"

He came right up to her now. "You know, I think we should kiss and make up. What do you think about that, kitten?"

She thought it was a very bad idea.

From behind her back, she whipped out the knife and plunged it into Ray's chest. She pulled it out and slammed it in again. She didn't even give him the chance to register surprise. She plunged it in over and over again, until she was sure that he was good and dead.

It was easy. She wasn't even grossed out by all that blood. She was very calm and efficient about it. It was just the way things had to be, the way nature intended it. She was helping him out, that's how she saw it; that's what made it so easy for her. She was simply putting Ray out of his misery.

After all, he had already suffered so much, and now he didn't have to suffer anymore at all.

30

His eyelids twitched. That's how it all began again. It was such a tiny, imperceptible quivering that it was easily overlooked by the fancy sensors that were supposedly monitoring his every movement. But these tiny, involuntary twitchings were, in fact, nothing short of momentous, for Eamon Wearie was returning to the land of the living.

At first he had no idea where he was.

His first guess was the county morgue. Maybe it was the eerie, radium-like glow of the room. Or maybe it was the antiseptic smells and the cool, sterile air. Or maybe it was just the fact that the last thing he remembered was Ray Duffy turning on him with that monster hunting rifle of his. After that, it was one big, dark blank.

Okay, he was in a hospital room somewhere. He was laid out on a bed, not on some hard slab. Then there were all those monitors, all those funny little bleeps, not to mention the intravenous tubes. How long had he been out, anyway?

He couldn't seem to move a muscle. His chest felt like it had an iron anvil sitting on it. His vision was a blurry mess. He tried lifting his head off his pillow.

No dice. He needed a nurse or a doctor, just to find out what the story was. Where was the buzzer or intercom or whatever? Where was everybody?

"Damn," he said, frustrated and sounding all rusty and hoarse. "Anybody hear me out there?" he called out weakly.

His reply came in the form of a sleepy "What? What was that?" from beyond the foot of his bed somewhere. He couldn't prop himself up to see. "Oh, my God," the familiar voice said. "Oh, my God."

"Mary," he said, full of recognition now.

Then she was standing beside him, clutching his hand. "Oh, my God," she said, weeping. "My prayers have been answered."

She was a beautiful, black-haired blur. "I love you," he said. "I love you."

"I'm supposed to get the doctor," she said, still crying. "That's what they told me to do when you came out of the coma."

"Not yet," he pleaded. "First tell me how long I've been like this."

"Over a week," she said, trying to compose herself. "They didn't know if you'd ever snap out of it."

"The girl?" he said, remembering. "What happened to her?"

"Jill Winters saved your life," Mary said. "She dragged you into Duffy's Jeep and went for help."

"She okay?"

"They say she's fine physically. Nothing that couldn't be stitched up. Mentally, I don't know. She's been through some ordeal."

"What about Duffy?"

"Burning in the fires of hell, most likely," she said. "I think I'd better get the doctor now."

"That can wait. Just get me a glass of water. My throat is parched."

Movement was starting to return to his body. He was able to lift the glass to his lips himself. It still felt like he had a damn anvil on his chest, though. And everything was still really out of focus. But no water had ever tasted more delicious—chlorine and everything.

"What's the damage report?" he asked, handing her back the empty glass. "What's the prognosis?"

"The big thing is that you've emerged from the coma," Mary said. "That's what everybody was worried about. And it doesn't sound like you've suffered any brain damage."

"How would you know? I was never very smart to begin with," he joked.

"You've had some internal damage," Mary said seriously. "But I think I should let the doctor explain about that."

"Is there anything else I should know now?"

"Well—" She hesitated. "I guess maybe I should be the one to tell you. You were dead."

"Nothing I can't live with," he said lightly.

"No, you don't understand; you were really dead. You lost a lot of blood. You were DOA at the hospital. They speculate you were gone for maybe twenty minutes, all told. Somehow they revived you. The doctors think you have the extreme cold to thank for that. They're not sure how, but they think the freezing weather that night played a role—put you in some kind of suspended animation."

He needed a minute to take it in. If he'd been dead, then there was nothing. Then it really was the blackness of eternity. Because all memory and sensation stopped a minute after Duffy blasted him. There was nothing, nada, zip. It was just like he'd always feared.

"Did you see the warm light?" Mary asked. "Is that what happened? Did you have one of those afterlife experiences? Were you greeted by your dead relatives and friends?"

"That's exactly what happened," he lied. "Just like you read about. All that warm, embracing light. The overpowering feeling of love and goodness. It was amazing."

"I'm so glad," she said. "I've always wanted to believe that those stories were true. It makes me feel good to know that God is watching over us."

"Exactly," Eamon said.

She began to cry again. "I'm just so glad you're back with us, that it wasn't your time yet. I need you so."

She squeezed his hand, and he squeezed it right back, as reassuringly as he could. It's what they were left with in the end.

"You sure smell good," Eamon said, catching a whiff of his wife's perfume now. "I've always loved the way you smell."

"Don't tell me you're horny now."

"It's about the only part of me that's still functioning," he said, trying to bring her into clearer focus and failing. She was still a beautiful vision, even if he couldn't quite make her out at the moment. "I wish I could make love to you right now."

"You will."

"You bet I will."

"You've always been so full of confidence," she said.

"I've lost some, believe me."

"You'll get it all back—I know you."

He said, "Don't be so sure."

"I'll help you," she said, squeezing his hand harder.

"You already have."

"I have something to tell you," she said. "I was going to save it. But I think, strangely enough, this might be the right time for it."

"What is it?" he said, hearing the gravity in her voice.

"I'm pregnant," she said. "We're going to have a baby."

"That's wonderful, absolutely wonderful. Oh, darling, that's the best news I've ever heard. I . . . I . . ."

He just stopped jabbering and started to cry from the sheer joy and relief and wonder of it all. Oh life, sweet, joyous life! His whole body seemed racked with happy sobs. It had been so long since he last cried. He welcomed these tears like they were raindrops visiting an arid land. It was just that his world had been shadowed by violence and death for such a terribly long time now. Death was his beat, death was his lonely bugle call. But now this, this miracle.

Eamon cried not only for the joy of becoming a father—which was wonder enough—but also for the miracle of simply being alive. His tears were for himself, for his fallen comrades, for Pinkus and Sanchez and Frank Shoe, for all the dead and soon-to-be dead. Nobody gets out alive, as Bunko once told him. Nobody gets out alive.

But for now, it was enough to know that they were bringing life into this mad, chaotic world, to know that they would live on in the genes of their child, and in the genes of his children, and on and on for infinity or as long as human beings roamed the earth.

Everlasting life was theirs. It was a truth that every father knew, that every new father discovered.

Jill had totally shed her fear of flying. As the jet started to gain momentum on the runway, she felt calm and serene, of all things. She would probably never be scared of anything again.

It was funny to think how petrified she used to be of flying across the country. It had nothing to do with logic; logically, she knew the chances of going down were infinitesimal. A pilot friend had once taken the trouble of giving her a private tour of a 747 that was in the hangar for a routine inspection, just so that she could see for herself how safe these big birds really were. He took pride in showing her all the backup systems and telling her about the kind of rigorous training the pilots underwent and the experience they had to have, not to mention the kind of expense and trouble the airlines went to maintain the aircraft. Jill was duly impressed. Not that it did any good, of course; on her very next flight, she went back to popping Xanax with her double Stolis.

Jill now understood that her former fear of flying was really a fear of dying. The fearful are always unhappy people, and Jill was no exception. She had been ashamed of her meek, obedient, conforming, obsequious little life. She had not yet learned how to be true to herself, or even how to truly love others, and so she had been scared of dying. Deep down, she must've realized that her life would never have stood up to the ultimate scrutiny of Judgment Day.

For the first time ever, Jill enjoyed a takeoff. This morning, she loved the feeling of raw mechanical power as the jet became airborne, knifing up into the stratosphere, leaving behind the antlike world below, full of its petty fears and temporal confusion. It was metaphoric, the way she was leaving it all behind her, going forward with her life, to someplace better, even if it wasn't exactly a new place.

California awaited.

In the month that she spent with her mother recuperating, she made some calls. At first, her old friends and business associates were surprised to hear from her, almost wary, but she was persistent because she really wanted to get her old Hollywood job back. Her post office days were over forever.

It took some doing, but she was finally able to convince an old director friend to give her another shot in the fabulous world of set design. He was at the helm of an upcoming serial-killer thriller.

"Babe, I don't think it's for you," he'd said. "It's going to be very bleak, very depressing. All pewter skies and clapboard houses and dismembered body parts. A real dreary shoot. I just can't see you doing this kind of thing. Let me tell you, it's not for the squeamish."

Fortunately, he caved in and hired her before she was forced to reel off the most recent addition to her résumé.

She couldn't wait to get back to work. And to start her new life. She had had four absolutely wonderful weeks in Muldeen with her mom. It was so great to get to tell her—without the embarrassment, without the old awkwardness—how much Jill loved her. And just to talk to her, to *really* talk to her for once. They must've hugged each other twenty times a day, trying to make up for lost time. A lot could happen in three years. It made Jill so sad to see the difference in her mother's face, the way the laugh lines had taken root, how much she had aged since the last time Jill had seen her. They had missed so much together that was rightfully theirs. Jill vowed that not even three months, let alone three years, would pass before she saw her mom again.

It hadn't been all that easy for her, either. At first her mom had acted just like the police and doctors had, overly cautious and overly protective, as if Jill were some fragile, entirely breakable piece of rare porcelain or something. It was not that she didn't understand and appreciate their concern; it was just that she wasn't a helpless invalid, or even, more to the point, some emotional cripple; the last thing she wanted was to spend her remaining days at some sanatorium crocheting oversize sweaters as well-meaning attendants patted her hand and said, "That's the girl, Jill."

She was going to be fine, absolutely fine. The hard part was over. The good part was just beginning. She was sure of it. She could feel it in the very warmth of the sun that was streaming through her little porthole on the world as the jumbo jet streaked over time zones and other people's harried lives. Yes, there was bright sunshine, over the cloud beds, at thirty thousand glorious feet.

"Do you mind pulling the shade down?" the passenger next to her asked. "The sun gets in my eyes."

Actually, she did mind a little, but in the interests of harmony and peace, she obliged.

"I hate to fly," he said, pulling down his tray as the flight attendant came around with the drink cart. He loaded up on the little vodka bottles and poured himself a triple brain-duller. "Can't get enough of this stuff when I'm in the air," he said. "Or when I'm on the ground, for that matter. You want one?"

"No, thanks," she said.

"Suit yourself," he said, sounding irritated by her refusal.

He was a large, pink-faced man with slicked-back hair, in a gangsterish, chalk-striped suit. He reeked of some designer perfume. Jill just hoped he would take a hint and keep to himself for the remainder of the flight.

"Business or pleasure?" he asked a moment later, interrupting her solitude one more time.

"Both, I guess," she said, trying to remain polite but indifferent.

"Is that a fact?" he said. "I happen to travel out to L.A. quite often on business. Love it out there. Whereabouts do you live exactly?"

"I'm in the process of looking for new digs," she said, wishing she had just told him that it was none of his cotton-pickin' business.

"I'm in the advertising game," he said, taking his card out from his wallet for her. "Name's Will Harris. But just call me Big Bill."

He stuck out his big, furry paw for her to shake; she felt she had no other choice but to oblige him again.

"Now I didn't get your name," he said, not going away.

"Ruth," she said.

"You don't seem like a Ruth," he said, taking a moment to look her over. "Nice-looking girl, though, I'll say."

She was getting more uncomfortable by the minute. Big Bill was still staring at her. Check that—he was still staring at the scar that was left on her cheek from

Ray's shenanigans with the kitchen knife. She could've had more plastic surgery if she wanted, but she decided that she would leave it as it was, as a reminder.

"Some kind of accident?" he asked, pointing to the scar.

"I don't believe in accidents," Jill said cryptically.

"Gives you character," he said. "I like my women with character."

Jill ignored him. She just picked up the in-flight magazine and threw herself into an article about duty-free shops as if it were the most fascinating reading material ever.

"You're quite a looker, Ruthie," he continued, oblivious. "A real wholesome woman. I like that. I bet you used to be a cheerleader in high school. Am I right? I'm just good at reading people. You know, we ought to get together later on, after we land. Drinks or dinner, what do you say? My treat."

"I'm sorry, that's not possible," she said, not looking up from the magazine but still trying to keep it polite.

"Give me one good reason why not."

"Well, for one thing, you're married." She brought the full force of her contempt to bear on his wedding ring. "And for another, I don't much care for you, Big Bill."

"Don't tell me you're one of those uptight modern bitches who don't like men," he said, the vodka and the maleness starting to mix into a particularly potent combination. "You're not some kind of dyke, are you?"

"Excuse me," she said tightly, forcing herself to get up now. "I have to use the restroom."

He made way, reluctantly.

In the old days, she probably would've just sat there for the duration of the flight, cringing. But now Jill found the nearest flight attendant and explained her situation. "I'm sorry to bother you," she said, "but if you could just find me another seat anywhere on the plane, it would be a great relief."

"I'm sure we can find you something," the young woman said sympathetically.

She led Jill into the mostly unoccupied first-class section, to a plush leather window seat that was serenely removed from anybody else. "I hope you'll find this more to your liking," the flight attendant said. "You'd be surprised how often this happens. And you'd also be surprised how seldom anyone complains. Most people just sit there and take it. Well, enjoy the rest of your flight now."

Jill smiled back at her, just grateful for this small, lovely gesture of humanity. It was always the little things that you remembered and appreciated, anyway. She brought the window shade up and let the sun stream back in. It was bright and glorious at thirty thousand feet, high over the clouds and far above the trifling concerns of mere mortals, in league with the angels.